Detours and Designs

Matt  Josh
Fazio Malacki

Torchflame Books
An imprint of Light Messages
Durham, NC

Published 2018, by Torchflame Books
   an Imprint of Light Messages
www.lightmessages.com
Durham, NC 27713 USA
SAN: 920-9298

Paperback ISBN: 978-1-61153-282-1
E-book ISBN: 978-1-61153-281-4
Library of Congress Control Number: 2018932653

Acknowledgements

*D*etours and Designs would not have been possible without the encouragement and inspiration from those around us. To our parents, families, and friends, thank you. We are also eternally grateful for the invaluable insights of our early readers and the constant support of those who have been rooting for the book to succeed since long before its publication.

Most of all, we want to thank everyone who reads this book, from the young to the not-so-young.

Table of Contents

Finding Answers
in New Places

Drew Daley jolted in his chair and lifted his head, the way he often did when his mind had drifted and life snapped its fingers for attention. He looked around the classroom and saw that almost everyone had erupted with laughter. Drew smiled and did his best to laugh along, but he had no idea what was so funny. It wasn't that he didn't have a sense of humor – he enjoyed a good joke as much as the next kid – it was that he had been focusing on something else. Something that demanded his attention.

He hadn't uncovered a shocking clue about a mysterious murder. That would just be scary and dangerous.

He hadn't received a message from outer space. That couldn't happen, right?

A Babe Ruth rookie card hadn't fallen into his lap. That would be cool – of course, it was about as likely as receiving a message from outer space.

And the fate of the world did not rest in his hands. The world would be in trouble if it needed to be saved by an 11-year-old kid.

What he had just found was much smaller than all those things. But it felt just as big. And although he was sure he had never seen it before, it somehow seemed familiar. To think, he might never have seen it at all if he hadn't accidentally left his social studies book at his dad's house and brought his science book to class instead.

He blinked a few times to regain his focus and looked up at his teacher. It wasn't unusual for Drew to find himself on a different page from his classmates (in this case, literally), but this was the second year in a row he had Mr. Sawyer for social studies, and Mr. Sawyer was the one teacher who usually managed to keep Drew's wandering mind on track.

"Okay, everyone, we have a few minutes before the bell rings, and I want to tell you about your new assignment."

The class quieted down so Mr. Sawyer could continue.

"Next week you are going to give a presentation on someone you greatly admire. Your role model, if you will."

Nearly half the students' hands shot into the air. Mr. Sawyer smiled, looking slightly amused yet also a little annoyed.

"No, you are not permitted to pick anyone in your family," he said. "We'll have an assignment that deals with them another time."

Several hands dropped.

"And yes, I mean entire family," Mr. Sawyer continued. "You already wrote an essay about an extended family member in language arts class last year."

Three more hands dropped.

"Also, no two students can choose the same person. There are twenty-three students in this class, and I want twenty-three different presentations."

Two last hands dropped, and Mr. Sawyer finally was able to continue.

"I want you all to take some time and really think about this. The question you should focus on is: 'What does this person do to *inspire* you?' Come in tomorrow with two choices. Everyone should have a backup in case someone else has the same idea. Today is Wednesday, and presentations will begin as soon as class starts on Monday. So that gives you, let me see ..." He feigned a confused expression and counted on his fingers.

"Five days," cried out several students.

"Five? Well, all right, I guess I'll take your word for it," he joked. "That's why I'm not a math teacher."

As he explained a few more details about the assignment, Drew looked around the room again. He saw nothing but expressions of certainty, as if everyone else already knew exactly who they were choosing.

Drew didn't know who he would pick. Nor did he know that what he had found in his book would soon change his life forever.

This was the first year Drew and his two best friends, Jeff Gray and Tommy Porter, were allowed to walk home by themselves. The school, Emerson Elementary, didn't have buses, and the boys' parents had always rotated driving duties. But this year was going to be different. Now that they were in fifth grade, they were finally awarded the freedom to walk home.

As the crossing guard stopped traffic and the boys crossed the street, Drew considered telling his friends about what he had seen while aimlessly flipping through his book. He wasn't sure how to explain it, though, so instead he asked his friends who they were picking for the social studies presentation.

"That's easy," said Tommy, keeping his coffee-colored eyes on his cell phone screen. "Bryce Harper. You see that homer he crushed last night? He did an epic bat flip. Let me find a video of it ..."

"Yeah," said Jeff, "he's awesome."

"Who you picking?" Tommy asked.

"I'm not sure," said Jeff. "I would pick my Pap, but since we can't pick family members, I'll just pick somebody on the Pirates."

"Oh," Drew blurted out. Even Jeff, who never seemed sure about anything, had a pretty clear idea of what he wanted to do. *Am I the only one who doesn't know who to pick?* Drew wondered.

"Who are you gonna pick?" Jeff asked.

"I dunno," said Drew. "I think – whoa, what's going on here!"

There was a short bridge between the school and the boys' houses that they would cross each day. But now there were several traffic cones lined across it, as well as an orange- and white-striped barricade with a flashing light and a big sign that said BRIDGE CLOSED.

"The bridge is *closed?*"

"Oh yeah, my mom told me about this," said Jeff.

"So what are we gonna do?" Drew asked.

"I guess we gotta go that way," said Tommy, pointing to the right before quickly turning his attention back to his phone.

"That's right," said the crossing guard from the other side of the road. She gave them directions and said it would take them a bit longer to get home while the bridge was out of order.

The boys thanked her and made their way around the bridge to begin their new route. Until now, they had left the school and walked straight down Emerson Boulevard and across the bridge, a direct shot to their homes. Their new route, however, was much more complex. They had to make a right and walk three blocks downhill, trek two blocks parallel with the bridge, and then go up a hill for another three blocks to circumvent the bridge.

"It's gonna take at least like fifteen minutes to get home now," said Drew.

But Tommy said, "Oh well," and Jeff simply shrugged.

The boys proceeded down an unfamiliar street. At one point, while checking out the new scenery, Drew saw a yellow-haired girl walking into a small, white house with light blue siding.

"Who's that?" he asked. "Does she go to Emerson?"

"Are you serious?" said Tommy. "You don't know who that is? It's Skylar Jansen. She's the most popular girl in sixth grade."

"Oh," said Drew, not particularly impressed. "Is that where she lives?"

"Either that or she's about to rob the place," Tommy joked.

A few minutes later, the boys were almost home.

"You guys ready for Saturday night?" asked Tommy. "My mom's taking me to get the new *Zombie Days* game in the morning, so we can have an all-night game sesh."

"Cool," said Jeff. "Can your mom make those pizza rolls like Drew's mom made when we slept over his house?"

"I'll ask," said Tommy. "But it still won't be as cool as Drew's. It's sweet how he can use the big TV in the living room or play video games in the basement, and he don't gotta worry about any brothers or sisters trying to kick him off."

"Yeah," Jeff nodded.

"Well, yeah, but Tommy's house is cool, too," said Drew.

"I dunno," said Jeff. "The last time we were over, Link slobbered all over me all night."

Tommy laughed. "That just means he likes you, dude."

Jeff rolled his eyes.

"Then I wish he hated me. But I'll see you guys tomorrow," he said, turning down his street.

Drew and Tommy continued walking. Their houses were on the same street, Ernest Way, two blocks from Jeff's.

"Ah, I'm bored," said Tommy as they approached his house. "I'm just gonna walk with you to your house to kill some time."

"Okay, cool."

As the boys neared Drew's house, Tommy swiped away on his phone, and Drew mulled over the social studies assignment.

"Hey, Drew, can you and your friend come help me a moment?" a voice yelled.

"Sure, Mr. Johnston."

Mr. Johnston lived in the house across the street from Drew.

"Ehh," Tommy groaned.

"Oh, c'mon, you said you were bored anyway," said Drew, motioning for Tommy to follow. The two boys entered the opened garage and set their book bags on the floor.

"I'm so glad you two were passing by. I couldn't keep this board straight for the life of me and I couldn't get these hinges in the right place ... Hi, I'm Mr. Johnston."

"I'm Tommy." He extended his arm for a handshake until he saw that both of the man's hands were occupied – one holding a ratchet and the other holding steady a big, wooden structure across a table.

"Nice to meet you. And if you don't mind, Drew, this piece needs to be held in place while I tighten it ... Very good, very good ... And Tommy, if you could hold from the bottom to make sure the whole thing doesn't slide right off the table, that would be great." Before Drew and Tommy even realized what they were holding, Mr. Johnston said, "Finished. Thank you, boys, you were fine assistants."

"Whoa, that was simple," said Tommy.

"Yes," said Mr. Johnston. "I had this whole thing set up, but I ended up losing a few things in this hodgepodge I call a garage." He paused and looked around. "That's life, boys.

Sometimes there are so many different things happening around you that you get lost in a hodgepodge."

Even though Drew wasn't sure what that funny-sounding word meant, he understood what Mr. Johnston was saying.

"Anyway, I have clips to hold everything around here somewhere, but I couldn't find the darn things," Mr. Johnston went on. "And I only have about twenty minutes until my wife gets home, so I needed to finish this part quickly."

Both boys looked confused, so the old man continued. "My wife and I are celebrating our fiftieth wedding anniversary on Sunday."

"You've been married for *fifty* years?"

"Sure have. Things were different back then. And we had a very simple wedding ceremony because we didn't have much money. Heck, we had no money. But the one thing I managed to surprise her with on our wedding day was hundreds of Ipomoea flowers. They come in different colors, but I went around to every florist in town until I found as many blue ones as I could. My wife absolutely loved them ..."

Tommy rolled his eyes and began scrolling through his phone. Drew nudged him with his elbow, but Mr. Johnston didn't seem to notice anyway. He was staring off to the side as he spoke, as if he were picturing the look of joy on his wife's face at the sight of the flowers.

"Inside the flower is a yellow center with a white outline, and all the petals are a deep, vibrant blue. They are just magnificent. Some say the Ipomoea stands for two people being together and holds the title 'I belong to thee.'" Mr. Johnston finally noticed Tommy's blank face. "Well, I'm sure you don't want to hear the ramblings of an old, hopeless romantic. Anyway, I decided to make this for our anniversary."

With a strenuous grunt, he lifted what looked like

a wooden fence with a crisscross pattern leaving diamond-shaped holes a baseball could probably just fit through. The structure was only about two feet wide, but it was at least seven feet tall. The fresh paint on the wood reminded Drew of his own time painting chairs, tables, and a swing set with his dad for a community project over the summer. Though he had never liked the smell of paint before, Drew cherished the hours spent working with his dad and now felt a connection with the familiar scent.

"I built it the same way I built the fence out back," said Mr. Johnston, dabbing the sweat on his tan forehead with his handkerchief.

"With power tools?" Tommy asked eagerly.

"No, just classic old handheld tools. I cut the wood, stapled it together, and painted it, and now it's ready for the flowers. This will hang along the side of our front porch and will be full of beautiful, blue Ipomoeas. That's why I needed the hooks."

"Won't it just fall over?" Tommy asked, apparently without fear of offending the man. "Flowers can't grow sideways."

"Oh, that's true. But, you see, the hinges are attached at an angle. I already have two studs to hang the base from. Also, I have a bottom section that connects to this fence, and that will hold the dirt and the water in. Now all I have to do is go pick up the flowers, plant them, then hang this whole thing up," Mr. Johnston said, admiring his work.

"Yeah, *if* it works, I guess it'll be cool," said Tommy.

Drew nudged him again. "I'm sure it'll work. And I bet Mrs. Johnston's gonna love it."

"Why did it take you so long to get home? I was starting to worry. And why were you and Tommy in the Johnstons' backyard?" Drew's mom asked as he approached the front porch.

"We were in the garage. Mr. Johnston was showing us this flower holder thing he made for Mrs. Johnston."

Mr. Johnston then yelled over from across the street. "Hey, Penny! Thanks for letting me borrow him. He was a huge help!"

Drew's mom waved and smiled. Her real name was Penelope, but just about everyone in Emerson, even some of the kids, called her Penny.

"And it took us so long to get home because the bridge is closed," Drew continued. "Can you believe that?"

"Oh, that's right. I hope it isn't closed for too long. It'll be a pain to get home. So, how was school?"

Drew's emotions were jumbled. Part of him was curious and excited about what he had seen in his textbook, and part of him was frustrated about not knowing who to choose for Mr. Sawyer's assignment. He considered showing his mom what he had found in his book, but he figured she was more interested in homework, so he explained the social studies assignment to her.

Penny suggested that he do his other homework, play outside for a while, and then come back to it. "If you still can't figure it out, we'll talk it through tonight before bed, okay?"

"All right."

Drew did his homework, threw a tennis ball off the garage for a while, ate dinner, played video games for half an hour, then got ready for bed. Instead of talking to his mom about the assignment, he told her he had figured it out and she didn't need to worry about it anymore. Something told him that he had to do this assignment on his own.

As he lay in bed that night, he repeated in his head what Mr. Sawyer had said in class: "What does this person do to inspire you?"

Inspire me. Inspire me. Who inspires me? Inspires me to

do what? Drew asked himself. He didn't want to let Mr. Sawyer down with a disappointing presentation, especially after all Mr. Sawyer had done for him. He thought back to a few weeks ago. It was the first day of school, and from the beginning it was a rough one. In math class, Drew had accidentally called the teacher by the wrong name – well, sort of. Mrs. Machado taught both math and Spanish. However, in math, students were to refer to her as Mrs. Machado, and in Spanish, Señora Machado. Because Drew only had her for Spanish in the past, he called her Señora Machado by mistake. Though it was just a minor misstep, it still prompted several classmates to giggle, and Abigail Linwood to pounce on the opportunity to correct him in front of the class.

He hoped to escape the rest of the day without any more issues, but he had no such luck. The science teacher, Mrs. Steinbeck, was known as the toughest, meanest teacher at Emerson Elementary. Everyone was silent as the bell rang for class to begin. Mrs. Steinbeck introduced herself and immediately turned to the chalkboard and wrote her name, sharply but carefully striking the chalk on the board.

"I don't like to waste time, which is why permission slips for science lab were mailed to your homes two weeks ago for your parents to sign. They contained instructions stating that you were to have them signed and prepared for me today. I need everyone to get them out and, quietly and orderly, pass them to the front of each row."

Drew felt a small rush of pride. His mom had signed the permission slip, and he had remembered to bring it to school. But when he opened his folder, nothing was there. *Where is it?* He checked his pockets. Nothing. He looked in the other folder he had with him. Empty. *That's right*, he remembered. The permission slip was in his daily planner, which was still in his locker.

All the other students quietly passed their permission slips to the person in front of them. The room resembled a fluent assembly line, with Drew being the one kink. He hesitantly raised his hand.

"Yes?" said Mrs. Steinbeck when she noticed the limp arm in the air.

"Mrs. Steinbeck, mine's in my locker ..."

Drew could sense the silent gasps all around him. Mrs. Steinbeck's eyebrows rose. She lowered her head slightly and peered above her stylish glasses at Drew. He gulped and smiled awkwardly. Mrs. Steinbeck started as if she were about to berate the forgetful boy, but something restrained her from doing so, and her expression calmed – barely.

"Go get it and return quickly," she said. She pointed to a small table against the wall next to the door. "Take the hall pass." After a short pause, she looked at the nametag on his desk and coldly added, "This is not a good start, Andrew Daley."

Drew hustled down the hall as fast as he could without running, hoping that a quick trip to his locker wouldn't put him on Mrs. Steinbeck's bad side. As he entered his combination, he noticed a small boy with neatly-combed, copper hair standing on the other side of the hall a few lockers down. Drew couldn't tell if he was waiting for something or if he was completely lost.

"Um ..." The boy was trying to muster the strength to say something.

Drew turned from his locker. "Do you need help with something?"

"Yes," he responded shyly.

Drew figured the boy to be in kindergarten or first grade. It felt strange to Drew that he himself had been so small and clueless just a few years ago.

"I have to go to art class," the boy continued, "but I don't know how to get there."

"Oh, I can help you with that," said Drew. Students that young had one main teacher and only went to other classrooms for special classes like art and gym. The boy must have gotten separated from his class somehow. *There are probably a hundred ways a kid could get lost and separated from the rest of the class*, Drew thought.

"Well, the art room is in the Garuba wing, down on the first floor at the end of the school. You can go down those steps to the first floor, and then make a right and go past the cafeteria to the end of the hall. You could cut through the cafeteria, but It's locked sometimes. So you go past it through the double doors at the end of the hall, then make a right and the art room will be the third, no, the second room on your left."

The young boy stood with glazed eyes, trying to commit this path to his memory. Drew saw the confusion in his face.

"I'll just take you real quick," he said. "It's actually pretty confusing if you've never been there."

On the way to the art room, Drew asked the boy about himself. His name was Brady, and it was his first day in the building. Drew intently listened as Brady explained his horror story of getting separated from his kindergarten classmates. Drew was acting like a seasoned big brother, even though he didn't have any siblings.

He waited outside the door as Brady rejoined his class. Peering into the room, he saw some of last year's art projects still hanging by string and clothespins. Drew wouldn't be taking art this year because at Emerson Elementary, all fourth-graders had art and all fifth-graders had music. He lingered at the doorway for a moment before reversing his path and heading back up the stairs to Mrs. Steinbeck's classroom.

He set the hall pass down on the table by the door and turned to quietly head back to his seat.

"Why were you gone so long, Mr. Daley? Was there a complication?" said Mrs. Steinbeck, standing in the front of the room but facing Drew.

A few giggles rose to the surface of the room, but Mrs. Steinbeck turned her head sharply toward the class and revealed an icy glare that suffocated the laughter. She turned back to Drew, and a horrible feeling shot through him. *Oh no!* What had he left the room for in the first place? Mrs. Steinbeck's enraged stare at his empty hands answered his question. *The permission slip.* He had forgotten to get the permission slip from his locker.

"You think you can just leave my class and do whatever you want, is that it? You think it is okay to *lie* to me and pretend your permission slip is in your locker when you actually forgot it at home. Is that it, Mr. Daley?"

Drew shook his head. His eyes shifted nervously around the room. All the students sat with their heads forward but slightly down. They didn't seem to know where they were allowed to look.

"Return to your seat," said Mrs. Steinbeck.

"But I –"

"Return to your seat," she snapped, stabbing toward Drew's desk with her index finger.

Drew bowed his head and slipped into his chair, his heart pounding and his cheeks beet-red. He had done the last thing a kid at Emerson wanted to do – he had gotten on Mrs. Steinbeck's bad side.

A cloud of embarrassment clung to him the rest of the day. But when it was time for last period, Mr. Sawyer's familiar face finally eased the tension.

"Six more months, right, Drew?" Mr. Sawyer had said as Drew entered the classroom.

"Huh?"

"You guys are still counting down until the premiere of that zombie movie, right?"

"Oh yeah," said Drew. "I think six months is right."

He, Jeff, and Tommy had made their excitement known last school year when the *Zombie Days* premiere date was announced. Even though the movie wouldn't hit theaters until winter, the boys couldn't stop talking about it the entire last month of fourth grade.

"What's it called again?" Mr. Sawyer asked. "*Zombie Dudes?*"

"Zombie *Days*," Drew corrected him and laughed. "Trust me, it's gonna be awesome."

"Well, I guess I'll have to see it when it comes out then."

Mr. Sawyer simply had a way of getting through to Drew, and, thanks to him, the first day of school hadn't been so bad after all. Now, though, just three weeks into the school year, Drew was already behind in his favorite teacher's class.

Disappointed in himself, he turned on the lamp next to his bed, pulled out his science book, and turned to page 139. Even now, after all the interruptions of the day, it brought him peace. His breathing eased into a soft rhythm. After a few minutes, he put his book away, turned off his light, and fell asleep without a worry in the world.

Despite the peaceful sleep, with morning came the reminder that Drew would disappoint Mr. Sawyer by being unprepared for the first big assignment of the year.

As he dragged himself out the door, his mom said, "Wait, here you go," and handed him a one-dollar bill. "You and Jeff and Tommy are stopping at Melia's after school today, right?"

Melia's Market was a small convenience store owned by a living legend, Mr. Melia. The old man ran the store with his wife, and he was one of the most beloved people in Emerson. Drew and his friends loved going there. In the past, they had to be accompanied by an adult, but this year they were granted collective parental approval to stop at Melia's once a week on their way home from school. The boys had vowed to go to Melia's every Thursday for the entire school year. And although it was only the third week of the school year, Melia's Thursdays were already becoming a sacred tradition for them. Melia's housed lunch meat, small grocery products, and a number of miscellaneous items, but Drew and his friends were only interested in the candy behind the counter.

Now, in the instant his mom handed him that dollar bill, Drew knew who he would pick for his social studies project.

"Oh yeah, I almost forgot. Thanks, Mom." He gave her a kiss on the cheek and darted out the front door.

"Yes! It's perfect! I'll pick Mr. Melia!" he nearly shouted as he headed down the street.

A minute ago he was dragging his feet, dreading the day ahead of him. Now he was practically running, full of anticipation for social studies class. He knew Mr. Sawyer would be impressed with his choice. And when he went to Melia's after school, he could tell Mr. Melia about it. His smile spread wider as he thought about how flattered the old man would be.

Drew eagerly awaited social studies class all throughout the day. He scribbled through his math worksheet, sprinted through the warm-up laps in gym, volunteered to pass out the science worksheets (which he did in record time), inhaled his lunch, impatiently tapped his foot through a language arts lecture, sang several notes ahead of everyone in music class, and recited translations in Spanish so fast that his classmates assumed he was speaking fluently, all in hopes that the clock would somehow match his pace. His haste likely had the opposite effect, and made the day feel longer, but, at long last, the bell rang for the final period of the day to begin.

"Here's how we'll do this. I think the fairest way is to put all your names in a hat, which I've already done." Mr. Sawyer held out an old brown fisherman's hat filled with small slips of paper. "When I call your name, you let me know who you're choosing for your presentation."

Drew sat with a proud smile on his face, barely able to wait for Mr. Sawyer to call his name. He had already asked several of his classmates earlier in the day who they were picking. The results were two singers, one baseball player, one hockey player, and two actors. He also over-heard Mitchell telling Erin that he picked a racecar driver, someone Drew had never even heard of.

"Without further ado, the first pick goes to ... Tommy."

"Bryce Harper," Tommy announced.

"All right," said Mr. Sawyer as he marked it down on his paper. He reached into the hat and pulled out the next name. Then another, and another, and another. Drew wasn't too worried at first, and no one had chosen Mr. Melia, but his foot tapped a bit faster each time someone else's name was called.

Please just be me, he thought to himself.

"Zobby, you're up next."

Drew's impatience lessened at the mention of his friend's name. Zobby was a friendly, brown-haired girl who lived across the street from Drew's dad. Drew and Zobby had been friends for years. He didn't spend as much time with her as he did with Jeff and Tommy, but he felt just as comfortable around her as anyone. He knew she would choose someone worthwhile for her presentation.

"I'm picking Miss Elisa. I take music lessons with her."

Drew smiled at the pick and turned his attention back to his teacher.

"All right. Caleb is next," said Mr. Sawyer.

"I'm picking, uh, Mr. Melia, from Melia's Market," said Caleb.

Drew could not believe what he just heard. He turned around to see Caleb Monroe sitting right behind him with an absent expression on his face.

"Nice pick, Caleb. I like it. Mr. Melia is a really great guy and a great choice for your presentation," said Mr. Sawyer.

Drew was infuriated. *Mr. Sawyer should be proud of me, not Caleb.* Two more names were called, but Drew didn't even hear them. He was still turned around, trying to stare a hole through Caleb.

"What?" said Caleb with a hint of irritation.

"Next is Drew," Mr. Sawyer declared suddenly. Drew turned back around and looked up at his teacher.

"I picked Mr. Melia," he said in a defiant tone that surprised even himself.

"He was already chosen. Caleb picked him a minute ago. Who's your backup?"

"Backup?" said Drew. He had a hard enough time choosing *one* person. "Um ..."

"You know you were supposed to have a backup choice for this very reason," said Mr. Sawyer.

"Uh ..." Drew tried to think. He couldn't pick his parents, and he couldn't pick Mr. Melia. He knew plenty of *nice* people, but he also knew none of them were right for this assignment.

"Drew," said Mr. Sawyer, "who is your backup?"

Drew opened his mouth, hoping a name would jump from his lips. Instead, all he could say was, "I couldn't think of one."

Mr. Sawyer shook his head in disappointment. "You're going to have to pick someone. See me after class."

Drew sunk down in his seat. Mere minutes ago he was excited for social studies class to begin. Now he couldn't wait for it to end.

After the bell rang and the other students had left the classroom, Drew walked slowly to Mr. Sawyer's desk.

"Drew, you are the only student in the class who wasn't able to choose a role model."

"I know, but I picked Mr. Melia. I really do look up to him. And you said we should pick someone who inspires us, and –"

Mr. Sawyer motioned with his hand for Drew to stop talking.

"That's great, Drew, but Mr. Melia was chosen by someone else. I understand that you had planned on choosing Mr. Melia, but you have to adjust. Being able to make adjustments is just as important as making plans. You understand, right?"

"Yeah," Drew murmured, facing the floor.

"All right, good," said Mr. Sawyer. "Come Monday, I don't want another situation like we had with the you-know-what."

Drew lifted his head. *Oh man*, he thought. That was the day he had learned firsthand that poor preparation leads to embarrassment. Toward the end of the fourth-grade year, each student was to give a presentation on one of the 50 states. But as Drew walked into the class-room on his day to present, he realized he had forgotten his notecards and poster he made at home. And he really needed those notecards, because he didn't practice his presentation one time. He felt humiliated just thinking of the debacle. "Texas is, um, a big state," was how he began. "Its nickname is, uh, well, it has lots of sports teams ..."

"Yeah," Drew said to Mr. Sawyer, "we definitely don't want that."

"So let's come in tomorrow with an idea," said Mr. Sawyer. "Think of someone who inspires you to be a better person. There's got to be someone besides Mr. Melia. Don't think of it as a painful assignment, think of it as an opportunity to talk about someone you really look up to."

"Yeah, I'll figure it out." And just like that, he was back where he began.

On his way down the hall, he spotted Caleb at his locker shoving dirty gym clothes into his book bag. Drew approached him with a sense of curiosity.

"Hey, Caleb."

"'Sup?" Caleb responded. He tossed his head back and to the right to flip the dark hair from his eyes, though he didn't look away from his locker.

"Nothing really. So you're doing your report on Mr. Melia, huh? That's pretty cool."

"I guess," said Caleb, still without looking up. He was searching for something in his locker.

"What made you pick him?" Drew asked. He was excited to hear Caleb's answer. Tommy had been hanging out with Caleb recently, and Drew was starting to think that maybe it was for good reason.

"Well," said Caleb, "I was just gonna take a hockey player, but when I told my mom about it she said to pick Mr. Melia. She said nobody else would pick him, and Mr. Sawyer would probably eat that up. So I was like, whatever."

Drew's anger returned even stronger than before. "You picked him because your mom told you to?"

"Yeah, I guess. I mean, it's just a lame assignment anyways. I didn't really care," said Caleb. He found what he was looking for in his locker and stuck it in his book bag. "Later," he added before strolling down the hall and out the door.

Drew lingered near Caleb's locker for a few moments. He couldn't believe how indifferent everyone was about the assignment. *Maybe everyone else is right,* he thought.

As he circled back to his own locker, he found Zobby waiting for him.

"What'd Mr. Sawyer say?" she asked, jumping into a conversation.

"Not much. Just that I have to pick someone," said Drew. He exchanged some books and filled up his book bag. "And he mentioned the States project again."

"Oh, that's rough. I'm sorry. So, do you know who you're gonna pick?"

"That's the thing. I wanted to pick Mr. Melia. He was the first person who made sense to me. Tommy and Jeff just picked sports stars, but I don't really feel like they inspire me. And then Caleb only picked Mr. Melia 'cause his mom told him to, not because he actually cares."

"That's stupid."

"Yeah, everyone thinks this is so easy and I should just pick a celebrity or something. I dunno, maybe I should."

"No," said Zobby, "I don't think it's easy. I get what you mean about not wanting to pick some person you see in movies or on TV. That's why I picked Miss Elisa. I actually know her, ya know?"

Drew nodded and added a half smile.

"Don't worry about it," said Zobby. "You'll figure it out."

The fact that someone understood him, even if it was just a little bit, really made him feel like he was on the right path.

The bright September sun hit Drew in the eyes as he stepped outside. He pulled his faithful Pittsburgh Pirates baseball hat from his book bag and put it over top of his sandy-blonde hair. The hat, given to him as a birthday gift from his parents years ago, had a white front panel, and the golden capital 'P' on the front was outlined in black.

Weathered from years of wear, the hat had begun to show its age. The capital 'P' had a stain on the top left corner, the white front had collected so much dirt that it looked more beige than white, and the rest of the hat, which used to be jet black, had noticeably faded. Penny had tried to clean the hat several times, but it was no use – the stains were too deeply seated.

Jeff and Tommy were waiting for Drew at the bottom of the school steps.

"What did Mr. Sawyer say?" Jeff asked.

"Did he yell at you?" Tommy added.

"He just told me to pick someone," Drew said, rushing past them without breaking his stride.

"Oh, wait up," said Jeff as he and Tommy caught up.

"Why didn't you just pick a baseball player like I did?" asked Tommy.

Drew didn't say anything. His pace was so fast that the walk around the unusable bridge didn't take much time at all.

"Well," said Tommy, "at least it's time for Melia's. I wonder what I should get today. I got two bucks!"

He and Jeff stopped and turned toward the store, but Drew kept walking.

"Where are you going?" Jeff asked. "It's Thursday, remember?"

"I don't have any money," he lied. "And I have too much homework to do, and we have that science quiz tomorrow. I'm just going home." It was only week three, and Drew was already missing out on a Melia's Thursday.

"Um, all right," said Jeff, shooting Tommy a confused glance.

Tommy shrugged and said, "All right, later, Drew." Jeff and Tommy went into the store as Drew disappeared down the street.

◆

"What are you doing?" Jeff asked as he approached Drew before social studies class the following afternoon.

"Nothin'," said Drew, leaning against the wall several feet from Mr. Sawyer's classroom door.

"Well, the bell's gonna ring in like ten seconds. Why are you just standing out here?"

"Mr. Sawyer's gonna kill me," said Drew. "I still didn't pick anyone for my presentation."

"Oh. Wait, I forgot to tell you!"

"Tell me what?" asked Drew. The bell rang before Jeff could respond.

"Just c'mon, get in the room," he said, grabbing Drew's arm and pulling him through the doorway.

Drew followed closely behind Jeff, his head down, trying to use his friend as a shield from Mr. Sawyer's vision. Maybe if Mr. Sawyer didn't see him walk in, he would forget to ask him about his presentation. Drew kept his head down as he slipped into his seat. He didn't look at Mr. Sawyer. He didn't even look in the direction of his desk. He slouched down as low as he could without sliding off the chair. Then, to his delight, he heard an unexpected voice.

"Well, there's good news, and there's bad news ..."

Looking up, Drew saw that Mr. Mayberry, the resident substitute teacher, was standing in the front of the room, reciting his trademark introduction.

"The good news is it's Friday," he continued, "the bad news is you have me for a teacher today."

Most of the students chuckled, aware that Mr. Mayberry was actually friendly and fair. Written on the chalkboard behind him in giant letters was a reminder from Mr. Sawyer: ROLE MODEL PRESENTATIONS ARE MONDAY. BE PREPARED!

Drew looked to Jeff, who was already smiling back at him, and breathed a huge sigh of relief. *The good news,*

Drew thought to himself, *is that I have more time to pick my role model.*

Figuring there was no harm in enjoying his weekend, Drew spent Friday night with his dad. They went to Rizzo's Pizza for dinner, and later that night they watched a movie. He thought about telling his dad what he found in his science book but wasn't sure if he'd be interested. *Maybe no one will care about it like I do*, he thought. He once again decided to keep the secret to himself.

He went to Tommy's on Saturday for the sleepover. Instead of choosing a role model, organizing his ideas, and rehearsing a presentation, he spent the night eating pizza, telling jokes, and playing *Zombie Days* with Tommy and Jeff.

He didn't get home from Tommy's until Sunday afternoon. As he dragged his feet through the front door, he was hit with the guilt of neglecting his assignment. Tired from a sleepless night, he tried to think of a way to get out of the presentation altogether. Realizing that wasn't an option, he began to concede to the idea of picking a big sports star or celebrity, just like most of his classmates had done. He picked up the remote and turned on the TV. This was where everyone else seemed to find their answers. But after a few minutes of flipping through the channels, he tossed the remote in frustration.

Feeling defeated, he walked outside and began throwing a tennis ball against the garage door. With his glove on one hand and the ball in the other, he flung the ball against the door and positioned his body, with knees bent, to catch the ground ball each time it bounced back to him. As he threw the ball, he continued to try to think of someone else he could choose for his presentation. Drew liked baseball just as much as his friends did, probably even more, but he didn't feel that his favorite athletes were his role models. Rather, they were just really fun to watch. He didn't admire them the same way he admired his dad for his creativity, his mom for her ability to help people with their problems, or Mr. Melia for the kindness he showed to everyone who walked into his store.

He threw the ball harder. How was it that he had spent more time thinking about this assignment than anyone but had made less progress than everyone?

After a few minutes, Drew realized he had missed the bouncing ball quite a few times, which was unlike him. He noticed how windy it had become, and that the tennis ball was being pulled to the right each time he chucked it against the garage. But even after picking up on the wind pattern, he continued to misplay the erratic ball. It snuck past him again and rolled into the street.

As he went to grab it, he looked across the street and saw Mr. Johnston's flower arrangement proudly hung on his porch. Though he helped with the project, Drew had not understood the concept of the flower holder. However, upon seeing the finished product, he was taken aback by its beauty. The Johnstons' house was on the corner of the street, and each time a car turned onto Ernest Way, people would see what looked like a hundred flowers filling the wooden base. He thought back to the story of Mr. Johnston's wedding flowers and how surprised and excited his wife would be.

Drew smiled to himself and walked back over toward his garage to resume throwing the tennis ball. He decided that he would play his game for about five more minutes. If he was still unable to think of something in that time, he would go to his room, defeated, and begin putting together what he knew would be a below-average presentation on an athlete he didn't truly feel inspired him.

Each time the ball connected with the old wooden

door, it made a loud *thunk*, which Drew was used to after years of practice. But after he threw the ball one last time, the *thunk* was followed by an enormous *crash* behind him.

He looked all around but saw nothing out of the ordinary. Then he did a more thorough investigation by squinting his eyes. With his eyes peeled, he saw the cause of the crash and shuddered at the implications: Mr. Johnston's leaning flower bed had fallen to the ground. The wind must have unhooked one of the hinges connecting the crisscrossed wood to the house. Drew froze. He knew he couldn't fix the flower bed. And, seeing that Mr. Johnston's car wasn't in its usual spot in the driveway, Drew knew the old man was likely on his way home with his wife. He recalled that today was their anniversary, and now the big unveiling of countless hours of hard work would be ruined.

Drew figured he should go tell his mom what happened, even though he doubted she would be able to do anything about it. But as he turned around, something caught his eye. There was movement near the Johnstons' porch. Drew stepped back beside his garage so he couldn't be seen. He didn't know why, but he felt like hiding. For the next several minutes, he peered across the street and watched something amazing happen.

A wizard hadn't appeared and fixed the flower bed with a wave of his wand. And a superhero hadn't swooped down from the sky to save the day. But what Drew saw was just as impressive – in a way, more impressive.

And at that moment, Drew finally knew what to do for his role model presentation.

It was Monday afternoon, and Drew was sitting quietly in his seat. Caleb stood in the front of the classroom concluding his presentation, which sounded suspiciously like someone else had written it for him (especially considering he read the entire speech from notecards, not looking away from them once).

"All right, thank you, Caleb," said Mr. Sawyer, in a tone that sounded to Drew much less enthusiastic than when Caleb had originally chosen Mr. Melia. "Let's see, next is Drew."

Drew got up and walked to the front of the room.

"Who will you be telling us about today?" Mr. Sawyer asked. Despite the disappointments from last week, Mr. Sawyer looked at Drew with confidence, as if he meant to show Drew that he still believed in him.

"Well, I'm not exactly sure."

"Drew ..."

"I mean, I just don't know his name," Drew continued.

Several students looked around at each other in confusion. A few giggled, anticipating another "50 States" disaster.

"But you do have something prepared for us," Mr. Sawyer said, nodding.

"Oh, yeah, I do. I just don't know this guy's name. See, my neighbor across the street, Mr. Johnston, built this big wooden flower holder thing for his wife for their anniversary ..."

Mr. Sawyer leaned back in his chair and listened.

"And he filled it with these blue flowers, I forget what they're called, they had a weird name, but they're the flowers he gave her on their wedding day. The same kind of flowers, I mean. He was showing Tommy and me the other day when he was still working on it. And he put a lot of work into it and you could tell he was so excited for his wife to see it. Oh yeah, this was for their fiftieth wedding anniversary. But anyway, last night the wind blew it over. I was outside and one minute it was hanging up, and the next minute it was on the ground and a bunch of the flowers had spilled out. I felt so bad, but I didn't know what to do. And then this guy came jogging by. I have no idea who he was. The sun was going down, and he was wearing a hat, so I couldn't get a good look at him. But he stopped and took out his headphones and looked at what happened.

"Then he walked right up to the Johnstons' porch. Some of Mr. Johnston's tools were still there, and so was a little ladder. Then, I couldn't believe it, the guy set the ladder next to the flower bed, grabbed one of the tools, and climbed the ladder. He sort of fiddled with pegs on the house – that's where the flower holder connected to the house. I think the wind unhooked it from the pegs. Then he climbed down the ladder and switched the tool for a different one and did something to the flower bed. Finally, he picked up the flower bed and walked it up the ladder. He sort of struggled – the thing is pretty heavy – but he hung it back up.

"Then he climbed down the ladder, he fixed the flowers, and he even swept the dirt off the driveway so everything looked nice again. Then he put his headphones back in his ears and jogged down the street. And like ten seconds later, the Johnstons came pulling into their driveway. They got out of the car, and Mrs. Johnston was so surprised she started to cry – but in a good way.

"And I just figure, that's what I want to be like. Because even though no one was watching – except for me, but he didn't see me – even though no one was watching, this guy did the right thing and helped someone out. It wasn't to impress anyone. It wasn't, like, an act. Mr. and Mrs. Johnston didn't even know what happened. They came home and everything was okay."

Drew stopped, realizing that he might have been rambling, and looked at Mr. Sawyer to see if he understood.

The rest of the students looked at their teacher as well. After a number of predictable speeches, they relied on Mr. Sawyer's reaction to show them the verdict of Drew's speech. They knew it was *different*, but they weren't sure if it was good or bad.

Mr. Sawyer smiled and said, "The deed is everything, the glory is naught."

A state of confusion momentarily consumed the class.

"Not what?" asked Abigail.

"Let me rephrase," said Mr. Sawyer. "The deed is everything, the glory is nothing."

The class was silent again until Drew said, "Yeah, I get it. You shouldn't do a good deed just to get credit for it. You should just do it because it's right."

"Exactly," said Mr. Sawyer. He looked to the rest of the class. "That's the lesson Drew's presentation has taught us. You should never forget that your true character is determined by what you do when no one is watching, when no reward is at stake, when there's a chance no one else will ever know what you did." He turned to Drew and nodded. "Very good work, Drew."

Drew smiled and returned to his seat. At the end of class, Mr. Sawyer handed each student a half-sheet of paper with his or her grade for the presentation. When the bell rang and the room emptied, he had given a sheet to everyone except Drew. Thinking he had done well, but now second-guessing himself, Drew fidgeted in his seat as Mr. Sawyer walked toward him. With the sheet facing the floor so Drew couldn't see the grade, Mr. Sawyer said, "Before I commented on your presentation, did you think there was a chance you would get a bad grade because your presentation was unlike everyone else's?"

Drew simply nodded.

"And did you care about your grade, or were you more excited to talk about this mysterious runner?"

"Well, my parents want me to get good grades, and I know that's important. But it wasn't all I cared about. I wanted to give a presentation that really meant something to me. You said we should pick someone who inspires us, so that's what I did. I don't know who that guy was, but I know he inspired me to be a good person."

"That's it!" Mr. Sawyer exclaimed, pumping his fist in excitement. "That's what this assignment was all about." He smiled and handed Drew the sheet of paper with the grade still facing down. "And do me a favor. If you do happen to see this mysterious runner again, thank him. Far too often good things go unnoticed."

Drew nodded. He slid the sheet of paper into his folder and went straight to his locker. He removed his science book, opened it to page 139, and stared down at a pencil-drawn picture of a sunset over an ocean shore. The drawing covered no more than a quarter of page 139, but he could see that tremendous effort had gone into it. Whoever drew the picture had been deliberate with every detail. It was as though each shimmer in the sky, each ripple in the water, each grain of sand, was carefully accounted for. There was even a small sandcastle in the bottom left corner of the drawing.

Drew wasn't sure if he would ever see the runner again. And even if he did, he might not recognize him, because he never got a good look at the man's face. But there was someone he could find: the person who drew the picture. The picture had brought him so much comfort over the hectic last few days, and whoever had drawn it deserved to be thanked. Drew flipped to the front cover. He scanned the names of the book's previous owners to give himself a head start. He was now on a mission: find the Mystery Artist.

Nobody Gets Hurt

"Your mouths should be silent. You have two more minutes to study, and I suggest you use your time wisely," said Mrs. Steinbeck.

As the fifth-grade science teacher for over 30 years, as well as the most difficult teacher at Emerson Elementary, Mrs. Steinbeck commanded the respect of her class in a seemingly effortless manner. Her voice was tender and smooth; it might have been soothing had it not come from such an intimidating source. Her attire was reserved yet fashionable, and always perfectly coordinated. Her short, silver hair looked as if she stopped at a salon every morning, as each strand lay in the exact same place every single day (this prompted rumors that she wore a wig, but there was certainly no one brave enough to try and find out). And she always smelled of perfume – a powdery fragrance that occupied her classroom and left a trace of itself wherever she went.

But no matter how angelic her voice sounded or how stylish her wardrobe was, Mrs. Steinbeck was seen simply as the old, mean teacher. She demanded absolute focus from her students, bell to bell, day after day. She was strict, consistent, and thorough, and she expected the same kind of perfection from everyone around her. Although she had been due for retirement a few years back, Mrs. Steinbeck returned year after year, continuing to be a nightmare for her students.

As soon as she spoke, the talkative mouths fell silent and the students tried to cram in a few extra bits of information before their weekly science quiz.

Unlike his classmates, Drew was not studying. Instead, he was fixated on the drawing of a sunset over an ocean shore in his textbook. *How do the waves look so real?* He ran his fingers across the textured wave ripples, hoping to feel the water. Since he first discovered the drawing a couple of weeks ago, he had marveled at it as though he were walking into an art exhibit every time he opened his book.

"One minute left," said Mrs. Steinbeck.

But rather than review his notes, Drew flipped to the front of the book to once again remind himself of his mission: find the Mystery Artist. Five kids had owned the book before him: Jason Porter, Stacey Janofsky, Alexus Ballentine, Mike Hudock, and Skylar Jansen. Which of these five people had drawn the amazing picture?

Two names on the list stood out. Jason Porter was Tommy's older brother. Although Tommy and Drew were good friends, Drew never thought of Jason as very approachable. Jason, now in tenth grade, was kind of a tough guy, and Drew figured it unlikely that he was the Mystery Artist.

The other name he recognized was Skylar Jansen. She was the yellow-haired girl he had seen on his new way home from school – the girl Tommy had referred to as "the most popular girl in sixth grade." Drew knew he would get a chance to ask her sooner or later. Although Skylar was in middle school, Drew would still have an opportunity to see her at lunch. The elementary school and the middle school were attached by a common cafeteria, and fifth-graders and sixth-graders had lunch at the same time.

Also, he passed her house on his new route to and from school every day.

It seemed important to find the artist, even though he wasn't sure what he would say if he did. He felt connected to the picture, as though he were meant to find it – almost like the picture had been drawn specifically for him. There was just something about that pencil-drawn ocean that eased his scrambled mind.

The nameless runner who fixed Mr. Johnston's flower arrangement could've been just about anyone, but the Mystery Artist had to be one of those five previous owners of the book.

"Time is up. Books away. The only thing on your desk should be a pencil. As always, you have ten multiple choice questions, and you have fifteen minutes to take the quiz. Today's quiz is on major bodies of water." Mrs. Steinbeck spoke with precision, enunciating each letter, consonant and vowel, as though she were interviewing for a broadcasting job. She walked up and down the aisles and placed a quiz on each student's desk, faced down. "When I tell you, you will turn your paper over and begin your quiz. Keep your eyes on your own paper. You have fifteen minutes, and your time begins ..." she said, with her eyes glued to her gold watch, "now."

Mrs. Steinbeck continued to pace steadily throughout the room, her hands clasped behind her back and her narrowed eyes searching for suspicious behavior.

After answering the first five questions, Drew lifted his head to check the time. As he glanced at the clock on the wall, he saw Trevor Lambert whispering something to Jeff. Immediately Drew looked for Mrs. Steinbeck. She would give both Trevor and Jeff detention if she saw them talking during a quiz. Luckily for them, though, she was on the opposite side of the room with her back turned.

Drew put his head down and covered his forehead

with his hand, as though he were concentrating on his quiz, but his green eyes were locked in on Trevor and Jeff. When Mrs. Steinbeck turned to face the boys, it looked as though nothing were out of the ordinary. But once she turned around again, Drew noticed Jeff dropping his left arm, which had been guarding his paper. Trevor, who sat next to Jeff (and in front of Drew), was now searching Jeff's paper to find his answers for each question.

"One minute left," Mrs. Steinbeck declared, sending a wave of panicky jitters through the handful of students still working. Drew still had three questions to go and knew he needed to focus all his energy to get through them in time.

"Time is up. Pencils down."

Drew had only finished nine of the ten questions, but he quickly filled in 'B' for number ten without reading it. He had imagined that, after the quiz, he would be focusing his thoughts on the unknown artist from his book, but instead he was consumed with what he had seen Jeff doing.

<hr />

After science class was lunch. Drew wanted to ask Jeff about what happened, but with teachers and other students hovering all around, he couldn't risk anyone overhearing, so he waited until they went outside for recess.

Tommy had a football he'd brought from home. He ran to the far end of the fenced-in pavement and yelled "Catch!" to Jeff. Jeff caught the ball on the run and passed it to Drew. The three usually split into a triangle while catching, but Drew walked over toward Jeff so he could talk to him. Tommy didn't seem to mind, as he simply alternated who he threw the ball to each time.

"I saw what happened during the science quiz. What was that all about?"

Jeff's cheeks reddened. "What was I supposed to do?"

"Jeff, this is Steinbeck we're talking about! You know

how much trouble you'd get in if she caught you?"

"I know," Jeff said sheepishly.

"Then why'd you let him copy?"

"Well ... did I really have a choice?" His words were meek, and Drew immediately felt bad for his friend.

"Couldn't you pretend like you didn't hear him or something?"

Jeff caught the ball and held onto it as he answered. "I did. But then we made eye contact. And he was telling me before class that he didn't have a chance to study."

"Come on, Jeff!" yelled Tommy.

Jeff chucked the ball to him and continued. "I just don't wanna get beat up. So I made sure Mrs. Steinbeck wasn't looking whenever I dropped my arm. I was real careful."

"Wait, did he say he would beat you up?"

"Drew, look at me. Trevor's a giant. He would've pounded me if I didn't let him copy."

"Have you ever *seen* him pound anybody?"

"I don't have to," said Jeff. "He's twice my size, he plays football, and he accidentally knocked Emma down in kickball last week running the bases, remember? She had to go to the nurse. And he didn't even *mean* to hit her. I'm sure if he *meant* to hit me, it would be way worse."

Drew pictured a fight between Jeff and Trevor and shuddered at the thought. Jeff was average-sized, and Trevor was by far the biggest kid in the fifth grade. Not only was he much taller than Jeff, but he might truly have weighed almost twice as much.

"Well, I don't know, man. You could've got in a lot of trouble."

"I know," said Jeff. "I just didn't know what to do. He was telling me about how he broke Kyle Olinski's wrist at football practice. At practice! Not even in a game. And Kyle's in sixth grade. Trevor plays on the older team 'cause he's so big. They don't even let him play with other fifth-graders. Then he said all this stuff this morning about not wanting to fail the science quiz 'cause he's already failing math. I'm telling you, I had no choice."

Drew spent the rest of the day trying to figure out a solution. He thought about confronting Trevor himself, or even telling Mrs. Steinbeck about it, but he figured either way it would result in a pounding.

Lying in bed that night, Drew finally made his decision: he would do nothing. After all, this was just a one-time issue. Trevor didn't study, so he pressured Jeff to help him cheat. Fortunately, they didn't get caught. Drew was able to rest his tired eyes knowing the problem was over. He could now concentrate on more important things, like the Mystery Artist. He fell asleep that night brainstorming how to go about asking Jason Porter, Tommy's brother, if he was the one who drew the picture.

A week passed, and it was time for another science quiz. Mrs. Steinbeck issued the same instructions she did every week. "Time is up. Books away. The only thing on your desk should be a pencil. As always, you have ten multiple choice questions, and you have fifteen minutes to take the quiz ..."

A few minutes into the quiz, Drew lifted his head to check the clock and saw Jeff's head turned slightly to the right, in the direction of Mrs. Steinbeck. She had her back toward him, so he dropped his left arm, and Trevor leaned over to copy his answers, just like the week before.

The rest of the afternoon was a daze. Drew barely ate his lunch and chose not to play basketball with his friends during recess. He figured other students tried to cheat sometimes, but he never thought Jeff would. Most kids are taught that cheating is wrong, but Drew had been taught *why*. He always remembered his lesson on cheating because of how his dad had explained it to him.

About a year ago, his dad was having a conversation with Ken, the neighbor who lived with his wife in the other half of Mr. Daley's duplex. The two men were talking about performance-enhancing drugs in baseball. Drew loved baseball, so he moved from the swing on the front porch toward the steps to hear what they were saying. Though he didn't know the technical terms his dad and Ken were talking about, he could tell that both men were frustrated. After they finished talking, Ken went into his garage and Drew stood there, silent, hoping his dad would continue. Mr. Daley could sense Drew's curiosity and tried to explain the situation the best way he knew how.

"It's not just the drugs, it's what they stand for. Baseball's a pure game, or at least it was, and those guys who used those drugs took away from the game being pure. And any records they break aren't truly theirs, you see?"

"Well, I guess so."

Seeing the look of confusion on his son's face, Mr. Daley continued: "Here's the thing, as a person, you've gotta be ... you've gotta be authentic. Being authentic is just being you. It's natural, it's genuine ... it's *real*. See what I'm saying? When you cheat, whether it's in a game or on a test in school, you aren't being you. You're being someone else. You know why I never yell at you when you don't do great on a test?"

Drew shook his head side to side.

"It's because I know it's you taking that test. I don't know about you, bud, but I'd rather get a C that I earned than an A that I didn't. So when you have your own baseball cards one day with your picture on the front, the numbers on the back will be yours, nobody else's."

Drew replayed that scene in his head while his classmates played basketball until the bell rang. Jeff, one of the kids playing, looked over at Drew every few seconds, but

Drew wouldn't meet his eye line.

He felt like he would explode if he talked to Jeff, so he avoided him all afternoon. He tried to pack and repack his book bag in hopes that his friends would begin walking home without him, but they were waiting for him at the bottom of the school's steps. As Drew emerged from the building, he thought of all the things he wanted to say to Jeff: how stupid he was being, how he was going to get caught, and why cheating was wrong. But he didn't get a chance to say any of those things, because Jeff spoke first.

"Listen, Drew, I talked to Trevor before homeroom this morning. He asked me if I studied for the quiz and I told him I did. He was like, 'Aw, good.' Then he started talking about Kyle Olinski again and how he broke his wrist. Kyle can't play the rest of the season. I know he did it by 'accident,'" said Jeff, framing the word in the air with finger quotes, "and everything, but I think he was giving me a warning: 'If you don't let me copy, you're next.'"

Tommy looked up from his phone. "Whoa, whoa, whoa, what are you *talking* about?"

"You didn't tell him?"

"No, I figured you did," said Drew.

For the first time since the bridge had closed, the long walk home was convenient. Drew and Jeff needed the entire 15 minutes to fill Tommy in. They were still discussing it when they reached the end of Jeff's street.

"It's like he has nothing better to do than ruin my life," said Jeff.

"Maybe he don't have time to study 'cause he's trying out to be an extra in *Zombie Days*," said Tommy. "The kid's so pasty white he *looks* like a zombie!"

The boys laughed at Trevor's expense while Tommy stuck out his tongue, rolled his eyes back, and dragged his feet through the heaps of golden leaves piled along the curb.

"Well, what are you gonna do?" Drew asked Jeff.

"I dunno," Jeff murmured.

Drew sighed. He realized now that Jeff was stuck in a situation beyond his control.

"So ..." said Tommy, raising his thick eyebrows in uncertainty.

"Well," said Drew. He didn't have a plan, but he sensed Jeff and Tommy were relying on him to figure out the next step. "My dad's picking me up in a little to go out to dinner. You two are hanging out tonight, right?" The boys nodded. "Try to think of something over the weekend. I'm not sure if I'll be home tomorrow or not. Either way, we gotta figure out a way to help Jeff get out of this. But remember, let's make sure we don't talk about it in school. No use getting caught *that* way."

"Yeah," said Tommy, "that'd be the worst way to get caught cheating – when you're just talking about it and not even doing it."

That night, Drew and his dad went to Rizzo's Pizza, Drew's favorite place to eat. He considered asking his dad for advice but wasn't sure how to do so without telling on Jeff. He brought up baseball, hoping to nudge his dad toward the topic of the "authentic," but it never came up. Still, the two of them had a good evening.

But later that night, as he tried to fall asleep in his bed at his dad's place, one thought was racing to the next. *If we don't do anything to stop Trevor, they'll eventually get caught and Jeff will get in big trouble. If I tell Mrs. Steinbeck and she confronts Trevor, Trevor will think Jeff told on him and then he'll beat Jeff up the next day. Jeff would never forgive me. If I tell Dad, he might tell Mr. Gray, then Mr. Gray would tell Mrs. Steinbeck and Trevor will still think Jeff told on him. We can't risk Trevor thinking Jeff told on him. Could Mr. Sawyer help?*

No, he'd still have to go through Mrs. Steinbeck …
Everything seemed to lead to Jeff getting in trouble, and Drew knew he couldn't let that happen. Besides, Trevor was the one doing something wrong. If only there were a way to get Trevor to back off without him thinking Jeff had anything to do with it.

After an hour of tossing and turning, the picture from the science book popped into Drew's mind. He sat up and turned the key-shaped knob on the light next to his bed. He looked around his room before remembering that he hadn't brought his science book to his dad's. Disappointed that he couldn't look at the picture before he fell asleep, he shut off the light, closed his eyes, and tried to actually hear the waves in the drawing. Within minutes, he drifted asleep.

Instead of hanging out with Jeff and Tommy, he decided to spend the weekend at his dad's. On Saturday afternoon, while they were playing catch in the front yard, Mr. Daley invited Zobby to join. When Mr. Daley went inside to get some drinks, Drew considered asking Zobby for advice about Trevor but decided against it. He knew he could trust her to keep the secret, but he felt like he would betray Jeff by letting anyone else in on it.

On Sunday, Drew and his dad finished up their volunteer work at Emerson Park. Over the summer, Mr. Daley had decided to help with a community project to renovate the old park. He was an architect's apprentice. He once had an office job but found himself unsatisfied. About six years ago, before he and Penny divorced, he changed his career entirely, planning to one day become an architect.

Due to his architectural background, he was given the job of constructing the swing set, and he asked Drew to help. The two of them worked on building the swing set all summer long, and Drew even got to paint it after they finished. When they were at the park on Sunday, Drew snuck a peek under the tarp that was covering the swing set, and he was filled with mounting excitement for the reopening of the park at the upcoming Fall Festival.

The weekend with his dad was just what Drew needed to escape all the anxiety caused by the cheating incident. He went to school on Monday feeling refreshed. For the first time in almost two weeks, he was able to greet Jeff free of awkwardness.

"What's up, man? How was your weekend?"

Jeff looked slightly surprised at the casual greeting. "Um, good. Me and Tommy and Caleb went to the mini golf course on Saturday. It was okay, even though Caleb acted like he was playing hockey instead of golf and we almost got kicked out."

As the boys retrieved their books from their lockers, Drew saw Trevor lumbering toward Jeff with a big grin across his face.

"Hey, how was your weekend?" the burly bully asked Jeff.

"Uh, good."

"Yeah, I had to study for this math test all weekend. I hate math. I'm way better in language arts. And you know I'm pretty bad in science sometimes, too," Trevor said with what appeared to be a laugh. Surprisingly, his laugh was squeaky and high-pitched, the last thing Drew expected from a big tough guy.

Jeff forced an awkward laugh. "Ha, yeah, well, I gotta go. Almost time for homeroom."

"All right, see ya, buddy," said Trevor, and he gave him a hard pat on the back before departing. His big paw landed heavily between Jeff's shoulder blades, causing him to stumble forward and nearly drop his books.

Now, having seen Trevor's intimidation tactics firsthand, Drew felt even worse for Jeff than before. Something had to be done. He spent most of the morning drawing pictures in his notebook and trying to come up with ways to get Jeff out of this dilemma, but every solution seemed to lead to the same inevitable conclusion: the big bully pulverizing Jeff into a fine powder. By the time Drew got to science class, he couldn't think of anything except that good-for-nothing Trevor, and how he was ruining his best friend's life.

"Mr. Daley? I said Mr. Daley." Mrs. Steinbeck had called on him, but he hadn't even heard the question.

"Um ..."

As Drew tried to stall, Trevor leaned back in his chair, stretched his huge, pasty arms as if yawning, then turned his head to cover his mouth with his shoulder as he whispered, "Condensation."

"Uh, condensation?" said Drew.

"Correct. Now stop daydreaming and start taking notes," said Mrs. Steinbeck, holding her glare on him for an extra second before moving on.

Drew and Jeff exchanged baffled glances. How could Trevor, the cheater, know that answer?

After class they ran to the cafeteria, shoveling down their meals so they could get outside to talk. Tommy had brought a basketball. Even though a pickup game was forming on the near court, the three boys traveled down to the far court for privacy.

"So, did you tell him my plan?" Tommy asked Jeff.

Jeff clearly didn't like Tommy's plan. "No, I didn't get a chance. But I –"

"Come on, man," Tommy interrupted. "It's awesome. So listen to this, Drew. Jeff can't tell Mrs. Steinbeck 'cause then Trevor will pound him. He can't tell his parents 'cause his parents will tell Mrs. Steinbeck. And he can't talk to Trevor 'cause Trevor will just pound him and keep copying off him ..."

Drew was impressed. It seemed like Tommy had contemplated the problem just as much as he had.

"So the best idea is to change seats," Tommy continued. "That way no one knows Trevor was cheating, and Jeff don't get his face rearranged."

Drew ran that idea through his head. "Yeah, maybe that'll work."

"No," said Jeff, "wait for how I have to do this."

"Yeah, well, the thing is, we always gotta sit in the assigned seats Mrs. Steinbeck gave us, right?"

"Right."

"Yeah," said Tommy, "so all he has to do is tell Mrs. Steinbeck he needs a seat near the door 'cause he got explosive diarrhea, so he might have to run to the bathroom at any second." He was laughing so hard he could barely get the words out.

Jeff rolled his eyes, obviously unamused by Tommy's bright idea.

"Well," said Drew, "maybe you *should* try that. I mean, we don't have a better idea."

"No, man, I'm not saying that! Besides, Mrs. Steinbeck would probably call my mom to make sure it's true. She'd probably want a note from my doctor or something."

"Yeah, you're right," said Drew. "But changing seats might not be a bad idea. Maybe there's another way ..."

"I dunno, man. Mrs. Steinbeck's so strict about everything, you know? If I ask her to change my seat, she'll still need to know why, right? Besides, the whole class is full, so there's no extra seats. Someone else would have to move too, and she'll never let that happen."

"Eh, good point," said Drew. "I just don't know what to do. And what was up with him knowing that answer today?"

"I dunno."

"He probably accidently learned something copying off you," Tommy joked.

The boys laughed and began shooting basketball. A few others came down to play along, and without a word, the boys knew their conversation was over.

A few more days passed. The Trevor issue continued to weigh on Drew's mind, but he couldn't imagine what Jeff was going through. Thursday night, as Drew told his mom he was up in his room studying, he was actually plotting how to get his friend out of this mess. After hours of brainstorming, he finally figured it out: the perfect plan. Mrs. Steinbeck wouldn't know Jeff was helping Trevor cheat, Drew's parents and Jeff's parents would never find out, and Jeff wouldn't get thrashed by Trevor. The problem would be eliminated.

And best of all, Drew thought, *nobody gets hurt.*

He took a deep breath and exhaled slowly. He rubbed his thumb and index finger together, as though he were trying to feel the sand from the drawing in his science book. Though he didn't understand how, the picture continued to soothe him. With the picture in his head and the imaginary sand between his fingers, he fell asleep.

The next day, just before Mrs. Steinbeck began her pre-quiz ritual, Drew walked to the front of the room to grab a tissue. Many students had their ears covered and their eyes glued to their books. Concentrating on getting a few extra minutes of studying in before the quiz, his classmates didn't even seem to notice that he had stood up. Even Trevor appeared to be studying.

With his pencil in his left hand, Drew blew his nose and walked back toward his seat. But before reaching his destination, he dropped the pencil. He quickly scanned the room and saw that nobody was paying attention to him. So, as planned, he knelt down to pick up his pencil with his left hand, and with his right hand he slid a small piece of paper onto Trevor's chair next to his leg. Drew's heart started beating hard. He quickly sat down and tried to collect his wits before anyone noticed.

"When I tell you, you will turn your paper over and begin your quiz. Keep your eyes on your own paper. You have fifteen minutes, and your time begins ... now."

Drew's nervous hand trembled. He could barely fill in the bubbles without scribbling outside the lines. Mrs. Steinbeck circled the room like a hawk.

To Drew's dismay, she didn't see the paper sticking out from under Trevor's pant leg on her first round. Once her back was turned again, Jeff dropped his left arm. Trevor didn't react, but Drew assumed he was just being careful. *The big bully's been cheating so much that he's actually getting pretty good at it.*

On Mrs. Steinbeck's second lap, she stopped next to Trevor's desk and said, "Mr. Lambert, a word."

Trevor looked stunned.

"Uh, yes, Mrs. Steinbeck?" he said in his most polite voice.

By this point, most of the other students' attention had shifted from their quizzes to Trevor. Drew, afraid of arousing suspicion from Mrs. Steinbeck, did his best to look as confused as everyone else. His heart was pumping so hard that he half-suspected she could hear it.

"What is under your leg, Mr. Lambert?"

"My leg?" Trevor felt around on his seat and found the little piece of paper. He picked it up, looked at the words written on it, and closed his eyes. Drew could see the giant's oversized hands shaking as he held the paper.

"What, may I ask, is that?" said Mrs. Steinbeck. Her words hung in the air, demanding to be answered.

"It's ..." Trevor's desperate eyes searched the room for a lifeline. His classmates stared back at him, amazed at the horror of the situation. Drew looked out the window, afraid that eye contact with the bully would give him away.

Mrs. Steinbeck held out her hand, and Trevor placed the crinkled paper in her palm. She took the paper and examined it carefully. Then she scanned the room herself, looked back down at Trevor, and said, "Thank you for not making this any more difficult. At least you didn't *lie* about it, too. Go to the principal's office, Mr. Lambert."

Trevor's mouth opened but his vocal chords continued to betray him. Finally surrendering, he gathered his things, averted his watery eyes from his classmates, and left the room.

The last remaining sound in the room was the reverberation from Trevor shutting the door. The students' heads turned from the boy, to the door, and now to the only person standing. Mrs. Steinbeck once again cast her gaze over the rest of the students, this time for several awful seconds. Then she picked up the cheater's quiz from his desk, held it in front of her by pinching the top with her index fingers and thumbs, and tore it in half. The ripping of the single piece of paper shattered the silence and struck fear into every student in the room. Then Mrs. Steinbeck simply looked at her watch and said to the class, "Six minutes left. I suggest you continue with your work."

Drew couldn't believe it. His plan had worked. He was filled with a mixture of feelings: pride, relief, and also confusion. When he envisioned how the events would unfold, he figured Trevor would make a scene and lash out. It was strange that he didn't put up a fight. But as puzzling as that was, Drew was too satisfied with how wonderfully things turned out to worry about it. Now, Jeff wouldn't get beat up or get caught cheating, and no one had to know how the cheat sheet ended up with Trevor. Drew had decided the night before that he wouldn't tell anyone – not even Jeff – that he was the one who planted the cheat sheet on Trevor. He felt like the runner who had helped Mr. Johnston, not needing the recognition to do the right thing. *Like Mr. Sawyer said, the deed is everything, the glory is nothing.*

At lunch, the boys couldn't wait to get to the playground to talk, so they whispered at the lunch table.

"Can you believe that big dummy? He's so stupid that he tried to use a cheat sheet on top of copying," said Tommy.

"I'm just glad I'm out of this mess," said Jeff. "Now that he got caught cheating, Mrs. Steinbeck and every other teacher will watch every move he makes. Even Trevor wouldn't be dumb enough to cheat again."

Drew barely contributed to the conversation. His joy was in knowing that he had saved Jeff from serious trouble. He did stop to think that he didn't study last night because he was concentrating on his plan, but he was okay with it. A failed quiz was worth helping out his best friend.

The three boys ended up playing video games the majority of the weekend. Things were finally back to normal. The tension and worrying of the previous few weeks was gone for good, and Drew knew it was all thanks to him.

Monday morning, Drew settled into his seat in science class, his body still overheated after an intense game of capture-the-flag in gym class. As Mrs. Steinbeck began taking attendance, he noticed that Trevor's seat was empty. *He wasn't in gym, either,* he realized. Then he turned his attention to his science book. He opened to the drawing of the ocean shore and wondered which of the previous owners could have drawn the magnificent picture. He was paying just enough attention to Mrs. Steinbeck to say "here" when his name was called.

He thought he'd better copy the five potential artists'

names onto another piece of paper so he could carry it around with him. But before he could do so, he heard Mrs. Steinbeck say something strange: "Trevor ... well, obviously he will not be with us today."

The heat that had disappeared from Drew's body came flooding back. His nerves were on fire and his heart was beating fast, similar to when he had planted the cheat sheet on Trevor's chair. He frantically tried to dissect what she had said. *If she emphasized "obviously" then she knows he'll be gone for a while, but if she emphasized "today," maybe he's just sick.*

Drew thought about talking to Jeff and Tommy about Trevor's absence at lunch but figured neither of them would care. Besides, he was desperate to keep his secret. He realized that he couldn't even tell this to his best friends – not ever.

Suddenly, a short, pudgy classmate named Jonathan came rushing over to their table.

"Tell me you guys heard," Jonathan said, out of breath yet still attempting to whisper.

"What are you *talking* about?" asked Tommy.

"About Trevor," Jonathan clarified. "He got suspended for cheating on that science quiz. He might even get kicked out of school for good."

"Are you serious?" asked Jeff.

"Yeah, he was using cheat sheets all year," said Jonathan. "Everyone knows it. He had to come to school over the weekend to have a meeting with Mrs. Steinbeck and the principal." Jonathan was obviously happy to find an audience for his gossip.

"Man, how bad would that be? My parents would kill me if they caught me cheating," said Tommy, laughing.

"Yeah," Jonathan continued, "and his parents aren't gonna let him play football anymore. Jada lives on his street, and she said she was talking to Trevor's sister, and

Trevor's sister said she had to leave the house because Trevor was getting screamed at so bad. But –"

"Boys," boomed a voice from behind them, "I didn't hear you talking about rumors, did I? That will not be tolerated, not even in the lunchroom. Mind your own business."

"Sorry, Mr. Barker," said the boys. Without another word, Jonathan waddled back to his normal seat.

Mr. Barker's words reminded Drew that the school had recently begun a new campaign against rumors. The entire school had an assembly at the beginning of the year. They watched a short video about the problems rumors can cause, and then a guest speaker, a young woman just out of college, talked about rumors. There were now flyers posted all over the school that said "Rumors Ruin Lives," and Drew knew this was important to remember. He also knew that at least one thing Jonathan said wasn't true. Trevor hadn't been using a cheat sheet all year long – he hadn't been using a cheat sheet at all.

As Drew ate his peanut butter and jelly sandwich at the silent lunch table – all the boys now afraid to make a sound – he looked around. He saw a yellow-haired girl walking to the lunch line from the middle school side of the cafeteria. In her left hand was a pink notebook on which the name Skylar Jansen was written in neat, sparkly letters. Every time Drew had seen Skylar, he had been with Tommy and Jeff. He hadn't had a chance to speak to her alone – until now.

"I'm gonna grab another chocolate milk," he said, hopping up from his chair. He had seen Jason twice since discovering he was a potential artist, but both times he chickened out and was unable to ask him. Jason was intimidating, but something about Skylar seemed friendlier to Drew. Besides, luck had been going his way.

"Hey, you're Skylar, right?" he said without an ounce of nervousness.

She looked down at her folder, which she was now holding close to her chest with her left arm. "How'd you guess?"

Her sarcastic tone may have thrown Drew off on another day, but not today. After all this time, he was still no closer to finding the Mystery Artist, and he wasn't going to blow this chance.

"I think I have your science book. I mean, the one you had last year."

"Is that so?" she said, sounding uninterested.

"Yeah, and I don't like science class, but I love the book. I don't know if you ever noticed, but there's this awesome drawing in there."

Skylar's expression changed. A glow seemed to flicker in her light green eyes.

"It's a drawing of a beach," Drew continued with growing excitement. "It's just in pencil, but it's one of the best pictures I've ever seen."

"I loved that picture," said Skylar, smiling. "When I got bored in Mrs. Steinbeck's class I would always flip to page ..."

"One thirty-nine," Skylar and Drew said in unison.

Drew couldn't believe it! His search was over. He had found the Mystery Artist.

"So, are you the artist?" he asked, positive the answer was yes. He was already preparing to thank Skylar for drawing the picture.

"Oh, no, I'm not an artist. But I did like the picture," she said, glancing over at her lunch table, as if she were checking to see if her friends were still there.

"Oh," said Drew. The simple words crushed him, but he decided to keep talking to Skylar. After all, she did like the picture, and it's always nice to find someone who likes the same things you do. They talked a little about the picture, and Drew told her about passing her house every day because of the bridge closure.

"Yeah, there are so many people passing by my house ever since they closed that bridge," she said. "It's kinda funny. I people-watch from my front porch sometimes."

Drew considered telling her about his search, but as soon as she paid for her soft pretzel, she said, "See ya," and hurried back to her table.

Drew was greeted at his table by the shocked faces of Jeff and Tommy. They couldn't believe he had just talked to an older girl. And not just any older girl – this was Skylar Jansen. Drew didn't see it like that, though. He was simply on his mission. And although Skylar wasn't the Mystery Artist, Drew was now one step closer to finding out who was.

During Spanish class that afternoon, he wrote the five potential artists' names on a blank notecard he found in his locker. Then he crossed out Skylar Jansen's name with a black marker. Without Señora Machado noticing, Drew pulled his wallet from his pocket. The wallet was one of his most prized possessions, given to him by his cousin Peter, who lived in Florida. Last summer, when Drew and his mom were visiting Drew's grandparents in Orlando, Peter bought a sleek new wallet at the mall and gave Drew the old one.

The wallet was worn and well-used, but it was still functional. The brown leather was smoother in some sections than in others. When the tri-fold wallet unfolded there was a small pouch on the right flap that could only be opened by a button-like snap. Drew had been keeping his loose change in the pouch, but he quietly removed the coins and slid them into his pocket. Then he put his list inside his wallet's hidden pouch. He wiggled the wallet back into his pocket and tried to refocus his attention on class, but all he could think about now was how much closer he was to finding the Mystery Artist.

Drew stowed away in his room until his mom called him down for dinner. The meal was already on the table as Drew sat down.

"We're eating a little early tonight because I have plans, remember?" said Penny.

"Yeah."

"And I was running a little late getting ready, so we only have about fifteen minutes before your dad comes to pick you up."

"That's fine."

"So what happened with Trevor Lambert?"

Drew stared at his mom in amazement, a string of spaghetti dangling from his mouth.

"Mrs. Gray called me to ask about the next PTA meeting and ended up telling me Trevor got suspended. That's why I'm running late." She leaned over and poured some milk into Drew's glass. Drew remained quiet.

"Well, are you going to tell me what happened?" his mom asked playfully.

"I don't know. I think he got caught with a cheat sheet or something."

Drew shoved more spaghetti into his mouth, hoping to avoid answering any more questions. He kept his eyes down, but he could feel his mom's gaze on him. He expected her to rattle off more questions, but none came.

"My friend Donna – you've met her – she and I are going to see a play tonight. I haven't been out with her in two years, and we've been planning this night ever since we heard *A Doll's House* was being performed downtown. We both love that play."

"If you've already seen it, why do you wanna see it again?" Drew asked, temporarily forgetting that they had been talking about Trevor seconds ago.

"Why do you watch your favorite zombie movies over and over again? Part of the reason is because it's simply enjoyable. But more than that, the play is different every time I see it. The first time I saw it I was about fifteen, and I thought it was about women's rights. Then when I was eighteen I thought it was about individuality and the pursuit of finding yourself. The last time I saw it, about five years ago, I thought it was about selfishness."

"So which one is right?" Drew asked.

"That's the beauty of it, Drew. It's all of them. I'm interested to see what I think this time. See, it depends what perspective you're looking at something from. Sometimes, if you look at a situation from one view, you think you can see who's good and who's bad. But then, if you look at it from another person's view, the roles are reversed. You have to think about something more than once if you really want to understand it. Maybe I'm not making any sense. Either way, finish up your dinner. Your dad will be here soon."

While Drew and his mom finished their spaghetti, Drew thought about what she had said. Maybe he needed to view this situation from another perspective. Maybe from Trevor's perspective, Drew was the bad guy.

As Penny was cleaning up the kitchen, there was a knock at the door.

"That's your dad. Let him in, then go upstairs and get everything you need for tonight. And your medicine is right here on the table. Don't forget it."

Drew did as he was told and quickly ran upstairs to grab his things while his dad stepped into the kitchen. He wasn't often privy to conversations between his parents, so he tried to listen when he had the chance. He crept halfway down the stairs so he could eavesdrop.

"Excited for your big night out?" Ryan was asking.

"Very much," said Penny. "Thanks for looking after

Drew tonight. It really helps out."

"Don't mention it. I'll hang out with Drew anytime you want. In fact, I think you should go out with Donna more often," Ryan said playfully.

"Still, thanks," said Penny. "But before Drew comes back down ..." Her voice changed to a whisper, but Drew could still make out what she was saying. "I think something's bothering him. A boy at school, the big kid, Trevor, got caught cheating. When I asked Drew about it, his face turned red, so I dropped it. It might be nothing, but if you can talk to him about it, that'd be great."

"Yeah, no problem."

"Don't pressure him, though. He always gets defensive when we try to push him."

"I know that."

Just then Drew decided to head downstairs, stomping loudly enough for his parents to hear him coming.

"And I'll go over his homework with him tonight and have him in bed at a reasonable hour. And I don't start work until ten tomorrow, so I'll just take him to school," said Ryan. "Hey, have fun tonight, and tell Donna I said 'hello.'"

"I will."

"Give your mom a hug, bud. We gotta get rollin.'"

Drew went to his dad's place that evening. After he finished his homework, the two of them watched a movie. His dad asked him questions about school, but Drew avoided saying anything about Trevor and answered each question as if everything were fine.

He knew his mom was still concerned, so over the next few days he did his best not to let on that anything was weighing on him. But there was still something he needed to do. It would be risky – maybe even crazy – but he knew curiosity would gnaw at him until he did it.

Monday was Trevor's first day back from his suspension. The anti-rumor campaign hadn't been very effective, and the news about Trevor had spread through the halls of Emerson Elementary like Mrs. Steinbeck's perfume. Everyone was steering clear of the big bad cheater, but Drew marched right up to him at his locker, tapped him on his shoulder, and said, "Hey, I know what you did."

"Yeah, dude, so does everyone else," said Trevor, his meek words projecting into his locker. "I got caught with a cheat sheet, and I got suspended."

"Not that," said Drew. "I mean the other thing you were doing."

Now Drew's words captured Trevor's attention. He turned from his locker and looked down at Drew. "What?"

"I saw you copy off Jeff!" Drew whispered harshly.

An angry look came into Trevor's pale face. He slammed his locker shut, grabbed a fistful of Drew's shirt, and yanked him into the computer lab entranceway, blocking them from everyone's view.

"Listen, we can't talk about this. At least not here," Trevor said through gritted teeth. He stuck his head out into the hallway to make sure no one was within earshot. "Let's meet behind the jungle gym at recess."

Drew nodded, and Trevor released his grip.

When Drew got to his locker, he was met with a barrage of questions from Jeff and Tommy, who had seen him emerge from the computer lab entranceway with Trevor. Was he talking to Trevor? Was it about the cheat sheet? Why was his shirt collar stretched? But he dismissed them all and went to class as if it were just a normal day.

As he sat through the morning classes, he thought about what his mom had said during dinner the previous week. He realized that he had never stopped to think about things from Trevor's perspective. And while Drew was pretty sure he had done the right thing for his friend, he still needed to know why Trevor cheated in the first place, and, more importantly, why he didn't deny the cheat sheet was his.

But while Drew stared at the back of Trevor's head during science class, he began to worry about his pending meeting with the giant. *Maybe this is a bad idea. If he doesn't want anyone to know, why is he willing to tell me? What if he thinks I'm gonna tell on him for copying, and he wants me to go behind the jungle gym so he can beat the snot out of me without any witnesses?* Beads of sweat formed on Drew's forehead, and he could feel his heart thumping hard and fast. He had come this far, though. He couldn't back down from Trevor now. He flipped to page 139 to sneak a peek at the picture, and he managed to calm down and regain some confidence.

Drew ate lunch at his regular pace and took his time getting to the playground. Trevor was at the jungle gym waiting for him. Drew rotated his shoulders back and puffed out his chest to show Trevor, and perhaps himself, that he wasn't scared. Trevor scanned his surroundings to make sure no teachers were around.

"Hey, dude, what's up?" he said.

His casual tone aggravated Drew. He stood with his arms crossed, staring up into the giant's eyes.

"Okay, here's what happened," Trevor began. "It all started a few weeks ago at football practice. I fell over on one of my friends and broke his wrist. It was Kyle Olinski. I don't know if you know him ... But it was an accident ... I swear I didn't mean to. And I didn't mean to do this all to Jeff either. So anyway, I ended up going to the hospital with Kyle because I felt really bad about it. But the worst part was I had football right after school, then I went to the hospital, then Kyle's parents took me to get ice cream with them because they said it was nice that I came to the hospital with them. Then Kyle asked me to come to his house and hang out for a little. And what was I supposed to tell a kid in a cast? So I didn't have time to study at all. To be honest, I was kind of okay with failing the quiz. I even told Jeff during the quiz that I was gonna fail. But then Jeff was trying to be nice because we're friends, so ... I copied off him."

He paused and took a deep breath, and for the first time all day, Drew almost detected a smile on Trevor's face. He seemed relieved to be talking about it, as if carrying around the weight of the lie had become too heavy, even for the biggest kid in class, and he needed to tell someone the truth.

"Anyway, my mum always says this thing at home. It's stupid and everything, but she always says, 'Every time you don't get caught for something you did, you will get caught for something you didn't do.' And ... I guess the cheat sheet was my way of getting caught for something I didn't do. I don't know, I mean, I didn't even make the cheat sheet. But I still felt bad because I was cheating, even if it wasn't the way Mrs. Steinbeck thought."

Drew could not believe his ears. As he listened to Trevor's story, he tried to find some gap, some flaw, to make it a lie. He wanted Trevor to be lying now more than ever.

"But the bad part is that I didn't cheat just once," said Trevor, dropping his head and drawing a circle in the mulch with his foot. "I don't know how much you saw, but I guess Jeff is cool with cheating, so he's been opening up his paper to me for a while now. And I know he's your best friend and everything, and he was just trying to be nice, but I didn't even *want* to cheat. I almost always study. Sometimes I get bad grades, but, I mean, I do try. But even though I studied, I still checked my answers with his. It was stupid, I know.

"So then, after I got caught with that cheat sheet,

I was so surprised. I was waiting in the principal's office, trying to figure out how to show them I was innocent, but all I could hear was my mum's voice in the back of my head: 'Every time you don't get caught for something you did, you will get caught for something you didn't do.' So I decided not to say anything. After all, I *had* been cheating. So I figure it was coming to me at some point anyway. And I'm glad it all ended before I got Jeff in any trouble."

"But why didn't you tell Mrs. Steinbeck the cheat sheet wasn't yours in the first place?" Drew blurted out.

"I tried, but I couldn't. She was staring at me, and she looked so mad, and I just ... I froze. I'm scared to death of Mrs. Steinbeck."

"You are?" said Drew.

"Yeah, who isn't? I dread going to her class every day. Remember when she yelled at *you* on the first day of school? That was so scary. I felt so bad for you."

Drew continued to stand in amazement as he listened to Trevor's story.

"But anyway, it all worked out. I mean, my parents were really mad at me at first. I got yelled at for a long time that first night. But after my dad cooled down, he told me everyone makes mistakes. 'The good ones just find the good in the mistakes,' he said. So I studied a lot all week and my neighbor, she's like a math whiz, she tutored me, and now I finally understand all the decimal stuff we've been doing in math."

After a period of silence, Drew said, "But aren't you curious to find out how that cheat sheet got on your chair?" Immediately regretting his question, his eyes grew wide as he waited for Trevor's answer.

"Nah, not really. It could be anyone. Maybe someone made a cheat sheet and got scared before the test, and it somehow landed on my seat. It's over. Now I just need to tell Jeff to stop giving me a clear shot at his paper and letting me cheat."

At this point, Jeff and Tommy emerged from the corner of the building where they had been hiding. They had walked around from the inside so they could sneak up behind Drew and Trevor to hear the conversation. Jeff and Tommy only caught the end of the conversation and were obviously lost, but Tommy's frustration got the best of him.

"Wait, what did you say?" he almost shouted. "Jeff *let* you cheat?"

"Shhh. Stop, or they'll hear," said the cautious Trevor.

"Stop, you really don't understand," said Drew, stepping between Trevor and Tommy.

"What don't I understand?" Tommy snapped. "This is all so stupid and it don't make sense."

"Just *listen* for a second," started Trevor, stepping toward Tommy.

"What, are you gonna beat us *all* up now?" Tommy said sarcastically, though he took a small step back. Tommy had a thick build and was one of the taller kids in class, but Trevor still towered over him.

"What? Why would I wanna beat you up? I was just telling Drew ..." said Trevor, and he explained everything again.

"So you weren't gonna beat me up?" Jeff said weakly.

"No way, dude. You're my friend."

"Wait, this story makes no sense," said Tommy. "If it wasn't your cheat sheet, then who planted it on you?"

"I was just telling Drew, I don't think anyone 'planted' it on me. I bet someone was gonna cheat and got scared. They probably threw it or something. Maybe I sat on it somewhere else and it stuck to my pants. Oh well, who cares, it's over now," Trevor said with a carefree grin.

Tommy's entire demeanor seemed to change instantly. "No way, dude, you gotta figure it out. Maybe someone was trying to get you in trouble!"

No, Drew thought, if Trevor looks into this, he'll probably figure out it was me!

"You got suspended for something you didn't do," Tommy continued. "That's not fair."

Drew suspected that Tommy cared less about fairness and more about prolonging the conflict, but he wasn't sure if he should say anything.

"I'm not worried about it anymore," said Trevor. "It's over. I'm back at school, and I just wanna forget this ever happened."

Drew breathed a sigh of relief. He couldn't have chosen better words himself.

The bell rang again, and it was time to go back into the school. Before departing, Trevor said to Jeff, "I'm sorry you thought I was gonna beat you up. Sometimes I hate being big. Everyone thinks I'm some tough guy. I'm totally not." He laughed at himself, but only for a moment.

Jeff nodded. "I'm sorry, too. Maybe we can all hang out this weekend and play football ... two-hand touch, not tackle," he said, laughing.

"Yeah, that sounds cool," said Trevor. "I'll see you guys. I gotta go to the bathroom before class," he added, and he turned and ran clumsily toward the building.

The three boys continued to walk slowly. The once terrified-looking Jeff was gone, and Drew's best friend was back.

"Crazy, right? I had nothing to worry about at all. And Trevor's actually pretty nice. I mean, we were always friends when we were little. His grandma used to live next door to me. He'd be there sometimes and we'd play together. So it'll be cool to hang out this weekend," Jeff rambled.

The boys stopped at their lockers and proceeded to math class. Drew thought about telling Trevor he was the one who planted the cheat sheet on him but figured nothing good would come of it.

Even though it wasn't science class, he pulled out his science book again and opened to page 139. He thought of the beautiful picture, Skylar's smile, and Trevor's mum's saying: "Every time you don't get caught for something you did, you will get caught for something you didn't do."

Tears in a Storm

Drew's heart sank as each rumble of thunder clenched at his stomach and each flash of lightning turned his worried face pale white. He paced across the living room, back and forth, back and forth.

"Honey, calm down," said his mom. "I didn't know storms scared you so much."

Drew paused. "I'm not *scared*. It's just ..." Unable to find the words, he shook his head and resumed pacing.

"I understand. But it'll be okay," said his mom. As she spoke, there was another modest grumble of thunder, as if the sky were clearing its throat in preparation to roar.

"How do you know, Mom? What about all that work I did? All that work Dad did? We've been waiting for tomorrow *forever*. What if everything gets ruined?"

"Worrying won't do you any good," she replied. "We can't control Mother Nature."

Drew let out a frustrated sigh and peered out the living room window. Everything was darkening by the minute. Drew was no meteorologist, but as another threatening gang of smoky clouds glided across the sky, and as the distant rumblings grew louder, he knew the storm was coming. Just yesterday a perfect, golden sun had hung in the bright blue sky, radiating warmth and pleasantness throughout Emerson. There were a few clusters of puffy white clouds, but they only made the scene that much more picturesque. Now, only one day later, the sun had gone into hiding, and the sky was a dark, murky gray, with clear intentions of destruction.

Drew looked straight out the living room window and watched as the gusting wind scooped leaves from the ground and sent them down Ernest Way in a spiraling frenzy. The half-bare elm tree in the front yard shivered. Emerson Township was well-known for its trees. Many homes had wooded areas for backyards, and almost every home had at least one tree in the front yard. Drew was staring at the elm tree when his gaze was interrupted by the sudden appearance of wet spots on the window.

"It's raining!" he cried out.

Penny didn't respond, either because she couldn't hear him from the kitchen, where she was removing some pork chops from the oven, or because she felt no need to respond to such an obvious declaration. Considering that the forecast called for a 100% chance of rain, and the sky was now the same color as the Johnstons' freshly paved asphalt driveway, there was no need for someone to announce the arrival of the rain. Drew saw just a few droplets at first, but within a minute they were scattered all over the window. He cringed as the rain pattered on the glass.

"Dinner's almost ready," said his mom from the kitchen. "I want to eat now, finish up a few emails, then go down to the basement while it's bad out. I'm sure everything will be fine, but I'll just feel better if we're down there. There'll probably be some hail, and they said on the news that some areas could even see tornadoes."

"Tornadoes? Seriously?"

"Honey, we'll go downstairs and we'll be fine. It's just a precaution, that's all. It's very unlikely there will be anything like that here, but there will be some strong winds. Better safe than sorry, right?"

"You don't understand," said Drew. "I'm gonna call Dad."

He grabbed the phone from the kitchen and dialed his dad's number. It rang five times and went to voicemail: "You have reached the voicemail of Ryan Daley, Architect Apprentice at Ewing, Jones, Parker, and Silverman Designs. Please leave your name and number, and I will get back to you as soon as possible."

Drew hung up without leaving a message. "Mom, Dad's not answering."

"Did you call his cell phone or his work phone?"

"Work. He said he'd be there late tonight so he can have more time for the unveiling tomorrow."

"Try him on his cell."

But there was no such luck. *Why isn't he answering? He always answers.* Drew began to think of possible reasons why his dad wouldn't have picked up his phone, but they only made him feel worse.

<hr/>

The rain continued tapping on the windows as a constant reminder of its presence. As Drew sat at the dinner table, barely touching his food, all he could think about was the swing set at Emerson Park, and all the time he had spent working on it.

Earlier in the year, Mayor Garcia had announced that the township would renovate Emerson Park. For years the old park had been unusable. The grass had died; the merry-go-round was rusted; the pavilion had a leaky roof; the basketball hoops had bent rims and shredded nets, and weeds sprouted from large cracks in the court; and the crown jewel of the park, the swing set, had to be removed after its collapse. Many older Emerson residents talked about the beautiful swing set that once stood proudly in the middle of their little town's park. But the area was now a taped-off void with rusty pegs emerging from the earth as the only vestige of a swing set. With roads to pave, snow to plow, leaves to collect, and other more practical jobs to do, there hadn't been much money left for anything else. However, after enough town members spoke up at board meetings, Emerson would finally get a new park.

Mayor Garcia announced that a construction company would coordinate the majority of the work, but volunteers would be needed because of the town's limited budget. When Drew's dad offered to help, he was given the revered duty of constructing the new swing set. The afternoon he accepted the job, he called Drew to see if he wanted to help. An enthusiastic Drew agreed.

The construction company and the volunteers worked on the park throughout the summer. For Drew and his dad, that meant painting the picnic tables and building the swing set. They decided to paint everything orange, white, and black, the official colors of Emerson. They spent hours working at the park on weekends and even some weekday evenings. Several times Drew turned down offers to hang out with his friends. He knew he was missing out on a lot of fun, but nothing seemed as important as that swing set.

It held three swings, and on each side of the structure two six-by-six wooden beams formed a triangle. Between those beams (which looked like giant, orange A's) was a wooden panel. On one panel, just last week, Drew carefully painted "Emerson Park" in black letters outlined in white. Because he was so mesmerized by the drawing in his science book, he decided to try something more artistic himself. So, with the help of a sketch by his dad, he also painted a silhouette of the park on the other panel, outlining the pavilion, basketball hoops, trees, and the swing set itself.

Knowing the swing set would stand in the center of the park for all of Emerson to see, he was attentive to every detail. Even the tiniest mistakes resulted in him wiping off the paint and beginning again.

But now, all that hard work was in danger of being washed away for good, and Drew and his mom were sitting helplessly in the basement as an onslaught of rain pounded down on Emerson.

"Isn't it funny how when you were little, you were scared to death to be in the basement at night, but now you're down here to feel safe?" said Penny, smiling and lifting her head from the book she was reading.

Drew rolled his eyes, both at the accusation that he used to be scared of the basement (this was something he didn't like to admit) and at the fact that his mom seemed to think he was scared of this storm. He *had* been afraid of the dark when he was younger. And, like most little kids, loud thunder and bright lightning strikes had been frightening to him. But now, as the storm worsened, it wasn't the darkness or the loud noises that scared him. This was a new, different fear. This fear was based on the realization that everything he had worked for could be ruined – and there was nothing he could do about it.

He walked to the back door and peered out its circular window. It was too dark to see much, but he could hear the rain surging and the wind whistling like a tea kettle.

"Drew, sit back down," said Penny. "Standing there isn't going to solve anything. Besides, we're in the basement to stay safe, yet you're standing in the one area that could possibly be *un*safe."

Too frustrated to respond, Drew slumped back down on the basement couch. He wasn't worried about his own safety – he was worried about the park. There was no basement for the swing set to hide in during the storm.

ZAP!

The TV and lights snapped off. Drew and Penny were surrounded by blackness. Penny turned on the two flashlights she had next to her and handed one to Drew.

"I figured," she said. "Well, it's getting late anyway, so we might as well call it bedtime. Sleep down here on the couch, where it's safe and a little quieter."

Normally Drew would remind his mom how much he hated when she used the word "bedtime," but on this night he simply said, "Whatever."

He lay on the couch in the basement, unable to fall asleep. He was kept awake not only by the noises of the storm outside but also by the whirlwind of worries inside his head. *What if the wind lifts the tarp off the swing set, and then the rain washes away the paint? What if the whole thing gets ripped from the ground? Will all that fresh sod be okay? Could the pavilion collapse?* His thoughts were interrupted by a fierce boom of thunder. Then the basement was lit up for a brief moment by a lightning flash. *What if something gets struck by lightning?*

He closed his eyes and gripped the couch pillow, trying to think of anything besides the storm or the park. The first thing to pop into his head was the drawing in his science book, but that was no comfort. The drawing was the reason he had painted on the swing set to begin with, and he needed to think of something different. Also, the idea of finding the Mystery Artist was losing its appeal. He still cherished the picture just as much as the first time he saw it, but his lack of detective skills made him want to give up on the case. Out of the five previous owners of the book, he still only knew who two of the people were: Jason Porter and Skylar Jansen. He was still uneasy about talking to Tommy's older brother, so he hadn't gotten around to it. And even though Skylar liked the picture, she wasn't the Mystery Artist. As for the other three people on the list (Stacey Janofsky, Alexus Ballentine, and Mike Hudock), Drew had no clue who any of them were. *Maybe it's easier to give up on my search and just be happy I found the picture at all.*

He continued to search for something, *anything*, to take his mind off the storm. *How about baseball?* He thought about the home run derby he and his friends had discussed having next week, but that just reminded him that the field would likely be too muddy. *Video games?* No, he quickly realized that wasn't an option with the electricity out. *What about Dad?* But this only worried him even further. *Why hasn't he called back? He always calls back. Is there a problem? Did he get caught in the storm?*

Drew literally shook his head to chase away the bad thoughts, and the drawing once again settled into his mind. Though it reminded him of the swing set, it did seem to have a calming effect on him. It could still help, even if he had given up on his mission. He closed his eyes and tried to immerse himself in the image, but for the very first time, he couldn't do it. Instead, he could only envision rough waves crashing violently onto the shore, uprooting beach umbrellas and leveling sandcastles.

There was a loud crash. Drew shot up from the couch. The crash had sounded like glass shattering. He turned on his flashlight and waved it around the basement. Everything looked intact.

He went to the back door and looked out the window. The rain was still pouring, and it was too dark to see what could have caused the noise. He tried to use the flashlight to see outside, but it only illuminated his own reflection in the glass. Another thunderclap barreled through the darkness, but the noise he had heard couldn't have been thunder. The sky began to flicker, and a staggering bolt of lightning struck down and split the sky in half. For a moment, everything seemed quiet and motionless, as if the lightning had the power to briefly make time stand still. Drew gazed in awe at the electric sky. Each time it flickered it seemed to reveal the world in a different hue: shades of purple and white and blue that Drew had never seen before.

Finally he snapped out of it and remembered why he had gotten up in the first place. Guided by his flashlight, he went upstairs and inspected the first floor of the house. He saw nothing out of the ordinary, but he could've sworn he heard glass breaking. *Maybe it was just a dream.*

But a moment later Penny came down the stairs and dispelled that theory. She too had heard the crash but said there was no damage anywhere on the second floor.

"How about we both go back down to the basement?" she said. "I think we'll feel a little safer."

With Drew on the couch and Penny on the old, chocolate-brown leather recliner, the two of them tried to fall asleep, still wondering what the loud crash could have been.

Drew's eyes opened slowly. Hazy gray light floated in the quiet basement. He could sense that it was morning, though he wasn't sure what time it was.

He sat up, tossed his blanket aside, and headed straight to the back door. Looking through the window, he saw that the downpour had eased to a lighter but steady shower. His old shoes were on the floor by the door, but he didn't bother to put them on. He opened the door and stepped outside barefoot (he had gone to sleep with socks on, but they must have come off during the night). The sky was steel-gray. The air had that earthy, after-storm smell. It was as if the storm had washed away the old world and replaced it with a slightly different one. Drew took a few steps into the backyard but stopped due to a sharp pain in the bottom of his foot.

"Ouch!" He looked down and saw that he had stepped on a branch. As a matter of fact, branches were scattered throughout the yard. He limped back into the house and went upstairs to find his mom. She was standing on the front porch, surveying the damage from the storm.

"Good morning," she said. "Power's still out."

"I know," said Drew. "I have to go to the park and check out the swing set. And my foot hurts. Look, I stepped on a stupid branch in the backyard." He showed his mom the bottom of his foot. It was scratched and red but not bleeding.

"Are you okay?"

"Well, I guess. I mean, it kinda hurts."

The truth was that it didn't hurt much at all, but he was so frustrated that he felt like everything should hurt. He found himself trying to urge pain into the foot, as if it would in some strange way make him feel better.

Penny knelt down to examine her son's foot. "It doesn't look too bad. I'm sure you'll be okay. Why weren't you wearing shoes, though?"

"I dunno. It doesn't matter. Can we please go to the park now? What time is it? The unveiling's at noon ..."

Penny frowned. "It's still raining, honey. I don't think there will be any unveiling today."

"It's barely drizzling," said Drew.

Penny paused. The determined look on her son's face told her that he wasn't going to take no for an answer.

"All right, I'll take you down. But don't you want some breakfast first?"

"I'm not hungry. Let's just go."

"Okay, get some shoes and socks on. And a jacket. We'll walk down. I'd actually feel safer that way, with all the water and everything else all over the road. I wouldn't be surprised if some areas flooded. I think we were actually the lucky ones. Well, except for the Zim –"

But Drew was already halfway up the stairs. He threw on a hoodie and some socks, mashed his feet into his shoes, grabbed his Pirates hat, and ran back downstairs.

"Let's go," he said.

The park was just three blocks from their house, in the opposite direction of the school. Penny grabbed an umbrella for each of them, and they headed down the street.

Mrs. Goyle was standing on her front porch as they passed her house. Mrs. Goyle was like the neighborhood information center. She was the person who always knew what was going on with everyone in Emerson. She knew all the gossip and loved spreading it around. Drew doubted Mr. Barker would approve.

"Hey, Penny, can you believe this?" said Mrs. Goyle, sounding more excited than concerned. "I heard some streets are flooded pretty badly. Main Street, Coelho Drive, a couple others. The Bucci house always has flooding problems in the basement, but I bet they're really in for it now. Their basement flooded in 2004, you know, and they had just put all new flooring in. At least then their son Michael was around to help. I haven't seen him in years. They're saying the power should be back on today, but we'll see. Oh, and I heard what happened at the Zimmers' ..."

The old woman's words seemed to spout out of her mouth automatically, regardless if anyone wanted to hear them or not. As she spoke, Penny's footsteps slowed, perhaps reluctantly, and she proceeded to do one of Drew's least favorite things: she stopped to talk. Drew rarely went on walks with her anymore because of the inevitable pit stops. He hated standing around waiting while she talked *forever* with someone about grown-up topics. It seemed like adults would stand around discussing the weather just to have something to talk about.

Drew heard a few words from their conversation, like "flood" and "electricity," but he wasn't paying much attention. He noticed that the rain had lightened and the sky looked a bit friendlier than it did mere minutes ago. He almost smiled but caught himself. Now scowling, he remembered that this was the same destructive sky from just a few hours ago. He heard his mom say something else about the Zimmers, who were their next door neighbors, and then, "Right, Drew?"

"Huh?" he said.

His mom and Mrs. Goyle looked at him strangely.

"Can we please go to the park now?" he asked impatiently.

"Hang on, Drew. We can go in a minute," said his mom. "Did you hear anything about the unveiling at the park?" she asked Mrs. Goyle. "Drew has been worried sick about it since the sky turned gray yesterday."

"Ah, yes, good old Mayor Garcia," began Mrs. Goyle, as if she were an authority on the subject. "First the park was to be done for the Fourth of July, then Labor Day, and then she pushes it back to a random Sunday in early *November* when weather here gets dicey and calls it 'Fall Festival.' For someone always bragging about being a lifelong Pittsburgher, you'd think she'd understand the weather here a little better. But I tell you, it would be nice if she would ever stick to her word. Just once! That's all I ask."

Her rant was lost upon Drew, who waited for her to actually answer his mom's question.

"But yes, the unveiling was postponed indefinitely. They made the decision before the rain started falling. It'll be too muddy, too messy, although it does appear to be clearing up. We just might have a nice day after all. But as for the park itself, I haven't talked to anyone who has seen it. On your way back, stop here and let me know if things are okay there."

When they reached the park, Drew sprinted across the marshy grass, through the cool, misty air, to the swing set. He passed the pavilion, which appeared unscathed. But when he got to the swing set, he let out a gasp. The giant tarp that had been covering the swing set was nowhere in sight. The wind had been so powerful that it must have lifted the tarp and carried it away like it was as light as a tissue. The exposed swing set was snapped in half, collapsed under the weight of a big, thick, buckeye tree. Two of the swings were wrapped around the post, while the third was on the ground about 20 feet away.

"No ... no!" Drew looked at the side panel where he had painted "Emerson Park." There was a wide scratch across it. It looked as though a tree branch had been thrown against it by the violent wind. Drew ran his fingers across the blemish. He had spent hours painting those letters, trying to make each one perfect. Now something had come along and mercilessly scratched them out. He looked all around, and, suddenly, the park seemed a lonelier and sadder place than when it was empty. It had been useless before, but at least it hadn't been disappointing.

His mom walked over and put her arm around him. "I'm so sorry, honey. It looks like you guys did a great job. You painted this yourself, right? You're turning into a real artist."

"It's all ruined," said Drew, ignoring her compliment and wiping tears from his eyes. He hadn't even realized he was crying. "And no one even gets to see it. Everything was perfect, and now it's ruined."

"Drew, nothing is ever ruined," said his mom. Drew still did not react to her words. "Let's just go home now," she said a few moments later.

"No," said Drew, pulling away from his mother's embrace. He ran to the other side of the swing set to see the real artistry, hoping that it had somehow escaped the storm's terror. Instead he saw that the silhouette had a crack down the middle of it. The meticulous outlines he had worked so hard on were now blurred from snapped

wood. He looked up at the sky and saw that it had lightened up a bit, but that didn't matter. Not anymore. He
turned to his mom, his watery eyes strawberry-red, and
they left the park.

When they got home, Drew went around the house
to the backyard. He didn't feel like going inside yet –
the dreariness outside was more in agreement with his
mood. As he tugged his hat down over his eyes, bristles
of his sandy-blonde hair peeked out all around, especially
between the arch and the adjustable strap in the back.
The once-oversized hat was fitting more snugly than ever.
Drew ignored it, but he knew he was beginning to outgrow
his favorite hat. He grabbed one of his tennis balls hiding
in the grass and repeatedly threw it against the back of
the garage, similar to when he was trying to figure out his
social studies presentation.

The weather changed with each passing minute. Soon
the rain had reduced to an almost invisible dribble, and
the sun shone faintly through the clouds. *What's the point
of clearing up now?* Drew thought as he whipped the ball
against the garage. *The damage is already done. It might as
well stay dark forever.* But the sky was soon emitting shades
of bright orange and soft blue, and Drew again caught
himself admiring the scene. *No,* he said to himself as he
felt his mood improving. He wasn't ready to move on yet.

After pulling his hat down even lower, he reared back
and threw the ball as hard as he could – so wildly that
he missed the garage completely and the ball soared over
the fence and into the Zimmers' yard. The fence was just
a couple of inches taller than Drew. He got on his toes
and peered over it, and he couldn't believe what he saw.
How didn't I see this before? A huge pine tree was leaning
on his neighbors' house. The tree had snapped and splin-

tered halfway down the trunk, and the top of the tree had crashed through a second floor window and was *inside* their home.

"Wow," Drew mouthed slowly. A nameless jogger certainly couldn't fix something like this.

Mr. Zimmer was standing in his backyard and saw Drew peeking over the fence. Drew hadn't noticed him until that moment. He wanted to hide. His eyes were still watery, and he was pretty sure they were red. He didn't want his neighbor to see him crying.

"Hey, Drew," said Mr. Zimmer somberly.

"Hi," said Drew, shifting his teary eyes back and forth between his neighbor and the fallen tree. Mr. Zimmer looked so sad, so disgusted. Drew still couldn't believe what he was looking at.

"What a day," said Mr. Zimmer, switching his gaze from the fallen tree to Drew. Drew felt strange, though. Mr. Zimmer was looking right at him, just a couple feet away, but his expression did not indicate in any way that he realized Drew was crying.

Mr. Zimmer then noticed Drew's tennis ball on his lawn. He picked it up and handed it to Drew.

"Thank you."

Mr. Zimmer began to walk away but stopped and said, "You remember when me and my brother painted this house?"

Drew shook his head side to side.

"Yeah, was probably ten years ago, now. The house used to be a putrid green, something I hated for years. And instead of gettin' a professional to paint it, me and my dumb brother thought we could do it. Took us almost a month and it didn't look too great afterwards, but boy do I love the house being anything but that awful, putrid green. My brother passed away a few years ago, remember? Guess he won't be helping me this time." The words didn't seem to be meant for Drew, even though he was the only person there with Mr. Zimmer.

Without saying goodbye, Mr. Zimmer walked toward the front of his house. Drew continued to stare at the catastrophe. After a few minutes, he wiped his cheeks again and went inside.

A peanut butter and banana sandwich was on the dining room table. His mouth watered for it, and he felt his stomach clench and grumble. He knew his mom had left it there for him because it was his favorite sandwich, but he resisted the urge to pick it up and take a bite. He saw that his mom was sitting on the front porch, and he stepped outside to join her.

"Mom, did you see what happened next door?"

"Of course I did. *That* was the crash we heard last night. I feel so bad. I'm just relieved no one was hurt."

"What are they gonna do?"

"Oh, I don't even know. It's so much damage, I don't even know where they begin."

Drew shook his head and looked out at the street. Water was still streaming along the curb, and newspapers were scattered all around. Some neighbors were outside, examining the damage and picking up items that had been tossed out of place.

Moments later Mr. Daley's white pick-up truck pulled into the driveway. He got out, walked over to the edge of the yard, and began talking to Mr. Zimmer. After a handshake and a pat on the back, Mr. Daley made his way to the front porch.

"Dad!" said Drew.

"Hey, bud, what are you doin' out here?"

"Are you okay? Why didn't you call back?"

"It's just been such a mess," said Mr. Daley. "We lost power at the office last night, so I went home. Problem was, I had no power at my place either, and my cell phone died, and of course I couldn't charge it, so I couldn't call, it's just a real mess. I was gonna stop over last night, but I figured your mom had things under control. Didn't mean to scare you, bud."

"How are things looking out there now, Ryan?" Penny asked. "We only saw the park."

"Not great. Main Street's flooded. Joyce Drive is closed off. There's a cop down on Coelho directing traffic, but that's not helping much."

"It's such a shame," Penny said, shaking her head. "Hey, why don't we go inside? It's still a bit chilly out here."

Mr. Daley took off his muddy boots, and the three of them went inside and sat down at the dining room table. Drew sat in the chair by the sandwich, but he still didn't touch it.

"Coffee?" Penny said to Ryan. She got up and walked over to the counter.

"Sure." He smiled and tapped Drew on the arm. "You think she'll figure it out?" he whispered.

Drew paused for a moment then smiled, trying not to laugh.

"What are you two whispering about over there?" Penny said, looking at Ryan and Drew skeptically as she scooped some coffee out of a canister.

Drew and his dad sat quietly with slight smirks on their faces.

"Ah – you two are the worst! Okay, okay, you got me," Penny said, realizing she couldn't make the coffee without electricity. "Hey, I'm just getting this ready for when the power comes back *on*, that's all."

Drew laughed, and for a moment he forgot about the storm. He looked back at his dad and, in a serious tone, asked, "Did you go look at the park, though?"

"Yeah, I did, bud. That's why I drove straight over," Mr. Daley said in a muffled voice.

"It's really bad," said Drew. "The swing set is ruined."

"I told him nothing is ever ruined," said Penny from the counter. Those words seemed eerily familiar to Drew, but he figured it must have been because she had said them at the park just a little while ago.

Mr. Daley put his hand on Drew's shoulder. "Well, we built it before, and we can build it again. We'll just have to make it even better. It's all we can do."

"Yes, and I know you didn't want to hear this when we were at the park," said Penny, returning to the table, "but your painting was really good. We need to get you more art supplies. I didn't know you were such an artist."

Drew fought the urge to smile. Then, as quickly as it had gone out, the power came back on.

"See," said Penny. "I told you both. You thought I didn't know what I was doing, but I did. The power is back on, and I'm number one!"

She began dancing around the kitchen with her hands in the air, singing "I'm number one, I'm number one!"

It wasn't often that Penny acted this way. In fact, Drew couldn't recall a time when she had seemed so lively.

Penny looked at Drew and motioned to the sandwich on the table. Drew smiled and, finally, picked it up. Bite by bite, he began to feel better. He wasn't sure why – maybe it was getting food in his empty stomach, maybe it was his parents' comforting words, or maybe it was his mom's zany behavior – but he felt reassured that things would be okay.

"I'll make some calls today and see what we can do to get back to work on the park," said Mr. Daley. "Remember, just because something might take a little bit of work, you know, a little elbow grease, doesn't mean it's not worth it."

Drew knew his dad was right. In a way, it was the hard work itself that made the swing set worth it.

"Well, I bet there'll be a ton of people to help with the

park again, right?" Drew nodded in answer to his own question. "So I was thinking maybe we can help Mr. Zimmer. I don't think he'll be able to fix his house by himself, so do you think we could see if he needs help?"

Mr. Daley smiled. "You're a good kid, you know that? Finish that sandwich, and let's get over there and see what we can do."

Drew knew helping the Zimmers wouldn't be as fun as building the swing set, but it seemed just as important, if not more. While sweeping pine needles out of the Zimmers' second-floor bathroom that afternoon, he thought of the Mystery Artist again. Originally, he had thought his search would be an easy task. Now that he realized it was never meant to be easy, he no longer wanted to give up. In fact, he was determined to complete his mission now more than ever.

A Lie Before Breakfast

"Sink your teeth into this," said Mr. Daley, sliding a bacon and egg sandwich along the coffee table. Drew picked up the muffin bun with both hands and paused.

"So, like I was saying last night, some of us are gonna go to the field to catch baseball later," he lied. He kept his eyes on the sandwich and took a massive bite. Nothing creates an appetite quite like a lie before breakfast.

Mr. Daley nodded but didn't say anything. He was more interested in Drew's sandwich verdict than his tall tale.

With a mouth full of eggs, Drew mumbled what was intended to be, "It's so good," and proceeded to devour his breakfast.

Mr. Daley smiled and stepped back into the kitchen to make a sandwich for himself. Then he sat down on the living room couch next to Drew, and the two of them enjoyed a quiet breakfast together. For the next few minutes, the only sound in the room was the soft ticking of the old wooden clock on the wall.

"Since we can't work on the park for a while, I was gonna go to the field today with my friends. That's cool, right?" said Drew, finally breaking the silence. "I talked to Mom about it already."

After the storm from a few weeks ago, the broken

swing set was removed from the park. Mayor Garcia announced that the park would be open for use, but the celebration was postponed yet again.

"Oh, good, yeah, that's fine, bud. You can go hang out with your friends. Can't wait to get back to the park, but it looks like we'll have to wait until summertime. But, hey, since you liked building the swing set so much, how about I help you with some homework, like your mom wants, and then you can help me with some sketches for a new building?"

"For real?"

"Yeah, you're the one with the artistic eye in the family. We can get some good work in before you leave."

They finished breakfast, reviewed the math worksheet Mrs. Machado had given for homework, and began to lay out some sketches for a building Mr. Daley's company was designing. The morning passed swiftly, and the old wooden clock was about to hit noon. When all three hands joined each other in pointing straight up, a soft bell chimed. Realizing the time, Drew rushed up the narrow staircase to get ready. It was almost time for the secret journey to begin.

"I didn't realize it was already noon!" he shouted on his way up the steps. "Tommy and Caleb will be here soon."

"Caleb?" said Mr. Daley, walking over to the bottom of the staircase.

"Caleb Monroe. You know him. He was on my baseball team last year."

"Lanky kid whose hair is always in his eyes?"

"Yeah, that's him," Drew answered from his room.

"What about Jeff?"

"He's doing something with his Pap today."

"So it's just the three of you?"

Drew wasn't sure if he was just being paranoid, but his dad seemed to be asking a lot of questions – more than he normally asked, anyway.

"Well, Zobby's coming, too."

"Oh, okay, good," said Mr. Daley. "You're just going to the field, right?"

"Yeah."

There was a brief pause, and Drew suddenly became nervous.

"And Mrs. Anscombe is gonna come down with us too," he blurted out. He hadn't planned on telling this additional lie, but he figured it would put an end to his dad's questions.

"Oh, that's good," said Mr. Daley. "Hey, if you wanna stay longer, I can come down and sub in for her if she wants."

"Um …" Drew was glad he was up in his room, because he could sense his own dishonesty written all over his face. "Well, she usually reads while we play, so she doesn't mind staying. I'll tell her you offered, though."

"Okay, good. And make sure to dress warm. It's get-sick weather out there now, you know?"

"Got it," said Drew.

He searched his dresser drawers for a pair of thick socks. After all, his dad was right. The temperature was supposed to drop throughout the day and hit the freezing point by night.

"Do you think it's gonna snow?" Drew asked. "Mom said it might."

"Well," said Mr. Daley, "they said there's a thirty per-cent chance this afternoon, and *some* areas *could* see *up to* three inches."

"What does that mean?"

"It means it's not gonna snow. But it will get cold."

Drew slid into his coat and instinctively put on his Pirates hat. Rolling his eyes at his own mistake, he replaced his favorite hat with a red beanie. Before leaving his room, he paused and grabbed his science book from his book bag. He had brought the book to his dad's even though he didn't have any science homework. He quickly leafed through it and stopped on page 139, viewing the drawing with mixed feelings. He still loved looking at it, but he was becoming frustrated that he hadn't made much progress in his search for the Mystery Artist. After recommitting himself to his search following the storm, he had decided a few days later to show the picture to Jeff.

"Look at the detail. It's like every single pencil stroke is perfect – like everything was supposed to be that way. Isn't it awesome!" Drew had gushed.

"Yeah, it's cool," Jeff had said, but Drew could sense his lack of enthusiasm.

Despite Jeff's lukewarm reaction, Drew still wanted to see if his friend could help him find the Mystery Artist.

"All you have to do is look up everyone online," said Jeff.

Before Drew could object, Jeff called Tommy to help with the search. In a matter of minutes, the boys were in front of a laptop at Tommy's house. As Jeff explained the situation to Tommy, Drew felt embarrassed, like everyone was talking about him and he had to sit and listen.

"Well, who's on the list?" Tommy asked with his fingers on the keyboard.

"Oh, uh, I left the book at my house."

"Then what are we gonna do? Why do you need to find this out anyways?"

"I remember one of the names – Stacey Janofsky. You can look her up."

Drew spelled out the name for Tommy, but he withheld the other four names. He didn't want his friends to know he had a list of the potential Mystery Artists hidden in his wallet. He didn't want them to know the picture was the reason he had talked to Skylar. And he didn't want Tommy to know his brother was on the list. Checking online might be helpful, but it felt like cheating, like it was somehow taking away from the search.

"I'm not seein' nothin'," said Tommy. "There's a Stacey Janofsky here, but she's old. So that can't be her. Look, she's from Virginia anyways."

"Oh well," said Drew. "It's no big deal." He regretted saying anything in the first place, and now he just wanted his friends to drop it.

"Sorry, man," Tommy said with a shrug.

"Wait," said Jeff, "what grade is this girl in?"

"Um, I think ninth, but it's not –"

"Then let's look her up in a yearbook!" said Jeff. Even though he had little interest in the drawing, he seemed to be excited about the search. "She should be in one of Jason's old yearbooks, since they're only a grade apart. At least you can find out what she looks like."

When Tommy went to find the yearbook, Drew became excited again. After all, until now Stacey Janofsky was just a name on his list. It would be nice to finally put a face to that name.

Tommy returned with Jason's eighth-grade yearbook and handed it to Drew. Drew flipped to the page with the seventh-graders whose last names began with 'J', and there she was: Stacey Janofsky. She had very red hair, she wore purple-rimmed glasses, and she looked quite uncomfortable having her picture taken.

"Hey," Jeff said to Tommy, "maybe Jason knows her. She's only a year younger than him. You should ask him."

Drew wished the words from Jeff's mouth could be picked up and shoved right back in. He didn't want Tommy to ask Jason about this! *What if Jason is the artist himself? Or what if he's not and he just laughs at me?* Drew knew he might have to approach the intimidating tenth-grader at some point, but he wasn't ready to do so yet.

"I dunno, man," said Tommy. "This girl looks like a

huge dork, and my brother's cool. He wouldn't be friends with her."

Since that afternoon, neither Jeff nor Tommy had brought up the picture. Maybe they thought Drew forgot about it, because he hadn't brought it up either. But it was that day that Drew decided he wanted to find the Mystery Artist on his own.

As Drew stood in his room admiring the picture, he heard chatter outside. He went to his window and saw that Tommy and Caleb had arrived. He knew if Jeff had been with them they would have knocked on the door and come inside, but instead they waited outside by the curb.

"Daaay-leee! Daaay-leee!" Caleb chanted.

Tommy chuckled but didn't join in the chanting.

"They're here, Dad, I'll see ya," said Drew, speeding down the stairs.

He normally would have given his dad a hug before leaving, but he knew the more time he spent in the house, the more likely it was that Mr. Daley would sniff out the kids' secret plan. So without giving his dad a chance to respond, Drew was already out the front door.

"I'm tellin' you, it's only like twenty minutes away," Caleb was saying. "I talked to three different seventh-grad-ers –"

"Whoa, my dad's right inside," said Drew. "Don't be so loud."

"Come on, he can't hear us."

"He's right, dude," said Tommy.

"Whatever," said Caleb. "We ready to go or what?"

Drew looked back to his front door to make sure his dad hadn't heard anything. "Yeah, we just have to get Zobby first."

Caleb tossed his head back and threw his hands in the

air. "You *got* to be kidding me. Why is *she* coming?" Caleb never made it a secret that he didn't care much for Zobby's company.

"C'mon, she's our friend," Drew bit back.

"She's *your* friend," Caleb muttered under his breath.

Drew considered firing back with a similar comment, but he decided it was better not to respond. He was well aware of Caleb's disdain for Zobby, but he invited her to come along anyway. The idea of being with just Tommy and Caleb made Drew a bit uneasy. He wasn't sure why, but Tommy sometimes didn't seem like himself around Caleb. So because Jeff was busy spending the day with his Pap, Drew invited Zobby. He knew she'd want to come anyway – Zobby was always up for an adventure.

"And it's not like I hate her," Caleb continued, "but it's like she's always trying to be one of the guys. I mean, it's stupid that our league lets her play baseball with the boys. She's a girl. What do you think they invented softball for? And she acts like she can do *anything*."

"Are you sure you just don't hate her because she's better than you at baseball?" said Drew.

Caleb spun toward him. "Are you serious? I'm way better than her."

"Well, she did strike you out last year," said Tommy.

"She – she did not. She got lucky anyways. That umpire was blind."

"You struck out *swinging*," said Drew.

"I guarantee I would crush a homer off her if I ever faced her again!" Caleb cried.

"Okay, just stop," said Drew as they began walking along the driveway of Zobby's house.

Although it was right across the street from Mr. Daley's duplex, the Anscombe house was much larger. Zobby had the luxury of having a big front yard *and* a big backyard. And best of all, she had a huge bedroom, probably bigger than both of Drew's rooms combined.

Mrs. Anscombe opened the door and greeted the boys. As Drew was answering Mrs. Anscombe's questions about how his mom was doing, Zobby came storming through the doorway, fidgeting into a puffy, navy blue coat.

"Sorry, Mom, we're already late. We have to go, I'll be back later."

"Elizabeth Margaret, get back here right now!" Mrs. Anscombe shouted.

Fearing that their secret plan had somehow been uncovered, Drew, Tommy, and Caleb exchanged nervous glances.

"Fine, Mom," she said reluctantly. She marched back up to the doorway, hugged her mom, and accepted a kiss on the cheek.

"Now that's better," said Mrs. Anscombe. "You're still not too old for that. Your sister thinks she is, too, and let me tell you, she's not. And remember, the reason you have that cell phone is so I can get ahold of you. So if I call, I don't care what you're doing, you better answer. Understood?"

"I understand, Mom."

As the kids made their way down the street, Drew began to question what he had told his dad. He wondered why he even lied about Mrs. Anscombe going to the park in the first place. He and his friends had gone to the park by themselves over the summer, so why would it be different now? Meanwhile, the others were captivated by Zobby's new cell phone.

"When did *you* get a phone?" asked Caleb, with an obvious hint of jealousy.

"Just last night," said Zobby, pulling the phone from the left pocket of her jeans. "My family was due for an upgrade, so I *finally* got my own phone. My mom wanted me to use my sister's old one, but I didn't want that. It has scratches all over it, and I can fit like ten times more music on this one! So I had to get an A in math and at least a B in science on my report card. I got an A in both, so I got to pick out any phone I wanted."

"Wow," said Tommy, leaning over and looking at the phone as Zobby swiped across the screen, showcasing all the phone's capabilities. "It's loaded. Aw man, you got movies on this thing, too? That's so sick. I wish I had that on mine," he said as he whipped out his phone.

"At least you two *have* cell phones," said Caleb. "I told my parents they better get me one for Christmas. Let me see yours," he said as he grabbed the phone from Tommy's hand.

"Yeah, just be careful," said Tommy.

Caleb's eyes were glued to Tommy's phone for the next several minutes. As the kids made their way down the winding hill that led to the baseball fields, Drew continued to turn around to make sure no one had followed them.

Tommy finally noticed Drew's apprehension. "What's goin' on, man? You think the zombie revolution's gonna start and we're gonna have to make a run for it?"

"Huh?" said Drew. "Oh, no, it's just that we're gonna get in so much trouble if anyone finds out where we're going. I don't wanna get grounded, that's all."

Caleb lifted his eyes from Tommy's phone and said, "If you're scared about something, it should be getting beat up, not grounded. If the older kids see us there, they'll kill us. Well, not *me*, since I'm on the hockey team."

Drew's eyes grew wide. Caleb looked at him with a cocky smirk. He had plugged a new and horrifying thought into Drew's head, and he didn't seem to mind.

Drew began to reconsider the whole plan. On top of having to lie to his dad about it, there was also a chance of getting pounded by older kids? Maybe this wasn't such a good idea after all. His feet must have been in agreement with his mind, because his steps had come to a halt, and he was now several paces behind the others. Zobby was the first one to notice.

"Wait, Drew, what's wrong? Do you not wanna go?" she asked. Her tone was concerned, not judgmental.

"No way!" Caleb exclaimed before Drew had a chance to answer. "You're scared to go? Are you kidding me?"

"Yeah, what's the big deal?" said Tommy.

"Well, what's the *big deal* about this place anyway?" Zobby asked.

"I'll tell you what's the big deal about this place," said Caleb. "Every kid at Emerson has heard about it, but none of us ever knew where it was or how to get there. Now we finally do, *and* we know nobody's gonna be there today, so we *have* to check it out."

"Wait," said Drew, "what do you mean you know nobody will be there? You just said we might get beat up by older kids!"

"No, look, man," said Caleb. "All the middle school hockey players had practice at seven this morning. I didn't have to go 'cause I only play with them part-time. But the coach was real mad 'cause he thought we slacked in our last game. Which I don't get, 'cause we won, so who cares?"

"Yeah, that's dumb," said Tommy.

"Yeah. Anyways, practice is always long when he's mad. And no one's gonna wanna walk this far after a long practice."

"But what about the people who don't play hockey?" asked Zobby.

Although it was a legitimate question, Caleb rolled his eyes simply because Zobby was the one who asked it. "No one goes there without Huddy. He's like, the leader. And most of the stuff there is his."

"Who's Huddy?" Zobby asked.

"Come *on*," said Caleb. "You really don't know who Huddy is?"

Zobby shrugged and waited for an answer. She was never embarrassed about asking questions.

"Everyone knows Huddy," Caleb explained. "He set a school record for goals when he was in sixth grade! He's like, gonna go to the NHL someday. His name's Mike, but everyone calls him Huddy since his last name is Hudock."

Drew's eyes lit up. "Did you say Mike Hudock?"

"Yeah, why?"

"Uh, no reason," said Drew, trying to act casual. "You know what, I think Caleb's right."

"You do?" asked a puzzled Zobby.

"Yeah, we've wanted to check this place out for a long time. Let's go for it."

The fear and regret had evaporated when he heard the name. Mike Hudock, one of the kids on Drew's list, frequented the very place Drew was on his way to. That meant there could be clues about him there, and that alone was enough for Drew to venture forward, regardless of the consequences.

The four kids continued on. Soon the baseball fields were in sight, but the kids would not be stopping there. They strode through the infield and across the grass of the big field, toward the deep, thick woods, each step that much closer to the forbidden hideout known as The Shack.

The Shack was a giant treehouse located somewhere deep in the woods. According to legend, it had been built over 20 years ago, it sat 30 feet in the air, and only those who were invited could hang out there. Over time, kids would leave valuable items there, especially ones their parents wouldn't approve of. In fact, if anyone made the mistake of mentioning The Shack around any adults, that kid would promptly be taught a lesson.

As Caleb and Tommy began discussing the goods that

could be found at The Shack, as well as the rumored methods of punishment for anyone who revealed the location to an adult, Drew found himself focusing on the baseball field. Walking through the infield dirt and the stiff, crunchy outfield grass, he was reminded how much he missed it. He could almost smell baseball – but it seemed dulled. The colder weather had a way of masking the scent of the game.

He thought about how the seasons seemed to change so quickly. The sun was hiding its head earlier each day, and the winter winds were approaching. Summertime always brought out the freckles on Drew's face, but now there wasn't a single one to be found. It was as though he physically changed each time baseball ended, but always returned to form the following spring.

When he rejoined the conversation, Caleb and Tommy were still discussing the treasure at The Shack.

"Everyone says they got paintball guns, fireworks, and a whole treasure chest full of cool stuff," said Caleb.

"Yeah, and most important, no parents know about it," said Tommy.

"How'd you guys find out where it is?" Zobby asked.

"Well, like I was saying before, I've been playing on the middle school hockey team," said Caleb. Now, because it allowed him to brag, he didn't mind Zobby's question.

"And a bunch of them were talking about it. Since I'm younger, they never woulda told me, but this one kid, Franky, he was talking about it all loud in the locker room. He said all you gotta do is go to the baseball fields and stand behind the right field fence, by the sign for Bo's Auto Garage. Then you put Drake's Car Wash into your phone's GPS. It tells you to go on a road, but if you just walk straight for Drake's Car Wash, it takes you right to The Shack."

"How does that work?" asked Drew.

"How does what work?"

"The GPS. How does it know where to go?"

Caleb looked at him strangely. "I dunno. Who cares? It just works. You sound like Mrs. Machado. She's always asking *how* you get the answer. As long as you get the right answer, who cares how you got there?"

"Yeah, who cares?" echoed Tommy.

"What if it's wrong?" said Drew.

"It can't be wrong," said Caleb. "It's a *machine*."

Drew shrugged. "Okay, just wondering." He was skeptical that the GPS would work, but he decided not to say anything else about it.

"Well, there better not be anyone else there, or we're gonna be in for it," said Zobby.

"You have no idea," said Caleb. "If the older kids catch you, they tie you to a tree and shoot you with paintballs. And then if you tell anybody where The Shack is, they hunt you down in school and give you swirlies every day."

"That's nothing," said Tommy. "My brother said some kid named Colin who went to our school a couple years ago, he found the place and tried to steal all the stuff there – you know, the fireworks, slingshots, gold coins, all that stuff. And the older kids caught him and ... they made him walk the plank."

"What's the plank?" asked Drew.

"Well, they say The Shack's up in a super tall tree. You gotta climb a huge ladder to get up to it and everything. And at the top there's a plank, like on a pirate ship, and it sticks out above a creek. There used to be a rope up there so you could swing out into the deep part of the creek, but it fell off or something. Anyways, the older kids made Colin walk the plank. He had to jump off it into the creek, and it's like thirty feet in the air. 'Cept here's the thing ..."

Tommy stopped walking and scanned everyone's face. Caleb tossed some hair from his eyes so he could watch as Tommy finished the story. "From up in The Shack, you can't tell where the water in the creek is shallow. With the rope you could swing across to the deeper end, but without the rope, you got nothin'. So when you jump off, you could land on rocks and break your legs. That's what happened to that Colin kid. He had to leave Emerson 'cause he was in a wheelchair after that, and everybody knew why."

"Wow," said Caleb, who seemed to hang on to every word of Tommy's story.

Drew and Zobby looked at each other, trying to read each other's reaction to the tale, but neither allowed their expression to reveal any fear.

The kids continued along the outfield fence of the big field. They passed the advertisement sign for Melia's Market, then the sign for Rizzo's Pizza, and a moment later they reached the sign for Bo's Auto Garage. They climbed over the fence, and the four of them stood gazing into the woods.

"Well," said Tommy, "here we are. I guess me and Zobby should put Drake's Car Wash into our phones, right?"

"Ye-yeah, that'll get us to The Shack," said Caleb, his voice shakier than before.

Tommy and Zobby set Drake's Car Wash as their destination, and the four kids entered the woods, a bit surprised at, but quite impressed with, their own audacity.

Moments later they were wading through brush, ducking under low-hanging branches, and maneuvering around giant trees, and Drew had forgotten about Tommy's horror story. Dragging his feet through the crumbling leaves, he soon found himself several paces behind the others, but they didn't seem to notice. They approached a huge tree that had fallen across their path. Drew wondered if this tree had gone down last month, another fallen soldier in the war waged by the storm. The other three kids climbed over the tree, not lifting their eyes from the phones, seemingly unaware that the tree was even there, and then veered to the right. *I guess the GPS is saying to go that way,* Drew thought, though he still doubted it would actually get them to The Shack.

After he climbed over the tree, he heard Zobby say something about a low battery, but he wasn't paying much attention. He realized the weather had turned out to be rather agreeable. The crisp, early-December air was cut swiftly by the bright sun. He removed his beanie from his head and put it in his coat pocket. The woods were becoming thicker, but the tree branches were bare enough to allow the sun to shine through, warming Drew's head and speckling the ground with patches of light. He felt the sun on the right side of his forehead and wished for summer again.

"Come on, Drew, we're almost there!" yelled Tommy from the front of the line.

"Yeah," said Caleb, who had also been staring at Tommy's phone, "we gotta be close."

Zobby shook her head and looked up from her phone. "No we aren't! My map says we're still eight minutes away. That's eight minutes if you're *driving*. That's at least like an hour walking."

"Are you serious? No way," said Caleb. "Let me see that." He grabbed Zobby's phone from her hand.

"Hey, give it back," Zobby snapped.

"Just a sec, I just wanna see it. You don't have to freak out about it. What ... are you a *girl* or something?" He laughed and looked to Tommy and Drew for support, but neither of them joined him. He rolled his eyes and handed Zobby her phone.

"Thank you," said Zobby. "And yes, Caleb, I am a girl. I'm surprised you were smart enough to figure it out. But I'm also a girl who can do this ..."

She thrust her arms out and pushed her hands into the fronts of his shoulders. Caleb tripped over a branch and fell to the ground. Drew came running up after Caleb hit the dirt. Caleb got to his feet, brushed his dark hair from his red face, and tried to lunge at Zobby, but Tommy stepped in the way.

"Whoa, whoa, whoa," said Tommy as he restrained Caleb.

"Are you kidding me?" Caleb screamed. "Why are we even hanging out with this ... this ..."

"Girl? Is that the word you're looking for?" Zobby taunted. "The same girl who struck you out in baseball and now the same one who threw your butt to the ground?"

"C'mon, Zob, not helping," said Drew.

"Well, as long as he doesn't touch my stuff, we'll be fine, okay?" she said, still glaring at Caleb.

"Whatever. Let's just keep going," Caleb said, stomping off.

"Guys, what if we really aren't close yet?" Drew asked once Caleb was out of earshot. "We left my house at like 12:15, and we've already been gone awhile. I told my dad we were at the field with Zobby's mom, but, still, I can't come home *too* late."

"Come on, man, we gotta be almost there," said Tommy. "And it's gonna be so cool. I even brought my mom's candle lighter so we can light fireworks."

Drew looked to Zobby for backup but didn't get the response he hoped for.

"Well, we *have* already come this far, right?" she said. "And the fireworks idea does sound cool. Hey, I have an idea."

She tapped and swiped on her phone and put it to her ear. A few seconds later she was talking to Drew's dad.

"Hey, Mr. Daley, it's Zobby. How are you? ... Nope, nothing's wrong. I just wanted to let you know we'll be hanging out a little longer than we thought. Drew didn't want you to be worried. ... Yeah, I got a new cell phone. Pretty cool, right? ... Uh, oh yeah, she's here, don't worry. ... All right, thanks. ... Um, yeah, we'll definitely be back before it's dark out. ... Okay, sounds good. Bye, Mr. Daley."

"Wow, I gotta admit, that was genius," said Tommy.

"I do what I can," said Zobby, smiling and taking a bow.

Drew was glad the journey could continue, but he wished he didn't have to lie to his dad *again*. As he thought about it, though, he figured that this wasn't really another lie. It was just an extension of the previous one. His dad already thought the kids were at the field with Zobby's mom anyway. *Besides,* he thought, *Dad isn't too worried about me. Mom would be mad if she found out about all this, but Dad isn't like that.*

The three quickened their pace and caught up to Caleb. They continued to trudge deeper and deeper into the woods, farther than any of them ever had before.

"We sure we'll find our way back?" asked Drew.

"Yeah, we have two phones with GPS," said Zobby. "I just need to hit a little button that says 'home' and it'll take us straight back."

"But isn't *your* phone gonna die soon?"

"No, Caleb, it's not. It's Tommy's phone that's close to dying. My phone has an extra-long battery life. This sucker won't be dying any time soon."

"Whatever," Caleb grumbled and looked the other way.

The four kids traveled in silence for the next several minutes. While the other three gazes were sucked into the little cell phone screens, Drew sauntered along behind them, admiring the scenery. He noticed that although most of the fallen leaves were brown, a few still had hints of green and gold and auburn in them. He also detected a unique pattern in the trees. For a while, the kids had been trudging through an area of towering pine trees with thick trunks. But now they had reached a stretch of pale, skinny, leafless trees. Looking ahead, though, Drew saw that soon they would be weaving between more lush, towering pines, grander than any they'd passed so far.

Shortly after they passed through the skinny trees, a small gully about 50 feet to the left caught his eye. Just beyond the gully was a hillside where big, moss-covered rocks barricaded what looked like a secret cave. Drew was tempted to go investigate it, but he knew The Shack was today's destination. He thought about asking Zobby to take a picture of the rocks with her phone but decided against it. *It would be cooler to try and draw them anyway,* he thought.

"Come on, man, what are you doing back there?" yelled Caleb.

"Oh, sorry," said Drew. Without realizing, he had again come to a complete standstill, and everyone was several yards ahead of him on the other side of a row of thick bushes. He slipped through the bushes and caught up.

"Oh no!" Tommy wailed. "My phone died!"

"Now aren't you glad I'm here, Caleb?" said Zobby. "Without my phone, we'd be lost."

Caleb simply sneered and rolled his eyes.

"Oh, then I guess it's not a big deal," said Tommy. "We can just use Zobby's phone. Besides, look!" He pointed to a ridge just above a thin stream in the distance.

"It's ..."

Zobby looked up from her phone and smiled. "It's The Shack."

Atop a small hill just beyond a clearing, three strong trees stood close together. In the grasp of their branches, as if it were being lifted to watch over the world, was the biggest treehouse the kids had ever seen. No longer were any of them staring at a cell phone. Instead all four were racing to The Shack.

Even in a full sprint, Drew tried to take in all the features of The Shack. The red paint was faded, weathered by frosty winters and baked dry by hot summers. The three trees holding the mighty structure each emerged from the earth in a slightly different direction, and their crooked but sturdy branches crawled from the trunks to form the perfect home for a treehouse.

Tommy reached the base of The Shack first, followed closely by the others, and climbed the wooden ladder. Within seconds they were all inside. Although it was immediately clear that some of the stories about The Shack were exaggerated – the treehouse was about 12 feet in the air, not 30, and there didn't appear to be a pirate ship-style plank anywhere – the kids still were in awe as soon as they entered. Even Tommy, the tallest of the four, could stand without ducking. From the inside, it was clear that The Shack had been built using several different types of wood, and a window had been cut into one of the walls with a handsaw.

The floor was lined with scraps of blue outdoor carpet. In one corner sat two lawn chairs and a little square table. In the opposite corner there was a CD player and a stack of CDs on the floor. Zobby went to that corner, searched through the CDs until she found one she liked, and put it in the CD player.

"CDs?" Caleb scoffed. "What are they, like a hundred years old?"

"Yeah," said Tommy, "I got all my music on my phone."

Zobby shrugged. "Your phone can't play it like this," she said, cranking up the volume.

The back wall was covered with drawings. Drew gravitated toward the artwork. He ran his hand over the pictures on the wall, trying to sense the time and effort that had gone into them. The biggest drawing was of the Pittsburgh Penguins logo. It appeared to have been drawn with a black permanent marker. The picture wasn't scaled well; the penguin's beak was too long, and one leg was shorter than the other. But Drew knew that everyone had to start somewhere. Maybe his silhouette he painted on the swing set wasn't perfect either, but he had still put a lot of work into it.

He turned around and saw that Tommy and Caleb were focused on something on the floor in the middle of The Shack. He had stepped right past it without noticing on his way to the decorated wall.

"We gotta get in there," said Caleb, staring down with eager eyes at the locked treasure chest.

"I know, but how?" said Tommy, trying with all his might to pry open the lid. "It's locked shut. Without the key, we can't do nothin.'"

"At least we made it here," said Drew. "This place is awesome."

"But there's no point in being here if we can't see what's in the treasure chest," said Caleb, crossing his arms.

"I hate to say it, but maybe Caleb's right," said Zobby. "Besides, there's probably a key around here somewhere. A bunch of different people come here, right? There's probably a key hidden somewhere so everyone who comes here can get into the chest."

All four kids searched every possible spot inside The Shack but didn't find anything.

"This is pointless," Caleb whined. "Zobby's probably wrong anyways. Everybody probably has their own key. Or Huddy keeps it. We're never gonna get it open."

Drew wasn't ready to give up, though. It made sense for the key to be hidden somewhere on site, the same way a key was hidden at his house.

"Wait!" Drew exclaimed. "I think I know where it is!"

He darted to the ladder and climbed down. He ran to the tree trunk in the back, dropped to his knees, and began tossing aside all the dirty leaves that were piled there. The others stuck their heads out the window and watched. Drew could hear Caleb whispering his doubts from above, but he kept digging until he felt something in his grasp. He snatched a little tin box from the earth and opened it. Smiling ear to ear, he raised his arm to reveal a brass key.

"No way!"

"How'd you know?"

"Get up here!"

Drew climbed back into the treehouse as the kids laughed and celebrated.

"Hurry up, open it," Caleb urged.

"Wait, seriously, how'd you know where to look?" asked Zobby.

"My mom told me a story once about these burglars who went around house to house, knocking on doors. If someone answered, they'd pretend to be salesmen and then just leave. But if no one answered, they'd search the front porch for a spare key. My mom said a lot of people have a spare key right on their front porch, like under a rock or something."

"Yeah, my family does," laughed Tommy.

"Yeah, and my mom said everyone knows people do that. So what you should do is hide the key *near* the front porch, but not on it. That's what these kids did. Instead of hiding the key *in* The Shack, they hid it *near* The Shack. I figured the tree in the back would be a good spot."

"Not good enough," said Caleb, rubbing his hands together. All his enthusiasm had returned as soon as Drew found the key. "Now stop wasting time and open it!"

Drew slid the key into the lock. It fit perfectly. The kids were so quiet that they could hear the inner clicking of the key going into its counterpart. As Drew turned the key, his stomach turned with it in anticipation. The treasure chest unlocked and Drew lifted the lid, revealing the contents: an assortment of fireworks, a box of matches, a stack of comic books, a pack of water balloons, a jug of water, a funnel, one container of green paintballs, one container of orange paintballs, a sling shot, two baseball mitts, a baseball signed by Cal Ripken Jr., a makeshift bow and arrow, four cans of root beer, an unopened bag of pretzel rods, a half-empty bag of Doritos, and a notepad with a list of names written on it.

"See, I told you this would be worth it," said Caleb, rummaging through the chest.

Drew held the autographed baseball, felt the laces, and wished it was his.

"Cool, they have pop in here," said Zobby. "My mom never lets us drink pop." She pulled one of the chairs to the middle of the room, sat down, cracked open a can of root beer, and took a sip.

Drew carefully placed the baseball on the floor and picked up the notepad. Near the bottom of the list was the name Mike Hudock. *He really does come here.* The notepad was filled with drawings. None of them were quite like the one from his science book, but they were good nonetheless. They definitely seemed different from the hockey-playing penguin drawn on the wall.

"All right, guys, it's fireworks time," said Tommy, pulling his mom's candle lighter from his pocket.

"Do you even know how to do it?" Zobby asked.

"Yeah, it's easy. I've seen my uncle do it a hundred times. See, this is called a Blue Blaster ..."

He took a small, blue firework from the treasure chest, placed it facing out on the ledge of the window, toward the clearing, and lit the fuse. Everyone took a step back as the firework began to hiss, and everyone but Tommy covered their ears. Seconds later, the firework blasted out of The Shack and exploded into what looked like millions of tiny blue specks.

"See! How sweet was that!"

"My turn, let me try," said Caleb. "I wanna use a bigger one. What's this one called?" He removed a larger, silver firework from the chest and presented it to Tommy.

"That's a Silver Salvo. It's way more stronger than a Blue Blaster."

"Awesome," said Caleb, grabbing the lighter from Tommy.

He set the firework on the window ledge just as Tommy had done. He lit the fuse and stepped back, but the firework began to wobble. The kids froze. It teetered on the window ledge a moment, and then, as if it had made up its mind, it fell backwards onto the floor inside The Shack.

"It's gonna explode!"

"Bail!"

The kids scurried down the ladder and jumped to the ground. An intensified *zing* echoed from The Shack, followed by a loud *pop pop pop*. Then the firework exploded completely, and the treehouse emanated a bright red light.

The kids sat on the ground, speechless, for several moments before standing up. A pink ribbon of smoke floated from the window of The Shack and disappeared in the still air.

"We should probably get outta here," suggested Tommy.

"Wait," said Drew, "let's check out the damage first."

The kids climbed with slow, trembling steps. Hesitantly, they lifted themselves into the smoke-filled treehouse. The music Zobby had turned on earlier was still playing, though now it seemed unwelcome. Once the fog cleared and the kids were able to see, their guilt worsened. The firework must have ricocheted off each side of the treehouse before exploding, as there were now black marks on all four walls. Most of the drawings on the wall were destroyed. A sharp pain pierced Drew's side as a physical reminder of the art the storm had destroyed just weeks ago. *After the swing set, I couldn't blame anyone. But these artists, they can blame us.*

There was a hole burned through the carpet where the firework had exploded. And worst of all, that hole was right next to the opened treasure chest. Drew carefully examined each item, one by one. Some didn't appear to have suffered any damage – the baseball gloves, paintballs, and sling shot looked fine. But some of the comic books were barely recognizable, and the autographed baseball had a burn mark that obscured Cal Ripken Jr.'s signature.

"Well," said Tommy, "at least the Silver Salvo didn't hit all the other fireworks and blow the whole place up."

But that didn't make Drew feel much better. He sifted through the remains to check for further damage. As he leafed through one of the comic books, a piece of paper fell out. It was slightly thicker than regular paper and had been folded twice. He unfolded it and found that it was a painting, perhaps completed in an art class, of a skeleton riding a big motorcycle. The only colors used were black and varying shades of gray, except for the skeleton's jacket, which was a bright candy apple red. The painting didn't impress Drew the way the drawing from his science book had, but he could still tell that this artist was talented. Like the drawing of the ocean scene, it was obvious that a lot of time and effort had gone into this picture. Could Huddy have painted it? And if so, did it mean that he had drawn the ocean scene, too? And why was Drew just now seeing so many works of art? Was it possible that they had always been around but he was just noticing them now?

"What are you looking at?" Tommy asked.

"Uh, nothing." Drew folded the picture and slipped it into his pocket.

"Listen, we'll throw everything back in the treasure chest and get outta here," Caleb said nervously. "It's getting late anyways."

"But maybe we should try –" began Drew.

"Oh no, you *got* to be kidding me," Tommy interrupted.

"What?"

But no explanation was needed. A murmur of voices was approaching. Drew peeked out the window and saw three older boys walking toward The Shack. Zobby turned off the music.

"I thought you said no one would be here, Caleb!" she said.

Caleb glanced at Zobby, and a sly smile formed on his face.

"Just follow my lead," he said.

The four hurried down the ladder as the three older boys inched closer.

"Isn't that Roey?" one of them said.

"Yeah, Kris, it is. Hey, Roey, I thought we made it clear The Shack ain't for little babies like you," taunted another.

"Uh, hey guys," said Caleb.

"Why are they calling him Roey?" Zobby whispered.

"Caleb Mon*roe*, so they call him Roey," Tommy whispered back. "It's just a dumb hockey nickname."

Now all seven kids were standing near the base of The Shack. One of the three older boys, tall with intense blue eyes, stepped in front of his two friends.

"These kids are trespassing," he said. "I guess we gotta teach 'em a lesson."

"Nah," said Kris, "it's not a big deal. Plus Roey's been

doin' good work for us on defense. I'd hate to see him outta the lineup."

Drew, Tommy, and Zobby smiled at each other and breathed a collective sigh of relief. Maybe Caleb could get them out of this mess after all.

"And look," Kris continued, "The Shack's still standing. It's not like they *did* anything to it. They probably just wanted to see if it was real."

The kids' smiles instantly morphed into awkward glances, and the change did not go unnoticed by the tall, blue-eyed boy.

"What was that? Did you see that?" he said. "They all looked at each other funny when you said they didn't do anything. They must've messed something up – or stole something. Empty your pockets ..."

"Relax, Huddy, these kids seem harmless," said Kris.

Drew straightened up when he heard the name. *It's Huddy.* Drew studied him, as if a clue would present itself if he watched him closely enough. His dark hair was shaved on the sides and spiky on top. Beneath his icy eyes was a small, turned-up nose. He stood with his fists clenched and his elbows flared away from his body, as if he had someone in a headlock in each arm. And he was the only kid there without a jacket. In jeans and a red t-shirt, he looked unbothered by the cold.

"Well, why's this kid looking at me like that?" Huddy said. His eyes seemed capable of burning a hole right through Drew. "You got a staring problem or something? Huh?"

"Uh, no, sorry."

Huddy glared at Drew for another second before curiously lifting his head in the air. "What's that smell? Smoke?" He quickly stepped toward The Shack and grabbed a rung of the ladder.

"It was Zobby!" Caleb blurted out.

Huddy spun around and charged toward him.

"What did you say?" he demanded, standing inches from Caleb. Every word he spoke stung the air like venom.

"Come on, cool it, man, we still don't know what happened," said Kris.

"Well, what *did* happen?" said Huddy, leaning down into Caleb with his arms still flared away from his body. "And who's Zobby? What kind of name is that anyways?"

"She's Zobby," said Caleb, pointing.

Huddy's head turned, and Caleb used the momentary distraction to take two quick steps backwards. Then he continued:

"It's a dumb name, I know. And, uh, we wanted to come to The Shack 'cause we heard about how the cool kids come here – like you guys, you guys are real cool. So, uh, one of us heard about how to get here and we just wanted to check it out. Then Zobby like, begged us to open the treasure chest, so she found the key and opened it. Then she wanted to light the fireworks. I didn't think it was a good idea, but she did. You know how girls are always messing stuff up. So she lit a firework and it blew up in The Shack. But it was an accident. We're sorry."

"You're sorry?" said Huddy.

"Yeah," Caleb nodded.

But Drew could tell that Huddy wasn't buying Caleb's apology. The situation was as combustible as the fireworks, and Huddy's fuse had been lit.

"You're sorry?" he repeated. "What are you talking about?"

"Yeah, what *are* you talking about, Caleb?" said Zobby. "I never even touched any fireworks."

"Oh, come on, Zobby," said Caleb. "We all know it was you. Stop lying about it."

Zobby couldn't contain her anger. She lunged at Caleb, but Tommy caught her before she got to him.

"You are such a snake, Caleb!" she screamed as Tommy held her back. "*You* dropped the firework in The Shack. *You* showed us this place to begin with! And *you* can't handle that I struck you out in baseball last year and that I knocked you down today! You're such a –"

"Stop!" said Kris. "Everyone needs to calm down. Let's just check out The Shack and see what the damage is."

"Yeah," said the third older boy quietly. He was standing behind Huddy and Kris.

As Kris stepped toward the treehouse, all eyes followed him – except for two blue ones. Huddy's gaze remained locked on Zobby. As Kris grabbed a rung of the ladder, Huddy charged at Zobby and tackled her to the ground. He wasn't looking for the truth; he wanted vengeance. His treehouse was ruined, and somebody was going to pay. He tried to grab Zobby while she was on the ground, but she rolled, hopped to her feet, and took off running. Huddy chased after her, and the rest of the kids did their best to keep up.

Huddy appeared to be faster than his prey, but she continued to change directions, making sharp turns around trees and zigzagging through the woods. She had no clue where she was going, but she knew she had to get away from Huddy. He was getting closer and closer, and Zobby tripped over a branch and fell to the ground, tumbling down a small hill.

After a fall like that, Drew figured Zobby would be hurt badly. But, as always, Zobby surprised him. She somersaulted, landed on her feet, and resumed a dead sprint. Huddy looked shocked, but he wasn't giving up. He caught up to her again. Just as Zobby's jacket was about to be in his grasp, Kris came flying in and tackled him to the ground.

"What are you thinking, man? Are you gonna beat up some girl? And we don't even know if she did it, remember?"

Kris had Huddy pinned to the ground so he couldn't move. Huddy was taller than Kris, but it was clear that Kris was stronger.

"Get off me, man," said Huddy, struggling to squirm free.

Zobby stopped running but remained several feet away from Huddy and Kris. Drew, Tommy, and the unnamed older boy were now surrounding Huddy and Kris. Caleb was gone.

"I'm not gonna do anything, I'm fine," said Huddy, in a much calmer voice than before. Kris finally unpinned him and helped him up.

"Besides, you're right," said Huddy, brushing dirty leaves from his shirt. "Maybe it wasn't her. Where's that creep Caleb, huh? Row-eeee, come out, come out, wherever you are!"

But there was no sign of Caleb anywhere.

"I guess he ran off," said Drew.

"You think? I don't think he'd do that," said Tommy.

"So, what now?" asked Kris.

"Yeah, what now?" said the third boy.

"I'll tell you *what now*," Huddy barked back, the rage in his voice rising again. "Somebody's gonna fess up and tell us what happened to The Shack. *Our* Shack. I don't care if it was Roey or not, none of you should've been in there, and none of you should've touched my stuff."

The third older boy finally spoke up. "C'mon, Huddy, it's not like we built The Shack, right? And most of the stuff in there is just stuff other kids left there, right? You've used other kids' stuff, too. I mean, we all have, ya know?"

"But they ruined it!" Huddy snapped back. "Did we ever ruin it? No!"

The quiet boy opened his mouth like he wanted to say more, but with Huddy's intimidating glare piercing into him, he simply nodded. Drew searched the boy's face trying to figure out what he wanted to say, but the only thing he could detect was uncertainty.

"Well, listen," said Zobby as she finally took a few steps forward. "It was all our faults. We all wanted to hang out in The Shack. No one meant for anything to get ruined. We really are sorry. We'll help you clean it up, and we'll even replace whatever we can."

Kris nodded as if to accept the apology and the offer, but Huddy spoke up again.

"No, you can't just say you're sorry and act like everything is okay. I had a baseball glove in there. And ..." His voice wavered, as if his anger was now joined by sadness, "and comic books. A bunch of my comic books are in there! Those can't be replaced. They're limited edition. They don't make those anymore!"

"What do you want us to do?" Zobby asked.

Huddy was seething. His sharp eyes darted all around, searching for an answer. Then they stopped abruptly.

"What's that?" he asked, pointing at Zobby's left pocket.

"What? Nothing." Zobby looked down and saw that she had been guarding her pocket with her hand without even realizing.

"It's your phone, huh?"

"Um, yeah," said Zobby, now pressing her hand tightly over her pocket. "So?"

An evil smile spread across Huddy's face. "Let me see it."

"No. My mom pays for it. You can't just take somebody's phone."

"Let me see it," Huddy repeated, motioning with his hand like a greedy child demanding a toy.

Zobby shook her head and continued to guard her phone.

"Fine, have it your way. Just wait until school. I bet

you all go to Emerson, huh? I'll track you down, and then you'll wish you gave it to me."

Zobby sighed and pulled the phone from her pocket.

"Wait," said Drew. "Don't. He'll break it."

"I'm not gonna break it," Huddy said immediately, as if he had been ready for the accusation.

"Come on, man, just let it go," said Kris.

"No. They ruined The Shack. All I'm asking is to see her phone. Now give it!"

Zobby looked at Drew and shrugged. "What choice do I have?"

After staring at her brand new phone for a few more seconds, she took a deep breath and quickly handed it over.

"Wow, this *is* a sweet phone," Huddy said as he examined it. "You can do a lot with it."

"Yeah, I know, thanks."

"Actually," said Huddy, "what I meant was you *could* do a lot with it … but not anymore."

He took apart the phone, the battery from the base, and threw them in opposite directions, flinging the phone to the left, then launching the battery down into a valley of bushes.

"Good luck finding that. I sure hope it's not ruined like my comic books. That would be terrible, huh?"

All the kids were silent. Huddy began to laugh but stopped when he realized his friends didn't join him. It sickened Drew to think that this kid could be the Mystery Artist he was looking for.

There was a rustle a few yards away, and Caleb emerged from behind a tree. Zobby's teary eyes turned toward him.

"Look what you did!" she screamed. "Why couldn't you just tell him the truth!"

Caleb simply sneered smugly back at her.

"Look, I don't care what the truth is anymore," said Huddy. "Somebody messed with our treehouse, so somebody's gotta pay. You were there, right?"

Zobby shrugged and quickly wiped a tear before it had a chance to slide down her cheek.

"So it's your problem, not mine," said Huddy, smirking.

Kris and the other boy looked astonished by Huddy's cruelty, but they didn't say anything.

"Let's get out of here, guys," said Huddy. "Roey, you comin' with us, or you gonna stay here with *them*?"

"Uh, ye-yeah, I'm coming with you, I guess."

"You guess?"

"I mean, yeah, I'm definitely coming with you."

He scuttled over to Huddy. Huddy then turned his attention to Drew, Zobby, and Tommy.

"And don't even think about following us," he said.

"But we don't know how to get home without my phone," said Zobby. "You can't strand us out here like this. We'll freeze."

"Yes huh. I can do whatever I want," said Huddy. "*I* have a phone, see?" He pulled a cell phone from his pocket and held it in front of Zobby's face. "If you follow us, if I ever even *see* you again, you'll be sorry. I'll break a lot more than your phone."

Drew looked to Kris. He had been reasonable throughout this whole ordeal. He wouldn't leave the kids stranded in the woods, would he?

Huddy walked off. Caleb and the quiet boy followed. Kris looked right at Drew, as if he had heard his thoughts. Drew sensed that his eyes were trying to apologize, like he was trying to say he wished things had been different. But as the others quickened their pace, Kris broke eye contact with Drew and ran off to catch up with them.

Maybe Kris doesn't know how to get back without GPS either, Drew thought. Within a few moments, the four boys had disappeared through the brush. In the distance, Huddy shouted, "Good luck finding your own way home, losers!"

Drew, Zobby, and Tommy stood in the middle of the woods. Shadows were beginning to drape over the forest. Every direction looked exactly the same. There were no street signs or crossing guards showing the kids which way to go. They felt trapped in a dark, inescapable maze.

Eventually, Tommy went to get the base of Zobby's phone. Drew could tell Zobby was doing her best to fight back more tears. This was the first time he had ever seen her cry, and he blamed himself. *He* had invited her to come along. *He* had dragged her into this mess in the first place. He wanted to console her but didn't know how.

Tommy brought back the phone and handed it to Zobby. It was scuffed and scratched, but it didn't appear to have suffered any major damage. Without speaking, the three of them walked in the direction the battery was thrown.

"Ahhh!" Zobby screamed. "Caleb is such a jerk. First he takes my phone, then he tries to fight me, and if that isn't bad enough, he tells those hockey jerks that *I* ruined The Shack. Is he serious? I could wring his neck. And then he leaves with them. He actually leaves with them. Who does he think he is?"

"Honestly," said Drew, "I still can't believe he went with them."

"I can. Jerks of a feather flock together," said Zobby.

"Actually, I think he told them it was Zobby 'cause she's a girl," said Tommy. "You know, he figured they wouldn't beat up a girl. He was trying to protect us."

"Yeah right," said Zobby. "You don't have to *always* take his side."

"Yeah, I think Zob's right," said Drew. "Caleb wasn't looking out for us."

"Seriously," Zobby added, "if he was trying to protect us, why did he leave with them?"

"I dunno. 'Cause you woulda tortured him the whole way home?"

"You know, maybe you're right. Maybe you should've gone with them, too."

"C'mon, Zobby, that's not what he's saying," said Drew.

"Yeah, I didn't go with them, did I?" said Tommy. "I didn't even ask to! So why are you jumping down *my* throat? I'm here looking for your battery, right?"

Zobby huffed. It was her way of acknowledging that Tommy was right, even though she wasn't in any mood to apologize to anyone.

Drew looked up and saw that the sun would be setting soon. "Guys, we're never gonna find this battery. We should go. It'll be pitch black before we know it."

Tommy shivered and put his hands in his pockets. "Man, I'm freezing ... and starving. Maybe we can find our way back to The Shack and eat the food in the treasure chest."

Drew realized that he was hungry, too. He would've done anything to be eating a bacon and egg sandwich with his dad right now.

"But Zobby ran around so much that I'm not even sure where The Shack is," he said. "We should just head home."

"Yeah, you're probably right, we should just go," said Tommy.

"No, he's not right, Tommy, he's wrong. How are we gonna 'just head home'? Without my battery, my phone doesn't work, and without my phone, we have no GPS. And your phone is dead. So we have no way to *get* home. The only one of us who *might* have known ran off like a baby."

"So you don't know how to get home at all?" Tommy asked.

"No!" said Zobby. "I was following my phone the whole time."

"Yeah, me too. I got no idea how to get back. But Drew wasn't following the GPS. Drew, do you know how to get back?"

Zobby answered for him. "Come on, Tommy. Drew was like a hundred feet behind us, staring up at the sky and moseying around. He wasn't paying any attention."

Drew didn't respond. He looked around and breathed in the brisk air, as if to inhale a solution and exhale uncertainty.

"Then what do we do?" asked a nervous Tommy. He shivered again and put his hood up.

"I don't know!" said Zobby, plopping herself to the ground.

"It'll be dark soon," said Drew. "Once it's dark, we might as well be trying to find our way home blindfolded."

"I'm guessing no one has a flashlight," said Tommy.

"My phone has a flashlight app," Zobby said somberly. "Not that that matters now."

"So we got no idea where we are," said Tommy. "Let's just start walking in a random direction. Like Drew said, it's gonna be dark soon, plus we'll freeze to death if we stay out here all night." He pointed directly in front of where he was standing. "Let's just walk that way. Maybe we'll luck out and get to the baseball fields. Or we'll come to a restaurant or a house or something, and we'll call our parents from there."

"Not mine," said Zobby. "My mom's gonna be mad enough about my phone."

"I can't call my dad," said Drew. "Zobby and I both already lied to him. I don't want him to know."

"My parents aren't even home," said Tommy. "They

were goin' out somewhere tonight."

"And if we walk the wrong way, we could just end up at the highway, or the edge of a cliff or something," said Drew.

"So there goes that plan," Zobby sighed.

Tommy shook his head and kicked at a branch on the ground. "At least I'm trying."

Drew had never seen Tommy so nervous. He turned to Zobby and watched as she stared down at the useless cell phone in her left hand. Her knees were pulled close to her chest as she hugged her shins. Her normally bright smile had drooped into a gloomy frown. With her right hand, she snuck another quick swipe at a tear that had escaped her watery eyes.

Both of Drew's friends were scared, confused, and abandoned. The GPS had gotten them to their destination, but it had stranded them there. Drew knew it was up to him to figure out a way home. But how?

As urgent of a situation the kids were in, something else was weighing on Drew's mind: Huddy. Drew was pretty sure now that Huddy couldn't be the Mystery Artist. He tried to picture Huddy, pencil in hand, putting the time and effort necessary into the beautiful picture, and it just didn't seem possible. When he got home, *if* he got home, at least he would be able to cross the name off his list.

He looked up at the sky. The low sun was growing paler. He thought about the sun shining across the ocean and wished he were somehow inside a drawing now, so that the sun would stay in one spot forever instead of setting.

"Wait, that's it. The sun is setting."

"Yeah, we know," said Tommy.

"Let's go. I can do it," said Drew.

"Do what?"

"I can get us home. Let's go."

"How?"

"Yeah, how?"

"Just trust me," Drew said. "I found the key, right? I can do this."

Tommy and Zobby exchanged unconvinced glances. But Drew grabbed Zobby's arm to help pull her off the ground, and the kids got moving.

The setting sun was what gave Drew the idea. His dad had told him several times before that the sun rises in the east and sets in the west. Drew remembered that it was early afternoon when the kids were on their way to The Shack and the sun had been high up in the sky, almost directly overhead. At the beginning of their journey, he had felt the sun on the right side of his forehead. So that meant the sun had already begun to set. Now, as Drew stared off at the setting sun, he realized it should be on his left side the entire way home.

Unlike before, when Drew followed behind the others, he now led them with poise and purpose. Instead of Tommy and Zobby urging Drew to keep up, they were trying to keep pace with him.

"Slow down, Drew," said Tommy, breathing heavily.

"Do you really know where you're going?"

"Are we just gonna get more lost?"

But none of their concerns broke Drew's gait. Within minutes he saw the moss-covered rocks he had seen hours earlier, only this time they were to the right instead of the left. Drew knew he was on the right path, and he picked up his pace to prove it. He sprinted through the area with the skinny trees, and Zobby and Tommy reluctantly did their best to keep up.

Moments later Drew saw an enormous pine tree he had noticed on the way. He remembered wondering why all the other trees lose their leaves for the winter but pine trees don't lose their needles. Then he saw a big pile of leaves that he had noticed earlier in the day because it seemed strange that someone would rake leaves in the middle of the woods. He continued to study his surroundings as he marched on, noticing the same details he had seen earlier in the day.

"He *seems* like he knows where he's going," Tommy whispered.

"I think he does," said Zobby. "He really does."

Drew could tell that Zobby was starting to believe in him. "We're almost there, guys," he said.

But soon he came to an abrupt stop.

"What's wrong?"

"Yeah, why'd you stop?"

"I – I don't recognize this area."

"Oh no, you mean we've been going the wrong way the whole time?" cried Tommy.

Drew searched all around for something familiar but found nothing. Panic shot through him. Everything was getting darker, and any possible landmarks were becoming less distinct in the shadows. In the distance a bird squawked, as if to give the kids one final warning to leave. Drew could feel the steady, rising breath of the forest. It seemed as if the forest had become aware of the intruders and was giving them until sundown to either leave or be swallowed up in the blackness.

"I trust you, Drew. I know you can get us out of here," said Zobby.

Drew could tell she meant it. He searched around once more. Then he realized what he was looking for. He went to the right about ten steps, then forward ten more.

"C'mon," he said, "this way!"

Soon the kids were climbing over the same huge, fallen tree they had come across hours earlier. A few moments later, Tommy cried out, "The fields! I can see the fields!"

The three kids charged through the brush and burst out of the forest. They had escaped. Tommy high-fived everything in sight – Drew's hand, Zobby's hand, the sign on the outfield fence for Bo's Auto Garage, everything. Zobby grabbed Drew and hugged him, holding him tightly for several seconds.

The three trudged up the hill as fast as their tired legs allowed. Feeling like conquering heroes, they each headed home.

Mr. Daley was waiting on the front porch as Drew approached the house.

"Yeah, one piece," he was saying to someone on the phone. "I'll have him call you when I'm finished with him."

He lowered the phone from his ear and looked sternly at Drew.

"That was your mom," he said. "I had to call her and let her know I found you. Anything you wanna tell me?"

"No, I mean, it's not a big deal. We just, we just went, uh –"

"No!" Mr. Daley shouted. "Don't lie to me again. You understand?"

He opened the front door and pointed for Drew to get in the house. Drew nodded his head quickly and kept it down as he walked inside.

"Do you have any idea how worried I was? I called Mrs. Anscombe at four o'clock to see if you all wanted to come have dinner here, and you know what she said?" He paused, but Drew knew he didn't need to answer. "You went to the field *without* her. So that's lie number one."

There was an angry quaver in his voice that Drew had never heard before.

"She said she'd call Zobby and call me right back. So

she calls back and says Zobby's phone went straight to voicemail. So I start to walk out the door to go down to the field myself, and do you know what I saw? I saw your mitt right next to the door. Now, it wasn't all that strange that you said you were playing baseball in this weather, because I know you'll play baseball any chance you get, but there's no way you would've gone to play without your mitt. Even if you forgot it, you would've come back for it!"

Drew remained silent with his head down as his father continued.

"So that's lie number two. Then," the volume of his voice continued to rise as he spoke, "I had to call your mother, and I'll tell you what, she is *not* happy. Look at me, Andrew! I'm not happy with you either. You get that?"

Drew looked up. His father's face was red and his hands were shaking.

"You lied to me at least twice today. Now you're gonna tell me the truth."

Drew broke down. The stress of the day finally got to him, and he began to cry. He buried his face in the pillow on the couch as his father waited. After a few moments, he lifted his head. The look on Mr. Daley's face alone could have extracted every last drop of truth from his son. Drew took a deep breath, wiped his tears, and began. He told his father about everything: The GPS; Zobby and Caleb's altercation; the treasure chest; the firework fiasco; Huddy and the older kids; Caleb placing the blame on Zobby; Huddy breaking Zobby's phone; Caleb leaving; and barely escaping the woods before darkness fell. By the time Drew neared the end of his story, the words were dripping out on their own. When he finally finished, he felt exhausted but better.

Mr. Daley had stood and listened to the whole story, not interrupting Drew once. When he finally opened his mouth to speak again, Drew assumed he would continue yelling at him. Instead, he asked a question: "You said Tommy's phone died and Zobby lost her battery, right? So how did you find your way home?"

"Well," said Drew, "on the way there everyone else was looking down at the phones. But I thought some of the trees looked cool, so I was looking at them. And I remembered how you're always saying the sun sets in the west and rises in the east. And when we started the sun was hitting this side of my face," he said, pointing to his right, "so when we were trying to get home, I knew the sun would be on the opposite side. So I figured out what general direction to go. Then it wasn't so bad. I ended up just looking for all the things I saw on the way there, like these big rocks, a pile of leaves, and a broken tree."

Mr. Daley's expression finally eased. He sat down and embraced Drew with both arms.

"You have to understand that you can't lie to me, all right? Your mom and I were scared today," he said, all while still holding his son. He finally broke their embrace but still clutched Drew's shoulders tightly and stared into his eyes. "Look at me. I hated today. You hear me?"

Drew nodded and, looking up at his father, he realized something for the first time. His beard, which Drew had always seen simply as reddish-brown, was actually speckled with gray hairs.

"This was one of the worst days I've had as a parent," Mr. Daley continued. "You lied right to my face. We had no idea where you were. You could've been hurt – or worse – and we wouldn't have known where you were. But I know you're a good kid. And I'm sorry I lost it on you, but I was mad. Hang on a second ..."

Mr. Daley went upstairs. A minute later he returned hiding something behind his back.

"You need to call your mom and get chewed out again. And, you know what, you've earned it. But, first, I have something for you. You know my father's father, your great grandfather, was in the Navy. Well, his whole adult life he wore this watch." He held out his right hand and revealed the watch to Drew. The face of the watch was round and silver. Inside, there were three hands: one for the hour, one for the minute, and one for the second. The forest-green straps on each side were made of a strong fabric, tightly bound and durable.

"He gave it to my dad, my dad gave it to me, and now I'm giving it to you. There's a compass built into it, see. My grandpa always used to say, 'No matter where you are, always know how to find your way home.' For him, that was coming home from the war. Maybe for you it was just getting home from the woods. But remember, you always have to find your way back home, okay?"

"Wow, this is awesome. Thanks, Dad!"

Drew tried to study every detail of his new present. The weight of the watch across his left wrist was heavy, but he knew he'd get used to it. As the father and son sat together for a peaceful moment, the only sound Drew heard was the faint ticking of the watch.

"You're welcome. Now, listen, I'm glad you made your way back home today, and I'm glad you're okay. I'm proud of you for figuring it out without the GPS. And I respect that you finally told me the truth. But, listen, you cannot lie to me like that. And not to your mom either. Did you see what happened once you lied the first time? You had to pile more lies on top of it. Even Zobby was lying to me. That's the thing about lying – it's a slippery slope. When you lie once, you end up having to lie again. Then things get out of control. It's like in baseball when one kid throws the ball when he shouldn't. Next thing you know, every-one's whippin' the ball all over the place, and you've lost control of the game. You get me?"

"Yeah, I get it. I'm really sorry, Dad."

"I know, bud. Now go get cleaned up. I'll make you something to eat while you call your mom."

Drew went to his room and took off his dirty clothes. Before calling his mother, he decided to cross Mike Hudock off his list. When he pulled his wallet from his pant pocket, a piece of paper fell to the floor, the same as when it had fallen out of the comic book earlier in the day. He picked it up, unfolded it, and studied the motorcycle-riding skeleton. Feeling bad that he had accidentally stolen someone's picture, he checked to see if there was a name on it somewhere. If there was, maybe he could return it to the person. He searched the picture for a few seconds and saw that there was indeed a signature in the bottom right corner. He hadn't noticed it in The Shack. At first it was hard to make out. But he examined it closer, and it became clear exactly what the name was. The person who painted the picture was Mike Hudock.

All Over the Place

Drew had suffered through three weeks of captivity. No video games. No TV. No hanging out with friends. No Melia's Thursdays. No staying up past 9:00, not even on weekends. Just three weeks of boredom and frustration. Three long weeks without any progress in his search for the Mystery Artist. Not that he was sure he still *wanted* to find the Mystery Artist, now that Mike "Huddy" Hudock, the meanest kid Drew knew, had emerged as the most likely candidate.

Three weeks to sit around and think about how he was so close to crossing Huddy off his list. Not only was Huddy still on his list, but he was also a good artist, which made it that much more likely he was *the* artist Drew was searching for. And, if he was, what would be the point of continuing the search? It would only be a letdown if Huddy really was the Mystery Artist. Besides, Drew could never ask him about it. Huddy had warned Drew, Zobby, and Tommy that if he ever saw them again, they'd be sorry. The only positive thing for Drew to dwell on during the three weeks he was grounded was that he could count the dragging minutes on the watch his dad gave him.

He stared longingly out the circular window of his basement door. It was a few days after Christmas and his first chance to hang out with Jeff and Tommy. A thick blanket of snow had dropped down the night before, as if the sky had decided to give him a present on his first day of freedom with his friends. Drew had a simple wish regarding the weather: If there isn't enough snow for sled riding, it should be warm enough for baseball; but when it isn't warm enough for baseball, there should be enough snow for sled riding.

Tommy sat on the old leather recliner, Jeff on the floor. Both were staring into the TV screen, their mouths slightly ajar and their thumbs tapping away on controllers. Drew had been trying to break them from their trances for the last half hour.

"Guys, please, let's do something else. Let's go sled riding."

"But this game is sick," said Tommy. "It's definitely my favorite Christmas present I got this year."

"Yeah, it got at least four stars in every review," Jeff added.

"That's great, but I've been stuck in my house forever."

The boys finally put down their controllers.

"I only got grounded for a week," said Tommy. "How come you got grounded for so long?"

Drew shrugged. "My parents grounded me 'til Christmas. They were really mad."

"Yeah," said Tommy. "My parents were real mad at first, 'specially my dad. But my brother stood up for me. He was like, 'Relax, Dad, he's just a kid, he didn't realize what he was doing.'"

"Jason stood up for you?" said Drew. "I thought he was a jerk."

"He is. Maybe he just wants to make sure my parents take it easy on him the next time he messes up. I dunno, sometimes he's okay, ya know?"

"Yeah, I know what you mean," said Jeff.

As Tommy and Jeff talked, Drew wondered about Jason. He was one of the names on his list – one of the names he had hidden from his friends. Drew hadn't given much of a chance to Jason being the artist. He had always imagined Jason as the type of kid who was spitting spitballs or flicking the ears of the kid in front of him during class, not drawing pictures.

"Drew?"

"Huh?"

"You wanna go sled riding, right?" Jeff asked.

"Yeah, we can go to school and sled ride down the hill into the parking lot. It's perfect for sled riding. You still have those sleds, right?"

"Yeah, they're in my garage. So I guess we can do that," said Jeff, looking to Tommy for confirmation.

"All right," said Tommy, "but we should have a snowball fight, too."

"Sure, fine," said Drew.

"Maybe we should find someone else to come with us," said Jeff. "If we have a snowball fight, it'll be better if we have even teams, right?"

"Good point," said Tommy. "I can text Caleb. He got a sick phone for Christmas."

"No way!" Drew snapped.

"Why not?"

"You know why," said Drew. "I'll call Zobby. She'll wanna play."

"Ugh, come on, man," said Tommy.

"What?"

"I don't wanna hang out with Zobby. If you don't wanna hang out with Caleb, I don't gotta hang out with Zobby. She's your friend, not mine."

"Well ..."

"Besides," Tommy continued, "Caleb will be on our baseball team again, so you gotta get along with him."

Jeff rolled his eyes. "Caleb thinks he's so good at baseball, but he's not."

"He's pretty good," said Tommy. "He hit two homers last year."

"And struck out about a hundred times," Jeff muttered.

"Zobby struck him out," Drew added.

Jeff chuckled, Drew began to laugh, and even Tommy couldn't help joining in. The fact that Zobby had struck Caleb out wasn't what was funny – she was a really good pitcher – but it was that Caleb could never get over it.

"Look," said Drew, "when springtime comes around, we'll invite Caleb to do baseball stuff. But not now."

"All right, whatever," said Tommy. "So who *can* we call?"

"I could call Trevor," said Jeff.

Drew winced at the suggestion. The boys had befriended Trevor since the cheat sheet incident, and now he sometimes sat at their lunch table, but Drew was still uneasy around him. He still felt guilty about what he had done, and he had a lingering worry that something would spark Trevor's curiosity and lead him to the truth about the cheat sheet.

"Uh, wait," said Drew, "wasn't your cousin staying at your house? Is he still there?"

"Yeah," said Jeff. "He was visiting someone else today, but he might be back."

"Let's invite him," said Drew.

The boys ran up the stairs and into the dining room. Penny was sitting at the table, eating an apple and working on her laptop. As a real estate agent, she could essentially make her own hours to cater to Drew's schedule.

"Mom, we're gonna go sled riding at the school."

Penny's expression stiffened as she lowered the apple from her mouth.

"I mean, can we go sled riding at the school?"

Penny still didn't respond. She cast a suspicious glare at her son.

"What?" said Drew. "I'm not grounded anymore, right?"

"Right, but I told you I'd be keeping a closer eye on you from now on."

"I know, I know. But I'm telling you the truth. We're going to school to sled ride down the hill and have a snowball fight. It's the truth, I swear."

"Don't worry, Penny, we won't do anything bad," said Tommy.

Penny stood up, "You go to the school and nowhere else. And be sure to stick together. No one goes off on his own." She looked at the clock on the stove. It was 2:02. "And I want you home by four o'clock, not a minute later. And I'm going to call both of your mothers to make sure they know where you'll be."

"Okay, but we have to go to Jeff's first anyway to get the sleds, plus we have to put on snow clothes. Can we make it four-thirty?" Drew asked.

Penny's response was in the form of a sterner look.

"Four o'clock sounds fair," said Drew. "But Jeff has to call his house before we go."

He looked down at his watch, which he hadn't taken off since his father gave it to him, to make sure he knew what time it was. Mesmerized by the firm, steady ticking of the seconds hand, he kept his eyes on the watch as Jeff dialed. For no particular reason, he felt like timing the call.

"Hey, Mom, it's me. ... Yeah, everything's fine. ... Is RJ back yet? ... Can I talk to him? ... Okay, thank you. ... RJ, do you wanna go sled riding and have a snowball fight with me and my friends? ... Yeah, at my school, it's real close. ... Me and two of my friends, Drew and Tommy. You met them before. They were at my birthday party, remember? ... Yeah, you did. Tommy's the taller, athletic one, and Drew's the one who's all over the place. ... Right, yeah. ... 'Kay, cool, we'll be there in like ten minutes to get you. ...

'Kay, see ya."

Drew's head had shot up. He was confused by what he had just heard.

"All good?" Tommy asked as Jeff hung up the phone.

"Yeah, he's in."

"All right, hurry up and get ready so we can stop at my house," Tommy said to Drew.

Disoriented from Jeff's comment, Drew nodded and went up to his room. *What just happened?*

As the boys made their way to Tommy's house, Jeff's words were running laps in Drew's head, circling his brain and constricting his thoughts. *Drew's the one who's all over the place. Drew's the one who's all over the place. Drew's the one who's all over the place ...*

Drew couldn't stop thinking about it. *All over the place. What does that even mean?* Maybe Jeff meant to say that Drew had a lot of hobbies. Or maybe it was another way of calling him energetic. But the more Drew thought about it, the more he realized it was not an endearing label. Jeff had called Tommy athletic. Why wasn't Drew athletic? Or couldn't he have said something else – nice, funny, outgoing, *something?* Why couldn't he have said Drew's the one who always wears the Pirates hat? Drew was sure he had been wearing his hat both times he met RJ. Or why not mention that Drew was shorter and thinner than Tommy? There were so many things Jeff could have said. Why did it have to be *all over the place?*

"Hey, what did that mean before?" he asked Jeff, interrupting Tommy's guarantees of "lighting everyone up" with snowballs.

"What did what mean?" said Jeff.

"When you were on the phone with RJ, you said I was 'all over the place' or something. What does that mean?"

"Yeah, all over the place? It means, uh, you know, all over the place."

Drew looked at Tommy, hoping to see a face as confused as his own, but Tommy just stared back blankly. It was the face he would make if Jeff had simply said, "Drew has green eyes."

"Do you know what he's talking about?" Drew asked Tommy anyway.

"Yeah," said Tommy, now looking at his phone. "It means sometimes it's like you're not paying attention." He shrugged nonchalantly. "It's not a big deal. Everyone knows it."

"Right, and, you know," Jeff added, "sometimes a teacher calls on you to read and you don't know where we are because you're looking at a different page. That's why I never call on you when we do popcorn reading."

Jeff didn't seem like he *wanted* to defend his comment, but rather that he *had* to because he had already said it. Still, it felt to Drew like he was just piling on.

"I ..." Drew started. The thoughts were swirling around in his head, but he wasn't sure how to slow them down and form them into the right words.

"Are you mad?" said Jeff. "I really didn't mean anything by it."

"Yeah, man. Who cares?" said Tommy. "It's just, whatever."

Drew gave a half-hearted smile, and they made their way through the Porters' front door. Tommy shouted his afternoon plans to his mom, who answered from one of the back rooms, and then he ran upstairs to get changed.

Drew and Jeff stood inside the doorway and waited. Jeff turned to Drew to say something, but Jason emerged from the kitchen and came toward them. Jeff seemed to choke on the words at the sight of Jason. He stiffened like a statue with his lips sealed shut, looking down at the ground.

Just ask him, Drew said to himself. But either because Jeff was there or because he still hadn't summoned the courage, Drew also found himself tongue-tied as Jason approached.

The boys instinctively parted like a double door. Jason passed through without breaking stride, slightly bumping into both boys, and walked out the front door. Drew watched as Jason hopped into a rusty Honda Civic that had pulled up to the curb. The exhaust was so loud that Drew could still hear it after the car disappeared up the street.

Jeff again turned to Drew to say something, but Tommy came running down the stairs.

"All right, let's go," he said.

◆

As the boys headed for Jeff's house, Drew continued to wonder about what Jeff had said. All over the place. Why would Jeff say that? And why would Tommy agree? It didn't make sense. He wasn't all over the place. It was just that other people couldn't see what was going on inside his head. *You can't judge someone if you don't know what's going on inside their head, can you?* he wondered.

Was it possible that all this time, the person Drew thought he was on the inside, the person he *knew* he was, was not the same person everyone else saw from the outside? It was strange to think about, like when you hear your own voice on a recording. Drew remembered the time he'd called home from his dad's and left a message on the voicemail. When he got home the next day and heard the message, he couldn't believe it was him. They were the words he had said, but the voice didn't sound like his – it sounded like a distorted, barely recognizable echo of himself.

And he thought about what Tommy had said: "Everyone knows it." *Everyone?* Did everyone really think Drew was all over the place? Zobby? His parents? His teachers? Maybe Mrs. Steinbeck, but even Mr. Sawyer? Did the whole world view him as nothing more than some kid with a little jumping bean for a brain?

Meanwhile, the boys were almost at Jeff's house. Along the way, Tommy listed everything he got for Christmas, and Jeff gushed about the golf clubs he got from his Pap.

"He always takes me mini golfing," he said, "but this summer he's finally gonna take me to the country club to play. Pap's the best."

When the boys arrived at the Gray house, RJ was sitting on the living room couch waiting for them.

"Hey, RJ, what's goin' on?" said Drew.

Realizing that RJ must have thought Drew was "all over the place" when he had met him before, Drew wanted to try and show him it wasn't true. He would show RJ that he was just as normal as any other kid.

"Nothin'," said RJ.

"That's cool," said Drew, trying to sound as "normal" as possible.

Almost as fast as Tommy changed, Jeff did too. He came back downstairs and the boys retrieved the sleds from the garage. As the other three boys walked down the front steps, Jeff snuck back and gave his mom a quick kiss on the cheek. Drew noticed it out of the corner of his eye but didn't draw attention to it. And with a slight waddle to their gaits, the boys were off.

The four boys made their way down the shovel-scraped sidewalks of Emerson Boulevard. The hill looked slick and untouched as it glistened in the sunlight. As soon as it was within their sight, the boys sprinted toward it. It was the only time kids could be seen running *toward* the school. There were stairs that led to the doors at the top of the hill, but the boys neglected to use them. Instead they stomped through the parking lot and began to clamber up the hill. After several minutes of their feet sliding from under them and causing them to slip back down, they finally struggled their way to the top.

Drew stood and looked out over the horizon of the neighborhood. He set his sled on the ground, sat on it, tucked his legs, and began his descent down the hill. As the brisk December wind blew against his face, he finally felt the exhilaration he'd missed while cooped up in his house. Tommy came gliding down soon after, then RJ, then Jeff, each boy toppling over at the bottom when his momentum ceased.

"Awesome!" said RJ. "Let's do it again! Race you guys to the top!"

The boys scrambled up the hill, flew back down, then repeated the act several more times. After a while, Jeff suggested the boys build a jump. Drew liked the idea. But just as they stooped down to begin building, Tommy scooped up some snow with both hands, packed it into a tight snowball, and whipped it at Jeff, striking him in the shoulder.

"I'm hit," Jeff cried.

"Man down!" yelled RJ. "I will fight for my fallen cousin!"

He formed a snowball of his own and threw it at Tommy, barely missing him. The snowball fight had begun.

"Ha! Me and Drew against Jeff and RJ!" yelled Tommy. He grabbed Drew's arm and yanked him over.

"You guys go over there," he directed Jeff and RJ, pointing to the other side of the parking lot. It hadn't been plowed, and there was just one car, a half-buried Jeep, parked anywhere in sight.

"Here," said Drew, standing up his sled in the snow to use it as a shield, "I'll make 'em and you throw 'em, then we'll switch."

"Yeah, cool, start pilin' 'em up."

Snowballs flew through the air. Tommy threw the hardest, but just like on the pitching mound, he was wild. Few of his throws connected with his targets, and he was getting upset.

He bent down behind his shield and said, "I think there's something funky with the snow. Mine keeps breaking. Find some ice and make some ice balls."

Before Drew could respond, Tommy was struck on the top of his head by a snowball RJ had lobbed over his shield.

"Yes!" RJ exclaimed.

"Let me throw for a little," Drew finally said.

Unlike Tommy, Drew was precise and methodical when it came to the art of throwing a snowball. He waited and waited while Tommy replenished the arsenal.

"What are you waiting for?" Tommy asked.

"Wait for it ..."

As RJ stepped out from behind his shield to gather more snow, Drew swiftly shot up, planted his feet, and fired, drilling RJ in the chest with a tightly packed snowball.

"Nice! Now let me try," said Tommy.

Now with a mountain of snowballs between them, Drew and Tommy unleashed. Tommy threw often and erratically, while Drew relied on patience and accuracy. He nailed his target on almost every throw.

As the battle continued, Drew noticed a girl passing by behind Jeff and RJ. She was walking a big, brown, fluffy dog along the sidewalk. It was fighting to come over to the boys, as if it wanted to join in on the snowball fight, but the girl tugged at its leash.

A flash of white came whirling at Drew. He tried to dodge but was too late. *Thump.* The snowball nailed him on his right hip.

"Gotcha!" Jeff cried out.

Drew regained his focus and packed together more snowballs. Tommy had been rapidly firing so many that their stock had quickly depleted. Drew popped back up to return the favor to Jeff but stopped before he could release the snowball in his hand. What he saw momentarily paralyzed him.

Thump.

Thwack.

One snowball hit Drew in the left shoulder. Another smacked him on his right cheek. The ice stung as it seeped into his pores. Tommy pulled him behind his shield before he was hit again.

"What are you *doing*, man? It's like you're not even trying."

Drew wiped at the slush dripping down his cheek, but his frosty glove only made it worse. He gritted his teeth and grabbed a snowball. He could hear Jeff and RJ laughing from behind their shields.

They probably think I wasn't paying attention because I'm 'all over the place,' he thought.

He stood up, and RJ hopped up at the same time, smiling, ready to launch another attack. RJ fired a snowball. Drew leaned to his right and it whizzed past him. He now had a clear shot at RJ, but he didn't take it. The girl and her dog were walking away, and he had to stop them. He reared back and launched the snowball over his enemy's camp. With a sharp *splat*, it landed hard against the capital letters on the back of the girl's jacket – letters that spelled the name BALLENTINE.

"Whoa," said Tommy. "Did you do that on purpose?"

Without answering, Drew ran over to the girl. He did the math in his head. Alexus Ballentine was the third name on the list, so that meant, if this really was her, she was in eighth grade. *Did I really just throw a snowball at an eighth-grader?*

"Hi, uh, sorry about that."

The girl turned around and looked at Drew with a slight grimace.

"We were just, um –" Drew continued.

"Having a snowball fight," she said. She gave a half smile that helped put Drew at ease.

"Yeah."

"Well, did you win?"

"Um, I dunno. We weren't really keeping score."

"Yeah, the score doesn't really matter in a snowball fight, huh?"

"No, I guess not," said Drew.

"Uh huh. Well –"

"What's your name?" Drew asked suddenly.

"Alexus."

"Alexus Ballentine?" Drew asked. "Um, just because your jacket says Ballentine on the back."

"Yep, that's me. I'm on the school dance team. They give us these jackets with our names on them."

It really was her. Alexus Ballentine. She had dark brown skin, big brown eyes, and a friendly smile that revealed a mouthful of braces. The rest of her was hidden, bundled up underneath the jacket, baggy sweatpants, and a white beanie pulled down over her head.

"What's your name?" she asked.

"Drew Daley."

Alexus held out her hand, clad in a black mitten. "Nice to meet you, Drew Daley."

Drew kept his gaze fixed on her as he shook her hand. Was he shaking hands with the Mystery Artist, the person who created something that changed his life? Was it the very hand that drew the picture?

After shaking hands, Alexus took a few steps backwards to continue her walk with her dog. It seemed like time was in slow motion as the potential Mystery Artist was leaving, and Drew was incapable of saying anything.

Before she left, though, Alexus stopped, somehow noticing Drew's curiosity, and said, "You look like you wanna ask me something." Her round eyes narrowed a bit, as if she were trying to read Drew's thoughts.

"Oh, no, I'm just sorry about hitting you with that snowball." *Just say what you really wanna say. This girl is nice. She's not scary like Huddy or Jason.*

"No biggie," said Alexus. "My brother does stuff ten times worse, and –"

"It's just that you look familiar," Drew blurted out. "Well, not *you* you, but your name. Your name sounds familiar, I mean."

"Hmm. Well, I'm not exactly famous. Maybe you have an older brother or sister who knows me? Or maybe you know my little brother, Adam. He's in fourth grade."

"No, I don't have any brothers or sisters, and I don't think I know Adam," said Drew.

Alexus nodded and shrugged. "I dunno then. I don't think I know you. Well, actually, I do now. You're Drew Daley, the kid who nailed me in the back with a snowball while I was walking my dog, Lucky." She finished her sentence with a smile to let Drew know she wasn't mad.

"Yeah, sorry again about that. Sometimes my aim isn't very good."

"It's okay. No big deal. See ya," she said as she began to walk away a second time.

"Wait ..."

"What is it?"

"Well, I think I just realized why your name sounds familiar," said Drew.

Alexus looked at him with a friendly curiosity. "Oh yeah? Why?"

Drew snuck a glance over his shoulder. His friends had disappeared, though the sleds were still on the ground. From the corner of his eye he detected some movement behind the snow-covered Jeep, which was about 20 feet to the left. He was pretty sure Jeff, Tommy, and RJ were hiding behind it, trying to listen to his conversation.

"Well, it's nothing really, it's just that, uh, I think I have your old science book, from Mrs. Steinbeck's class."

"Oh, that's cool. So you go to school here," she said, motioning toward the building. "Small world, isn't it?"

"Yeah, I guess so."

"So I'm assuming you know that because you looked at the names inside the front cover, right?"

"Well, yeah."

Alexus nodded. "I always do that, too. Don't know why. I guess just to see if I'll recognize one of the names."

"Really?"

"Yep. But I never remember the names later. You must have a pretty good memory, huh?"

"What do you mean?" Drew asked. No one had ever told him he had a good memory before (at least not that he could recall).

"To remember my name just because you saw it in your science book. That's impressive. I bet you're like the genius of your grade, huh?"

"Definitely not. I've looked at the names a bunch of times. I mean, not a bunch of times, but ..."

"There's that look again, like you wanna ask me something. What is it?"

"Well ... someone drew a picture in the book, and it's really good, and I was wondering if maybe it was you."

"Hmm. It's really good?"

Drew shook his head eagerly. "Yeah, it is."

"Then I doubt it was me," said Alexus. "I'm not much of an artist. All I can draw is stick figures."

"Oh. This picture is of an ocean shore. You can see the sunset and the sand and waves and everything."

"That sounds really cool," said Alexus. "But yeah, sorry, wasn't me."

"Oh, okay," Drew murmured. "No big deal," he added with sudden casualness, trying not to sound as disappointed as he really was.

"Then again, I guess it's possible it was me. It would've been like three years ago, so I could've drawn it and forgot about it. But if you said it was really good – and do you think it took a lot of time?"

"Oh yeah," said Drew. "There's so much detail in it."

"Then it definitely wasn't me, because I never would've had the guts to do something like that during Mrs. Steinbeck's class. I was so scared of her."

"Yeah, she's still scary!"

Alexus shook her head. "Back then I was terrified of her, but seriously, she was one of the nicest teachers."

"What? She used to be nice?"

Alexus laughed. "Well, maybe 'nice' isn't the right word, but think about it – she has a quiz every week, but she doesn't have any big tests. In other classes, they might only have like two tests for an entire quarter, and if you do bad on one, your grade is bad. But with Mrs. Steinbeck, you get nine quizzes each quarter, and homework, and science lab stuff. So one bad quiz doesn't kill your grade, ya know? And she never gave homework on weekends, which was so nice."

"Oh, yeah, that is cool," said Drew. Though he knew all those things, hearing them from Alexus helped him to see Mrs. Steinbeck in a new light. Mrs. Steinbeck might never be Drew's favorite teacher, but he felt like he understood her better.

"But anyway, what are the other names? Maybe I know one of them."

"Um, I don't really –"

"Don't pretend like you don't remember the other names," said Alexus. "You remembered mine."

"Okay, there are four others, but the only one I haven't found is a girl named Stacey Janofsky. I looked her up online with my friends, but we couldn't find anything."

"Stacey Janofsky," Alexus repeated. "It does sound familiar ..."

"She should only be one grade ahead you," said Drew.

"Yeah, I dunno. I think I recognize the name, but I don't know who she is."

"Are you sure?"

Alexus frowned. "I'm sorry, I really don't know her."

"Man, how am I ever gonna find her?"

"Maybe you can hit her with a snowball."

Drew blushed. "I –"

"It's okay. I think it's cool what you're doing."

"What do you mean?"

"Well, you're like, on a mission to find someone. You're pretty focused, huh?" said Alexus.

"Me, focused?"

"Yeah. Focused on a mission to find Stacey Janofsky ..."

"The girl with bright red hair and purple glasses," said Drew.

"Wait, she has purple glasses?"

"Yeah, at least she did in the yearbook picture I saw of her."

"Oh my gosh! That's why I recognized the name. I *do* know who she is. I just didn't know her name. Everyone always called her 'Red.'"

"Because of her hair?"

"Actually, no," said Alexus, shifting her weight uncomfortably. "I think it was because she had really red cheeks, especially when she got embarrassed."

The dog was getting restless and began pulling away.

"Settle down, Lucky," Alexus said. "Yeah, thinking about it now, I feel really bad. I never even knew her real name. Everyone called her 'Red,' not just me."

"Well, okay, so I can still find her, though," said Drew.

Alexus took on the expression of someone who had bad news.

"What?" asked Drew. "Now *you* look like you wanna tell *me* something."

"Well, she doesn't live here anymore."

"Oh. Well, was she an artist?"

"I don't really know. I know she was super smart, but she got made fun of a lot."

"Where'd she move to?" Drew asked.

"No clue. That's the thing. She kind of, you know, disappeared."

"Disappeared?"

"Yeah. Red was – I mean Stacey was really smart. Like really, *really* smart. She was always winning competitions at school, spelling bees and things like that. Then one day she just wasn't there. My friend Mara, she's a year older than me, was supposed to have a few classes with her. But on the first day of school, Stacey wasn't there. And she didn't show up the next day, or the next day, or ever."

"But she couldn't just disappear," said Drew. "People don't just disappear!"

"She kind of did, though. Some people say she went to a college prep school. Some say she left because she got made fun of."

"So what do you think happened?"

"I never really thought about it," Alexus answered. "I mean, I knew who she was, but I didn't know her or anything."

"And no one has seen her since?"

"Not that I know of – Lucky, hold on. Listen, it was nice talking to you, but I really have to get going. Nice meeting you, Drew Daley."

"Nice meeting you, Alexus Ballentine."

"Enjoy your adventure!" Alexus said as Lucky pulled her out of the parking lot and down the sidewalk.

As Drew walked back toward the other side of the parking lot, Tommy, Jeff, and RJ stepped out from behind the Jeep and hurled questions at him – much harder to endure than snowballs.

"You know that girl?"

"How old is she?"

"What were you talking about? We couldn't hear."

"Her name's Alexus," said Drew. "She's in eighth grade. We were just talking about some stuff."

"Wow," said Jeff. "It's like when you talked to Skylar Jansen at lunch. You shoulda seen it, RJ. Drew was talking to the most popular girl in sixth grade like it was no big deal. And now she always waves to him when we walk by her house."

"Really? That's impressive," said RJ.

"Wait," said Tommy, "were you talking to her about that dumb little picture or whatever?"

Tommy's question kicked Drew's pedestal out from underneath him.

"Why?" Drew asked, unsure how else to respond.

"I thought I heard you say something about Stacey Janofsky. Isn't she that ginger girl I looked up for you that one time?"

"Well –"

"I knew it," Tommy continued. "That's weird, man. Why would anybody care about –"

"Lay off," said RJ. "I don't know what picture you're

talking about, but if Drew's talking to all these older girls, whatever he's doing is working."

"Yeah, that's awesome," said Jeff.

Drew was grateful for RJ's interjection. He didn't want to explain why he was on this mission. That was why he had decided to do it on his own in the first place.

He pulled off his left glove to check his watch. It was 3:45. "Whoa, guys, it's almost four o'clock. I'm not getting grounded again."

Without another word, the boys bolted home. When Jeff and RJ turned down Jeff's street, they quickly said their goodbyes.

"Drew, that was awesome. I'll talk to you later," said Jeff.

"Yeah, Drew. That was sweet. And maybe I can check out that picture sometime," said RJ.

Drew and Tommy continued on to Ernest Way without any conversation, and Tommy darted off to his house. Neither boy said goodbye, but they were in a hurry and didn't have a second to waste.

Drew stormed through his front door and looked at his watch. It was exactly 4:00. His mom was in the living room on her laptop.

"Just in time," she said.

"I know, but I made it," Drew answered, smiling and catching his breath.

That evening, Drew was no longer concerned about being "all over the place." Instead of Jeff's words, it was Alexus's words echoing in his mind. "You're on a mission to find someone … You're really focused," she had said.

"That's what I need to do," Drew said aloud to himself. "Stay focused on my mission. In the end, it'll all be worth it."

He pulled out his list and crossed off Alexus Ballentine's name. Though he had made progress, today's developments also raised more questions. What happened to Stacey Janofsky? Where could she be? Drew looked at the three names that remained, two with dread, one with hope. The only problem was that he would have to place all that hope in someone who was practically a ghost in Emerson.

Zombie Days

The final bell of the school week rang, and the students scattered out of Emerson Elementary. Drew, Jeff, and Tommy scampered down the hall toward the staircase by the exit. That three o'clock bell on a Friday was always like music to their ears, but this particular Friday in February was *extra* special – *Zombie Days* had finally hit theaters. Drew and Jeff jumped down the bottom few steps while Tommy slid down the railing.

"Zom-bie Days! Zom-bie Days!" Tommy chanted.

"I can't wait," said Jeff. "It feels like a holiday."

"I know," said Tommy. "It's gonna be so epic."

"Yeah, the whole night's gonna be awesome," Drew added.

He was referring to more than just the movie. First, the boys were heading to Jeff's house for pizza and video games. Then, Jeff's mom was taking them to the movie. Finally, they would return to Jeff's for a sleepover.

The bridge was still closed, and no one, not even Mrs. Goyle, seemed to have any idea when it would reopen. The boys walked around it and headed down Emerson Boulevard. By now, the detour didn't feel like a detour at all. It felt natural, like it had always been there.

The boys were so excited for the evening that they practically ran to Jeff's house. Jeff opened the front door, and Drew and Tommy followed, staggering along limply and groaning in their best post-apocalyptic drones.

"Mom, we're here!" Jeff shouted.

Mrs. Gray stepped out from the family room. "Okay, Mr. Zombie Man. Are you boys excited for tonight?"

"Of course!"

The boys took their book bags and coats up to Jeff's room. When Drew unzipped his book bag to switch his beanie for his Pirates hat, his books were exposed.

"Why do you got your science book?" Tommy asked. "We had a quiz today. We don't got any homework."

"Uh, I guess I forgot to take it out," said Drew.

Truthfully, he had grown so attached to the drawing on page 139 that he had been bringing the book home every weekend, even though Mrs. Steinbeck never gave homework on weekends. Regardless if it were the best of times or the worst of times, Drew always felt better when he looked at that picture.

Tommy shrugged and shifted his attention to his phone, but Jeff seemed to be turning something over in his mind. Drew waited for him to say something, but he didn't. If Jeff did realize that it was no accident Drew brought his science book home, he let it go.

The boys went back downstairs and claimed the living room to play video games. Mrs. Gray said she would order the pizza soon and they would leave early for the 7:10 showing of *Zombie Days*.

"We gotta play *Zombie Days* on story mode this time," said Tommy.

The *Zombie Days* video game was the boys' favorite game to play together, even though most of the time two would watch while one played. The three of them took turns. As was the rule in all their single-player games, you kept playing until you lost. While one would play, the other two would give their expert opinions. It was the childhood equivalent to a backseat driver.

"Go in that building," Tommy implored Jeff. "No, not that one. Come on. The white one on the left ..."

"I know, I got it, man."

"Watch out, there's a group of them over in the corner," warned Drew. "They're coming for you."

"They're all over you!" said Tommy. "Die. Die. DIE!"

"I think I can ... still ... get ... out." Jeff was feverishly smashing the buttons on the controller. "Ugh, I'm dead."

"My turn," said Tommy, yanking the controller from Jeff's hands.

Another hour passed with the controller switching hands every now and again. Right as it was about to be Jeff's turn, Mrs. Gray summoned Jeff to the kitchen.

"Just a minute, Mom, it's my turn."

"No, Jeffrey. Now." Her voice was stern yet weak and scratchy.

Jeff groaned and set down the controller. Drew couldn't see Mrs. Gray, but he knew by the tone of her voice something had to be wrong.

Tommy grabbed the controller. "We're not waiting 'til you get back. I'm up now."

Jeff slowly backpedaled into the kitchen, his eyes remaining on the TV until he disappeared behind the kitchen wall.

"What do you think that was about?" Drew whispered to Tommy.

"What was what about?" Tommy responded, without taking his eyes off the screen.

"Mrs. Gray," said Drew. "She sounded ... sad, I think. Or maybe scared." Why would Mrs. Gray be sad or scared? She was her regular self when the boys got to the house.

"I don't know what you're *talking* about, dude. Everything's fine."

Drew nodded and said, "All right," but he couldn't shake the feeling that something was off.

"Man, I already died. But that was still Jeff's turn, so now it's my turn. I'm just gonna restart, dude," said Tommy.

"Okay," said Drew, now paying more attention to the kitchen than the video game.

A few minutes later, a red-eyed Jeff returned to the living room. Mrs. Gray stood to his right with her arm around him. Drew could see that she was clutching his shoulder firmly.

"Uh, guys," Jeff began, clearly trying to hold back more tears.

Tommy continued tapping on the controller until Drew nudged him.

"What's the matter, Jeff?" Drew asked.

"Um ..." Jeff looked to his mother for support. She gave him a slight nod, and he continued.

"My Pap died," he said, looking at the floor.

Drew and Tommy froze. Unsure where to look (or what to say or do), they joined Jeff in his staring contest with the living room carpet.

Picking up where her son left off, Mrs. Gray continued, "He'd been having trouble with his lungs for years now, and this winter has been terrible for him. And he had never been the same since Mom passed."

As heartbroken as she must have been, her tone was unwavering. It was as though by stating facts, she wouldn't have to think about the emotional side of her father dying.

"They're together now, where they belong," she said, nodding to herself.

"So ..." started Tommy.

"I have to go," said Jeff with a quivering chin. Without giving his friends a chance to respond, he ran up to his room.

"I'm sorry, boys," said Mrs. Gray, "but your big night will have to wait."

Drew figured he should say he was sorry for her loss,

but he found himself answering Mrs. Gray's question instead.

"Do you need me to drive you home?" she asked.

"No, it's okay, we'll walk," said Drew.

"Jeff was very close with Pap, and now he's ..." Mrs. Gray trailed off, as if the words were caught in her throat. The once strong and deliberate voice had cracked and now revealed her sadness. She stared out the living room window, as though she were looking for something she couldn't find. Then she suddenly regained her composure. She inhaled sharply and said, "Well, I have calls to make and arrangements to get in motion. Goodness, so many people to call, things to do. Would you boys mind letting yourselves out?"

"Okay, but our stuff's still in Jeff's room," said Tommy.

"Sure, sure, go up and grab it."

When they reached the top of the stairs, Jeff's door was closed and their book bags and coats were on the hallway floor.

"Should we say goodbye to Jeff?" Drew asked.

"Nah, his door's closed," said Tommy. "Let's get outta here."

Drew and Tommy silently walked down the street. Drew had never thought about it before, but he now realized that he had never known anyone who died. And even though he didn't really *know* Jeff's Pap, as much as Jeff talked about him, he felt like he did.

When they reached Ernest Way, Tommy looked up from his phone and broke the silence. "Hey, wanna come to my house? I think my mom can take us to the movie."

"Um ..."

"Come on, why not?" said Tommy.

Drew felt like there was a reason, but he couldn't explain it.

"All right," he said. "I'll just need to call my mom and let her know."

"Yes!" Tommy exclaimed. "Zom-bie Days! Zom-bie Days! Zom-bie Days!"

Mrs. Porter, dressed in workout clothes and holding a water bottle, opened the front door and let the boys in.

"Hey, guys," she said. She took a swig from her water bottle. "I got your text, Tommy. Everything okay?"

"Jeff can't go now," said Tommy. "His grandpa died."

"Oh, my goodness," Mrs. Porter gasped. "What happened? Was he sick? And how's Jeff taking it?" While she asked questions, she was checking her heart rate on her fitness watch.

"I dunno," said Tommy. "I think he's okay. He's sad, I guess. Hey, can you take us to see *Zombie Days* since Mrs. Gray can't? We've been waiting forever to see it."

"I guess I can. Your dad and I were planning on having a date night, but we can just go out to dinner somewhere near the theater during your movie. Then we'll pick you up right after."

"Then Drew's gonna sleep over," said Tommy. "He has all his stuff with him and we really wanted to have a sleepover tonight."

"It's fine with me," said Mrs. Porter. "But call your mom, Drew, and tell her where you are, okay? She made me promise to keep her in the loop, especially after your little excursion in the woods."

"Okay," said Drew as Mrs. Porter handed him her cell phone. He stepped into the den and dialed home.

"Hello," Penny answered on the other end.

"Mom, I'm letting you know that I'm at Tommy's now, not Jeff's."

"Oh. Okay. What happened?"

"Um, Jeff can't go to the movie."

"Aw, that's too bad. Why –"

"So Mrs. Porter's gonna take me and Tommy. She said she could and it's no problem."

"All right, are you sure she doesn't mind?"

"Yeah, she doesn't," Drew answered quickly. "And then can I sleep over Tommy's tonight?"

"All right, Drew, but again, only if Mrs. Porter doesn't mind."

"She doesn't mind, Mom."

Drew and his mom said "I love you" to each other, and she made him promise to call her first thing in the morning.

"Everything good?" asked Mrs. Porter, holding out her hand for her phone.

"Yeah."

About an hour later, Drew and Tommy hopped into the car with Mr. and Mrs. Porter, and the two boys were on their way to see *Zombie Days*.

"Man, that was so awesome," said Tommy as he shoved open the exit door from the theater. "There better be a sequel."

"Yeah, that would be cool," said Drew. "The part where that girl zombie popped out from behind the couch was ridiculous. I was so scared."

"I wasn't," said Tommy, "but it was awesome. I can't believe the ending."

"I know. I couldn't believe that one guy was bad all along."

"It was nuts. Plus that battle scene was so sweet. There were like a million zombies."

"Yeah, Jeff's gonna love it," said Drew. As soon as the words left his mouth, he felt awful. He wished Jeff were there with them.

Soon they were back at Tommy's house, setting up shop in the basement for phase three of the big night.

"I'm telling you, man, I already drank so much pop. I'm gonna be up gaming 'til like six in the morning. I might not fall asleep at all," said Tommy.

Drew hadn't been participating in much of the night-time conversation, though. And what was strange was that Tommy didn't even seem to notice. It seemed like it was just a normal night for him.

Drew took his book bag into the bathroom to brush his teeth. As he brushed, he grabbed his science book and quickly opened to page 139. He felt better as soon as he looked at the picture. Studying the details of the drawing, he began to think about something new: *Art never really dies. Even after the artist is gone, the art is left behind.*

He headed down to the basement, where the video games were set up. Tommy was slumped over on the couch.

"I'm up, I'm up," he said when he heard Drew coming down the stairs.

Ten minutes later, Tommy was snoring and Drew was wide awake and alone. He opened his book bag and pulled out his science book. As he turned to page 139, a loud car pulled up outside. The car door slammed shut, and someone entered the house. Footsteps scraped through the living room and into the kitchen. Seconds later, the microwave was turned on.

That's gotta be Jason, Drew realized.

Drew tiptoed over to the bottom of the steps. The TV in the living room shot flickers of light against the wall at the top of the dark staircase. It reminded Drew of watching the lightning strikes from his own basement during the storm. He knew now that the storm was the kind of thing he couldn't control. The same thing went for Pap – there was nothing Drew, or anyone else, could do to bring him back. But there were some things he *could* control, and this was one of them. He grabbed his science book and marched upstairs.

Jason was sitting on the living room couch with his feet on the coffee table, watching *SportsCenter* on TV. In one hand was a plate of steaming pizza rolls. In the other was his phone.

Drew took a few hesitant steps toward him. "Hey, Jason."

Jason's head jerked away from the TV. "Where's Tommy?"

"He's asleep downstairs."

"Pssh, what a wuss," Jason scoffed and swiped on his phone.

"Anyway, do you draw?" Drew asked.

"No," Jason murmured. Between his phone, the sports highlights on TV, and the pizza rolls, Drew was struggling to hold Jason's attention.

"Oh. Well, um, your name's in my science book."

"Huh?"

"Your name's in the front cover of my science book. I have the same book you had."

He held up the book for Jason to see.

"Wow, that's *so* awesome," said Jason, rolling his eyes and checking his phone again. "What do you want?"

Drew took a nervous gulp of air and continued. "Well, uh, someone drew this picture in here, and I was wondering if it was you."

"And if it was, what are you gonna do, tell on me or something? Go 'head, tell the principal, I don't care. Seriously, I don't care." He shoved a pizza roll into his mouth, but it was obviously still too hot. His eyes widened, and he took a series of quick breaths with his mouth open.

"No, no, uh, someone else was asking and I just thought I'd check," said Drew. He hadn't planned on lying, but he blurted out the words anyway. It was just easier.

He opened the book and showed Jason the picture. Jason's eyes passed over it without the slightest change in his expression.

"Wasn't me," he said. "If it was a picture of a car or something, maybe. But a picture of some dumb beach wouldn't be me."

"Okay, just checking, thanks," said Drew. "Uh, see ya."

He scuttled out of the living room and crept back down the stairs. He slid his science book into his book bag and removed his wallet from its side pocket. He paused and glanced over at the couch; Tommy was still out cold. He pulled the list from his wallet and examined it. Then he took a black marker from his book bag and crossed Jason Porter off his list. Now only two names remained: Mike Hudock and Stacey Janofsky.

Drew tried to call Jeff over the weekend but couldn't get ahold of him. On Sunday he checked the obituary in the newspaper and found the listing for Jeff's Pap, Jeffrey Joseph Shelley. Jeff's name was listed as one of the grand-children. Drew knew that under different circumstances, Jeff would have thought it was so cool to see his own name in the newspaper.

Pap's funeral was on Monday. When Jeff returned to school on Tuesday, he had to do make-up work in the library for most of the morning, so Drew and Tommy didn't get a chance to talk to him until lunch.

"Long time no see," said Tommy as the boys sat down at their table in the cafeteria.

Jeff smiled faintly. "Yeah, I know."

"I got a ham sandwich and chips," said Tommy, dumping everything from his brown paper bag. "What about you guys?"

"Peanut butter and jelly," said Jeff. "And vanilla pudding."

"I'm buying," said Drew. "I forgot my lunch this morning."

"Man, on Tuna Fish Tuesday? That's the worst!" said Tommy.

"Yeah," Drew sighed. "Oh well."

He went to get his lunch and returned in under a minute (the line was never long on Tuna Fish Tuesdays). As he sat down, Tommy was proposing a trade to Jeff.

"How about your pudding for my chips?"

Jeff considered. He looked to Drew. Drew nodded his approval, and the exchange was made.

"Good deal," said Tommy.

"Yeah, I like to put the chips on my sandwich," said Jeff.

Tommy turned to Drew, who was prodding his tuna fish sandwich as if it were a science experiment and not his lunch, and said, "Hey, that tuna looks pretty good, but I'd rather eat your BRAINS!"

The two boys broke out in howling laughter.

"What's that mean?" asked Jeff.

"That's what this one kid says in Zombie Days," Tommy answered.

"What? You guys saw Zombie Days?" said Jeff. He looked confused, but Drew couldn't tell for sure.

"Yeah," said Tommy.

"Without me? When?"

"Friday," Tommy mumbled, his mouth full of ham sandwich. "My mom took us since yours couldn't."

The confusion on Jeff's face was joined by anger. He dropped the bag of potato chips to the table.

"Because my ... you ... my Pap died!"

The boys sat in awkward silence for several moments. The rest of the cafeteria was bustling with lunchroom noise, but Drew felt he could have heard a pin drop. He waited for Jeff to say something, but Jeff just sat there with his arms crossed and his lips sealed.

Finally Drew broke the silence. "Jeff, you okay?"

Jeff didn't answer. He picked up his lunch, leaving the chips on the table, and moved to an empty seat at the next table over. He didn't talk to Drew or Tommy the rest of the day. When school was over, he quickly gathered his things and got a head start home. Drew tried to catch up, but it was useless. By the time he got to the closed bridge, Jeff was gone.

When Drew got home from school, his mom was waiting for him. He could feel her eyes on him as he walked through the front door and into the living room.

"There's something I'd like to talk to you about, Andrew."

Drew's stomach sank. He took off his coat and sat down on the other end of the couch. The strange thing, though, was that he wasn't sure what he had done wrong. Normally when his mom or dad called him "Andrew," he knew exactly why, even if he pretended not to. But this time was different. Something had felt off, especially since lunch, but he couldn't figure out why. He felt guilty, but at the same time he felt like he truly had done nothing wrong.

"I ran into Mrs. Goyle today," said Penny, "and she told me Mrs. Gray's father, Jeff's grandfather, passed away on Friday. Is that why Jeff couldn't go to the movie?"

Drew could tell she already knew the answer.

"Yeah," he said, almost in a whisper.

"Why didn't you tell me that when you called me on Friday?"

"I dunno. I ... I guess I felt weird telling you someone died. I didn't know what to do."

After a pause, Penny said, "And how's Jeff doing? Did he talk to you about it?"

"He was really sad on Friday. He was crying and everything – not in front of us, but we could tell he was. And then today he got really mad when we said we saw the movie. But I still don't get it. All I did was see a movie. And now Jeff hates me."

"I'm sure he doesn't hate you," said Penny.

"Was it wrong to go to the movie? I mean, I wanted him to be able to go, but he couldn't. So I guess I was wrong, huh?"

"No, going to the movie wasn't wrong. There isn't really a right or wrong when it comes to these things. It's ... it's just a tough thing to deal with, that's all. Jeff was, and still is, going through a difficult time. He's hurting, and you have to understand that."

"Well, now he's really mad at me, and I don't know what to do," said Drew.

"You could give him a call and see how he's doing," Penny suggested.

"But he won't talk to me."

"He'll appreciate if you still try. He's going through a process, that's all. Even if it doesn't seem like it, I'm sure he wants to have his best friend by his side during a tough time."

"Okay, I'll try," said Drew. He wasn't sure if it was a good idea, but he had to do something.

"Drew," Penny said before he walked out of the room, "you're a good kid." She stood up and hugged her son. "This is just one of those tough times. You two will be okay. I promise."

Drew went to the kitchen and sat there for several minutes. Finally he picked up the phone and dialed Jeff's number. He was nervous as he dialed, unsure if Jeff was still upset. Unsure if he would even talk to him. Unsure if he still wanted to be friends at all. A part of Drew hoped no one would answer. It would be much easier to face the impartial voicemail than the scornful rage of Jeff. But after two rings, the phone clicked. Drew's heart jumped into his throat.

"Hello?"

"Hi, Mr. Gray. This is Drew. Um, is Jeff there?"

"Sure, Drew. Hold on just a minute."

Drew could hear Mr. Gray calling for his son: "Jeff, Drew's on the phone."

Drew cringed. He almost expected to hear Jeff yelling back to his dad, expressing no interest in talking to his now *former* friend.

"I don't wanna talk to that jerk," he imagined him saying.

"Hello?" It was Jeff.

"Hey, uh, hey, Jeff."

"Hey, Drew."

There was a pause. Drew waited for Jeff to say something else, but he knew Jeff well enough to know that he was doing the same.

"What's up?" Drew asked.

"Nothing. What's up?" Jeff responded quietly.

"Uh, nothin'. I just, well, you seemed like you were in a hurry after school, and ... I'm sorry we saw the movie without you. You were hurting, and I should've understood that," Drew said, unsure of what it really even meant.

Jeff took a few seconds to respond. Drew braced himself. He was afraid of what Jeff might say, but the silent anticipation was even more unbearable.

"It's okay," Jeff said finally. "I was just sad about Pap. I didn't ... I just didn't think you'd see *Zombie Days*. Everything has just been so crazy, you know? I dunno. I didn't know what to do. But I guess I wasn't really mad at you."

Again Drew thought back to the storm. He remembered how, even though he had only been mad about the swing set, it had frustrated him into feeling anger toward everyone and everything else, too.

"Yeah, I understand," he said.

Another moment of awkward silence passed. Jeff *seemed* like he wasn't mad anymore, but Drew still wasn't sure.

"Oh, by the way," he said, "this one kid in *Zombie Days*, he's so cool. He reminds me of you."

"Really?"

"Yeah. A couple times I forgot what I was watching, and I was thinking like it actually *was* you. Do you wanna go see it on Friday? I mean, you still wanna see it, right?"

"I mean, yeah, definitely," said Jeff. "You wanna see it again, though?"

"Sure. I wanted to see it with you in the first place. Besides, I like seeing movies a second time. I always miss stuff the first time."

"All right, yeah. That'll be cool."

Drew was relieved. The phone call he had dreaded making had settled into a friendly conversation. Still, even if things were back to normal between the two boys, Drew knew things would never be quite the same for Jeff.

"Cool. So you and your Pap were really close, right?"

"Yeah, I mean, he was sick for a while. But we actually thought he was getting better. That's why it was so surprising. But I used to visit with him all the time."

"You liked to golf with him, right?" asked Drew.

"Yeah, we went mini golfing all the time. He loved golf."

Drew sat and listened. Somehow he knew it was exactly the thing to do.

"He'd always be winning by a lot," Jeff continued, "but

then on the last couple holes he'd mess up on purpose so I could catch up and I would end up winning. I never realized when I was little. I just thought he got tired or something. But then the last time we played, it was like, October I think, I realized he was letting me win. I don't know how I didn't realize it before. It just hit me all of a sudden. And sometimes he would swing and miss and say the sun was in his eyes. Even if it was cloudy or nighttime. He was always joking around."

"It sounds like he was really cool," said Drew.

"Yeah, he really was. Sometimes when he had a real easy shot, like the ball was only a couple inches from the hole, he would yell 'Fore!' like real golfers do when they hit the ball really far, and then he'd just tap it in real easy."

Both boys laughed. They talked for a few more minutes until Drew heard someone on the other end say something to Jeff.

"Hey, I have to go," said Jeff. "Someone beeped in twice already and my mom's been waiting for a couple calls."

"Oh, okay, I'll see ya tomorrow," said Drew.

"See ya tomorrow."

Drew hung up the phone. *Mom was right*, he realized. *Jeff wasn't really mad at me. He was sad about losing his Pap.*

After grabbing a granola bar from the cupboard and his book bag from the floor, Drew went up to his room. He sat down at his desk and turned to his affairs, which consisted of 15 long division problems in his math book and a worksheet on adverbs.

Hardball

It was a warm Sunday afternoon in late March. The air was soft and lazy and filled with optimism. The snow from the last few months had melted away, and the birds had returned home to sing songs celebrating its disappearance. Colds and coats were being replaced with allergies and sweatshirts. All evidence suggested that winter's grip had loosened and spring was ready to make its welcome return.

Drew was as excited as anyone for the seasonal shift, because the arrival of spring meant the arrival of baseball. Practice hadn't officially started yet, but, knowing the temperature would fluctuate throughout the upcoming weeks, Drew called his friends and suggested they take advantage of the warm weather.

He waited by the curb a few doors up from his house. He seemed to always be running late for school, but, miraculously, he was always early when it came to baseball.

"Hello, Drew."

Drew looked over and saw his neighbor kneeling on a soft pad on the ground, working in her garden.

"Hey, Mrs. McGrath, what's up?"

"Oh, cleaning up the garden. It's finally that time of year again. What are you up to?"

"I'm waiting for my friends. They'll be here soon," said Drew. He smiled and held up his baseball mitt. "Finally time for baseball, too," he added, smacking the palm of his mitt with the back of his right fist.

Mrs. McGrath smiled and continued yanking the weeds from her garden.

"How's school going?" she asked.

"Pretty good. The last quarter starts soon, so that's good."

"And how's your dad? I see him picking you up some-times, but I haven't talked to him in a while."

"He's good," said Drew. He stopped smacking his mitt so he could answer the question more thoroughly. "Well, he's really good. I think he might get a promotion at work. He works a lot – hey, what are you doing?"

"What do you mean?" said Mrs. McGrath. "I'm just gardening."

"Yeah, I saw you pull the weeds and turn over the soil. I get that. But why are you ripping the dandelions out?"

"Oh, because they don't belong there."

"Why not?"

"They just don't." She pointed to a group of red flow-ers and said, "I planted the tulips, and they're about ready to bloom." She nodded at the yellow flowers to her left. "And the daffodils, too. Oh, and those lavender ones, those are my crocuses. They're the first to bloom every year. I just love them. But the dandelions, they came up all on their own."

"But don't you think dandelions are pretty, too? Like, by themselves?"

"Well," said Mrs. McGrath, "I guess I do."

"Then why would you get rid of them?"

"You're just full of questions, aren't you," Mrs. McGrath laughed. "I guess because it just isn't the right place for them. I purposely planted my flowers where I did. All in a row, all in a line. But dandelions just sprout out wherever they feel like. They just ... they aren't planned, that's all."

Jeff appeared at the end of the street, a navy blue baseball hat on his head and his mitt on his hand. He waved as he made his way toward Drew.

"All right, my friend's here. See you later, Mrs. McGrath."

"Bye, Drew. Have fun."

Moments after Jeff arrived, a car pulled up and Caleb hopped out, his Emerson baseball hat from last year concealing his long dark hair. All three boys wore hats as a silent reminder that baseball season was around the corner. Drew wore his Pirates hat all the time, while the others reserved their hats for playing baseball or attending baseball games.

Drew had kept his distance from Caleb since their adventure to The Shack. The only times he had spoken to him were when Tommy would include him in a conversation at school. Luckily, Caleb sat with his hockey friends at lunch, and Drew did his best to avoid him otherwise. He still wasn't thrilled with the kid who had fought with Zobby and ditched them in the woods, but he figured it was best to put their differences aside and focus on playing ball. He decided it was probably best not to invite Zobby on days when Tommy invited Caleb. That way there would be less fighting.

Each boy had his mitt on his hand, and, just like always, Tommy brought the bat and ball. No one ever needed to ask who would supply those two items. It had become Tommy's duty long ago, and he embraced it. The three other boys stood by the curb as Tommy made his way toward them from his house. As soon as he was within throwing distance, he reached back and heaved the ball.

"Catch!"

The three boys jostled for position and reached out as the ball came toward them. It landed in Drew's mitt a bit harder than he expected.

"Wait, this is a hardball," he said.

"Yeah," said Tommy, now standing just a few feet away.

"But we're playing in the street, so we have to use a tennis ball. Our parents have told us like a hundred times."

"I couldn't find a tennis ball. I think Link chewed 'em all up," said Tommy, turning his hat backwards.

"Oh. I can go find one –"

"What for?" Caleb interjected. "Tennis balls are for babies."

"Yeah," said Tommy. "I don't wanna stand around while you look for a tennis ball. Don't worry, we'll be careful."

Drew felt convinced enough. If they were responsible enough to go to Melia's on their own, they were responsible enough to play a little hardball in the street.

"All right, let's play."

The four boys walked to the end of the street where there weren't any cars. Then they spread out and began to catch. Drew set his feet and threw the ball to Jeff, who in turn threw to Tommy, who reared back and fired to Caleb. Caleb's first throw to Drew bounced a few feet in front of him and skipped past.

As Drew sprinted down the street for the ball, Caleb yelled, "That was my curve."

The boys continued to throw in this square-like shape.

"Hey, did you save up enough money for your bike yet?" Drew asked Jeff.

Jeff had wanted a new bike for a while but didn't get one for Christmas. So now he had to save enough money to buy it himself.

"Almost," Jeff said excitedly. "I need two hundred forty dollars and I have two twenty-five. And my neighbor said she'd give me fifteen bucks to help her clean out her basement next week. And then I'll have a brand new bike."

"How'd you save up all that money?" asked Caleb.

"Bunch of ways. I traded in some old video games, and I got extra money for Christmas from my Pap."

Drew could see the pain in Jeff's face as soon as he said the words. It was as though Jeff, for just a second, forgot his Pap was gone.

The next few cycles of throwing were silent. Drew figured it was best to stay quiet – resuming the conversation or changing the subject seemed like it would be disrespectful to Pap – but Tommy picked up right where they left off.

"I always spend money as soon as I get it," he said.

To Drew's surprise, Jeff answered quickly and unoffended: "And that's why I'm gonna have a cooler bike than you."

"Yeah, yeah," Tommy said as he whipped the ball to Caleb.

"Ya know," said Caleb, "you might have a cooler bike, but so what? You're still not better at baseball."

"I'm just as good as you, Caleb," Jeff contended.

"Yeah, right. I guarantee I could strike you out."

"No way!" said Jeff. He fired the ball to Tommy much harder than before. The mitt popped like it was an exclamation point to Jeff's response.

"Yes huh! You're lucky we're on the same team, or I'd be striking you out all the time."

"No, I could definitely crush one off you!"

"Okay, prove it," said Caleb.

"How?"

"I'll pitch to you right here in the street."

"Yeah, right."

"Yeah. What's the matter? You scared I'll strike you out?" Caleb sneered.

"No. You still mad Zobby struck *you* out?" Jeff bit back. It was unlike Jeff to be so aggressive, but he seemed to have gained some mettle since his Pap's death.

"Man, you gotta be kidding me," said Caleb. "We've been over this. It was one time ..." Now he shot venom with his words: "Plus, I'm a better athlete than all of you."

All three other boys' eyes widened, and a moment of stunned silence passed.

"Stop being a baby and get up to bat. I'll show you up right now," Caleb continued.

"No," said Jeff, clearly agitated. "We're not even on a field. And the field at the park is still too muddy. We don't even have a mound, or a catcher, or an ump!"

"So? Here, this'll be the plate ..." Caleb grabbed Jeff's mitt off his hand and slapped it on the pavement. Then he walked several paces up the street. "I'll pitch from here. This is about the space from the mound to home plate. Tommy can catch and Drew can be the umpire."

"But we don't have catcher's equipment," Jeff argued.

"Yeah, I'm not catching without a mask ... or a cup," said Tommy. "I guess I shoulda looked harder for a tennis ball, huh?"

Caleb thought for a moment. "Okay, so Drew and Tommy can stand like ten feet behind the plate and call balls and strikes. And they can catch the pitches that get past. 'Cause trust me, they *will* get past. Three of 'em, right in a row. And when I strike you out, no more *Zobby* jokes. If you even hit *one* off me, I'll admit you're better than me – unless you just wanna admit now that *I'm* better than *you*."

Jeff was fuming. "Fine! Let's do it!" He grabbed the bat and got into his batting stance.

Caleb peered over the top of his mitt, trying to intimidate his opponent.

"Pitch it," Jeff demanded.

Drew and Tommy stood about 15 feet behind Jeff.

"Maybe this isn't such a good idea," said Drew.

"It's not a good idea for him 'cause I'm gonna smash one right over his head!" Jeff bellowed.

Caleb was already in his wind-up. He turned, reached back, and threw the ball as hard as he could. It landed a foot in front of the plate, but Jeff swung anyway. It bounced past him and into Tommy's mitt.

"Ha, that's strike one," Caleb boasted.

"C'mon, Jeff, that was way too low," said Drew. He forgot he had been opposed to this challenge, and he now found himself rooting for his best friend to blast one over Caleb's head.

Tommy tossed the ball back to Caleb.

"Pitch it again," Jeff growled, wringing the bat.

Caleb had a sly smile on his face. He wound up and pitched the ball. This pitch was a little faster than the first, but it was right down the middle. Jeff swung hard, but again the bat made no contact with the ball. It flew past him, bounced once, and Drew snagged it.

"Steee-rike two!" Caleb roared.

"Shut up. You're not the umpire," said Jeff.

Caleb laughed. "One more strike and you're out."

"Count's nothing and two," said Tommy.

Caleb took off his hat and ran his hand through his hair. With his glove tucked under his arm, he put his hat back on and rubbed the ball hard with his bare hands. "Sorry, Jeff, this will only take a sec. The ball's all scuffed up since it hit the street ... you know, 'stead of your bat."

Jeff waited in the invisible batter's box with the bat held high.

"What, no comeback?" said Caleb.

"Just pitch."

The next pitch was Caleb's attempt at a curveball. Just like when he threw to Drew, the ball bounced several feet before its intended destination. Jeff let this one pass him.

"Ball one. One ball, two strikes," said Tommy.

"That was my curve," said Caleb.

"Oh, good one," Jeff said sarcastically. "You might wanna stick to hockey."

"Shut up. I won't waste my time anymore. Here comes strike three."

Caleb wound up and delivered the pitch.

"C'mon, Jeff, you got this," Drew whispered to himself. He found himself rooting against Caleb just as much as he was rooting for Jeff.

The ball sizzled toward the plate. Jeff swung. *Ping!* The ball jumped from the bat and towered over Caleb's head and above the treetop horizon. The bat dropped from Jeff's hands. Each boy stood and watched, helplessly frozen by the soaring white dot. It descended toward a red-brick house up the street.

The unmistakable sound of shattering glass filled the air. Drew felt certain the entire neighborhood must have heard it.

"Oh, crap!" Caleb shouted.

Each boy's eyes darted around, first at each other, then at their surroundings. They ran toward the house but stopped as soon as they were close enough to see the damage. A rectangular window on the right side of the red-brick house was broken. Only jagged shards around the edge remained.

"Look what you did, Jeff," said Caleb.

Jeff's lips quivered, but no words escaped. His face was a mask of shock, fear, and guilt.

"We gotta get outta here," said Tommy.

Finally Jeff spoke. "I ... This is *your* fault, Caleb."

"Me? You hit it. And Tommy's the one who made us use a hardball."

"What? You can't blame me," said Tommy.

"You can't blame me either," said Caleb. "If I get in trouble for this, my parents will seriously ground me forever."

"But ..." Jeff started. He looked like he was going to be sick. He turned his pale face to Drew in desperation, and Drew knew exactly what he was thinking. If Jeff got in trouble for this, his parents would make him use his bike money to pay for the window.

A pair of headlights emerged from the end of the street.

"Someone's coming," said Tommy.

"Run! We'll go to Tommy's house," said Caleb, taking off down the street.

Without hesitation, Tommy picked up the remaining evidence – his bat – and followed Caleb.

"Come on, guys!" Caleb shouted back to Jeff and Drew.

Jeff looked to Drew. He gave an apologetic shrug of the shoulders, picked up his mitt, and took off after Caleb and Tommy. The car slowed down and pulled into a driveway several houses up the street. A woman got out of the car and walked into her house without even looking in Drew's direction. *And those guys ran away as if –*

"Hey!" Mr. Kaminsky had emerged from his front door. He lumbered toward Drew, clenching the baseball in his meaty hand.

"Drew? My kitchen window – did you see who did this?"

"I ... I ..."

He looked back, hoping his friends had decided to return to the scene of the crime and turn themselves in, or at least admit *some* fault, but no one was there. He was all alone. The only thing he could think to say was, "It was me. I broke your window."

Tommy brought the hardball, Caleb made the challenge, and Jeff hit the ball that smashed the window. So how did I end up taking the fall?

"Let's go talk to your mom," said Mr. Kaminsky.

When they walked through the front door, Penny was on the phone with a potential home buyer.

"If you want to put in an offer, I'd do it soon. There just aren't many houses like it in the North Hills area, so it won't be available much longer. But something just came up. Think it over, and I'll give you a call back first thing tomorrow morning. ... Okay, Nicole, sounds good."

"Hi, Penny."

"Hey, Mike. Everything okay?"

"Well," said Mr. Kaminsky, "my kitchen window is broken to pieces, and, well, your son apparently knows how it happened."

Why did Mr. Kaminsky say it like that? Drew wondered. *Why didn't he just tell her I broke the window?*

"Drew ..." Penny said with sudden anger in her voice. "What happened?"

"Well, we were playing baseball in the street, and –"

"But you were using a *tennis ball*, weren't you?" She hadn't noticed the baseball in Mr. Kaminsky's hand.

"We couldn't find one, so we used a baseball. But we were being careful."

"So how did Mr. Kaminsky's window happen to break?"

Drew thought one last time about telling the truth. He wanted to tell them exactly what happened: Tommy brought the hardball, Caleb initiated the confrontation, and Jeff hit the ball. He also wanted to tell them he was the only one who said using the baseball was a bad idea. But, for some reason, he found himself telling a different story.

"Um, the other guys went home, and I just wanted to hit one more pop-up to myself. I thought it would go straight up in the air. But I hit it too hard, and it ended up going through Mr. Kaminsky's window."

Drew had lied to his dad about The Shack, he lied to *everyone* about Trevor, and now he was lying again. Each time, it seemed to be the only option he had. Lying was the only way his friends would be safe and Jeff could still get his bike.

"So, is that how it happened?" said Mr. Kaminsky.

Penny shook her head side to side.

"Mike, we will obviously pay for the window," she said. "Let me know how much it costs and we'll take care of it. Drew, did you tell Mr. Kaminsky how sorry you are?"

"I'm really sorry, Mr. Kaminsky. It really was an accident, I swear."

"I know, Drew. Accidents do happen," said Mr. Kaminsky. He looked over at Penny as she sighed and rubbed the side of her face. He turned to walk out the door but stopped and said, "You like to paint, right, Drew?"

"Yeah, I guess."

"Well, the fence in my backyard needs painted. I'm not sure I'll have time to do it, and the arthritis in my hand has been acting up. I was gonna pay someone to do it next weekend, since this sunny weather is supposed to hold up for at least another week. But here's an idea – you could paint the fence for me, and then we'll call it even. Of course, I'd still expect you to do a good job."

Mr. Kaminsky was looking at Drew but seemed to be talking to Penny. "Of course, this is only if it's okay with your mom."

"Oh, Mike, are you sure about this?"

"Sure I'm sure. I got to see the mural Drew painted on the swing set at the park before the storm hit. I saw how hard he worked on it. If he puts that same effort into the fence, he'll do fine." He turned back to Drew. "I know it doesn't sound like as much fun, but whadda ya say? Do we have a deal?" He extended his hand toward Drew.

Drew looked at his mom. Her expression seemed to indicate approval. Feeling like there was no other option, Drew accepted the gesture and said, "All right, Mr. Kaminsky. It's a deal."

"Good. Be at my house Saturday at nine a.m." He stopped before he was out the door and turned back. "And Drew ..." He smiled and tossed the baseball to him, "Don't be late."

While Drew waited for his mom to start yelling at him, he wasn't thinking about the painting, the swing set, the window, or even the picture on page 139. Instead, he was thinking about Jeff's bike. Jeff had run so he wouldn't have to spend his bike savings on a new window. But, as it turned out, he never would've had to pay the money anyway. And now Drew was still left to bear the blame.

"Andrew, go to your room *now.*"

"But just –"

"No, none of that. I am *furious* with you." Penny picked up the phone from the table next to the couch.

"Who are you calling?" Drew asked.

"Your father."

"Oh, why?"

"Drew, enough. Get to your room."

Drew slunk out of the living room and grabbed the phone from the kitchen on his way. When he got to his room he turned it on, covering the end with his hand and breathing lightly so his eavesdropping couldn't be detected.

"I've told him a million times not to use a hardball in the street. It's like he doesn't get it," Penny was saying.

Drew heard what he recognized as a frustrated sigh from his dad.

"All right, how much is it gonna cost?"

"Well, actually ..." Penny explained Mr. Kaminsky's suggestion.

"I don't know about that, Pen."

Drew knew his dad would be unsure about Mr. Kaminsky's idea. Mr. Daley never liked to take shortcuts that would leave him feeling like he owed something to somebody.

"I think it would be good for him," said Penny.

"Do you think he learned his lesson?" Mr. Daley asked.

"I just don't know anymore. I thought the whole thing with the woods would have calmed him down. He seemed to be fine, but now this. It's starting to feel like one thing after another. And before you know it, it'll be summer, which is always difficult because then he has even more free time."

"He'll be all right."

"I know he'll be *all right*, Ryan. But I want more than that for him. Drew's a good kid, but he gets into some bad situations."

"Think that has anything to do with that Caleb kid?" Mr. Daley asked.

"I don't know, he seems harmless. Maybe just a little more outgoing."

"I dunno, Pen, he seems kind of like a schemer. I –"

"So are you saying you don't want Drew to paint the fence?"

After a pause, Mr. Daley said, "No, it's fine. He can paint the fence. I know Kaminsky's a good guy. If that's what he wants to do, that's fine. Wait, hold on ... yeah, that's my boss on the other line. I have to take this."

"All right."

"Tell Drew I'll catch up with him later."

Drew wished he'd never picked up the phone in the first place. He shouldn't have heard all that. The disappointment in his mom's tone. The irritation from his dad. It was too much to take.

For the first time ever, Drew resented his friends, even Jeff. Drew did nothing wrong, but he had to pay. It was *his* Saturday that was wasted, not theirs. It was *his* parents who were disappointed, not theirs. After all he had done for his friends, he felt betrayed.

He had trouble falling asleep that night. His head was filled with the sound of shattering glass, and he was still bothered by his parents' conversation. He turned on his light and opened his science book to page 139. The drawing of the ocean shore hidden away inside the book was a lot like Mrs. McGrath's dandelions – neither belonged. But Drew didn't care for Mrs. McGrath's theory.

Who gets to pick where something fits in?

After studying the picture for a few moments, the sound of breaking glass was replaced by the sound of breaking waves.

Monday morning began with a lecture. Penny admonished Drew about using a hardball in the street just as she had done many times before, but this time she spoke in the "I told you so" tone adults seem to relish.

"And you understand why I'm upset, right? It's okay to play baseball with a hardball at a field, but *not* in the street. The same way it would be fine to scream and yell at a ball game but not in school."

It was one thing to be punished for going to The Shack – he knew he deserved that. But Drew didn't have much interest in being scolded for something he didn't do, so this lecture fell on deaf ears.

To make matters worse, when he got to school he

didn't receive the hero's welcome he had expected. He thought Jeff, Tommy, and Caleb would be grateful for his sacrifice, but none of them mentioned the incident at all. And, because no one brought it up, the others didn't even know Drew had gotten caught, or that he'd be painting a fence on Saturday.

Instead, most of the conversation all week (especially during lunch) was dominated by the big birthday party Tia Cardiff was having on Saturday. The entire fifth grade was invited, along with many other kids. Tia's family lived in the biggest house in Emerson. On Monday everyone was talking about how they had a basketball court and a heated indoor swimming pool. On Tuesday everyone was talking about how a magician would be at the party. On Wednesday Skylar told Drew she was going to be there, which meant Drew would miss out on spending time with the only other person he had found who appreciated the ocean shore drawing.

By Thursday Drew couldn't take it any longer. He quickly ate his packed lunch and asked Mr. Frye, who was on cafeteria duty, if he could go to his locker to get his lunch card. He couldn't sit and listen to everyone talk about a party he wouldn't be able to attend.

As he loafed to his locker, Zobby came speeding up alongside him.

"Hey," she said, giving him a friendly nudge with her elbow.

"Hey, where are you going?"

"I forgot my lunch card in my locker. Gotta run and get it. I'll see ya in the cafeteria," she said as she passed him.

"Isn't lunch like halfway over?"

"That's why I'm running. I was talking to Mr. Barker for a while. He really wants me to start playing an instrument."

"That's cool. Can I walk with you?"

"Sure. What's up? Something wrong? Why aren't you still in lunch?" Zobby's line of questioning was as quickly paced as her gait.

"I dunno. It's just some stuff with the guys."

Zobby slowed down. "What happened?"

"Just some stupid stuff," Drew said.

"What *kind* of stupid stuff?"

"I dunno. It's nothing."

"Oh. Well, it happens. It'll probably blow over. Hey, on Saturday I got in a big fight with Mary Beth. I was over her house and her brother was playing wiffle ball with his friends and they needed an extra player. So I played because, why not, ya know? But Mary Beth wouldn't play. Then she was mad at me because I wasn't hanging out with her. I said she should've played, too. Then she said I wanted to be a boy. Like, just because I played wiffle ball doesn't mean I wanna be a boy, ya know? I'm just good at wiffle ball. I dunno. I guess she was just mad 'cause I was playing with them instead of her. But the next day she wasn't mad anymore and everything was back to normal. We never even had to talk about it, ya know? Sometimes we get mad at each other, but then things go back to normal. Maybe that's what being friends is all about."

"I hope you're right," said Drew.

Zobby snatched her lunch card from her locker. "Well, I'm starving, so let's go."

On their way back to the cafeteria, Zobby asked, "You excited for Tia's birthday party on Saturday? I think it's from eleven 'til three. Did you know they have a pool where music plays underwater? Isn't that like, the coolest thing ever? My mom can take us if you need a ride."

"I can't go."

"What do you mean you *can't go*? Your *girlfriend* Skylar Jansen is in the same dance class as Tia, so she's gonna be there!" She completed her mockery by making kissing noises.

"First off, she's *not* my girlfriend. We just talk sometimes. And second, I have to do something on Saturday."

"With your dad?"

"No, it's pretty much the reason things are so weird with me and the guys right now."

"Well," Zobby said as they entered the cafeteria, "you obviously don't wanna tell me what it is. But whatever it is, I'd try to get out of it. I wouldn't wanna miss this party."

On Friday afternoon, as social studies class was about to end, the students were gathering their things and getting ready to go home. Mr. Sawyer was standing near Drew, Jeff, and Tommy, while Caleb was talking to Danny a few feet away.

"Anyone have fun plans for the weekend?" Mr. Sawyer asked.

"Tia's having a huge birthday party tomorrow," said Tommy.

"It's gonna be awesome," said Jeff. He turned to Drew. "You're going, right?"

"No, I have to paint a fence tomorrow."

"Well, hey, painting can be fun," said Mr. Sawyer. "You like to paint, right?"

"Well, yeah ..."

"Where's the fence? Your backyard?" Mr. Sawyer asked.

"No, I have to paint a neighbor's fence 'cause I accidentally hit a baseball through his window," said Drew, as if that was what really happened. It was as if he had told the lie so many times that he forgot it was a lie in the first place.

Jeff and Tommy exchanged nervous glances, as if they

were wondering if Drew was tempted to tell Mr. Sawyer the truth. Caleb, oblivious to the conversation, was giggling and playing a hand-slap game with Danny.

Mr. Sawyer smiled. "I've been there."

"You've been to Mr. Kaminsky's house?" Drew asked.

"No, Drew, I mean I've broken some windows in my day."

"Really?"

"Yeah, really?" said Jeff.

"Sure. One time, I was about your age, maybe a little older, and my friends and I were having a snowball fight. We were firing those babies at each other. We were behind our fort, and my buddy was making them while I was throwing them. He handed me one and I threw it without realizing it was actually a big chunk of ice."

"Oh, man," said Tommy. "What happened?"

"Luckily for my target, he ducked. But it flew over him and smashed the windshield of a car."

"No way! You can't smash a windshield with a snowball," said Tommy.

"I did. Things can break pretty easily when it's very cold out."

"How much trouble did you get in?" Jeff asked.

"And how hard did you throw it?" added Tommy.

"I threw it about as hard as I could. Anyway, I thought a vein was going to pop out of my dad's forehead when he was yelling at me. But I ended up with a punishment similar to Drew's."

"What do you mean?" Drew asked.

"The car belonged to a woman named Miss Barr. I agreed to shovel her sidewalk and driveway every day for the rest of that winter. So every morning I got up early, and if it had snowed that night, I walked up to her house and shoveled. And if it snowed throughout the day, I went and shoveled in the afternoon."

"That stinks," said Tommy. "I'd never wanna do that."

"I didn't have much of a choice," said Mr. Sawyer. "But Miss Barr told me something that I've always remembered, even though it didn't mean much to me at the time. She said, 'When you have to do something you don't want to do, do it with a smile on your face. You'll find that it's not so bad after all.'"

The boys looked at their teacher blankly.

"I like that advice," said Mr. Sawyer. "Anyway, you said it was an accident, right?"

"Yeah, it was totally an accident," said Drew without looking at his friends.

"The way I look at it," the young teacher said, "every kid is allowed one broken window."

All three boys smiled.

"You gotta let kids be kids, right?" said Tommy.

"I think so," Mr. Sawyer answered. "You've got to let kids be kids. Otherwise, the balance of the universe is disrupted."

"Hey, Drew, hold up," Jeff yelled.

Drew was already heading out the door of the school.

"Listen, man," said Jeff, catching his breath, "I'm sorry."

Drew looked at his best friend without changing his facial expression.

"Okay," he said.

"I didn't know what to do, and I thought I'd get in a ton of trouble," said Jeff. "And I thought you woulda run, too. I didn't think you'd stay behind."

As they talked, Tommy caught up to where they were standing.

"It's okay," said Drew.

"No, it's not," Jeff went on. "I'm the one who broke the window. I should be the one in trouble, not you."

"Yeah, but if you say it's you now, we'll *all* get in trouble," said Tommy. "Plus Drew will get in trouble for lying."

It was clear that Tommy had already considered what would happen if the boys came clean.

"Drew's the man for not ratting us out," he said, putting his arm around him. "'Cept he does have a thick skull ..." He lightly knocked on Drew's head with his knuckles. "You gotta learn to run away, man! My brother taught me that when I was like five."

Drew shrugged his shoulder to get Tommy's big arm off. "Oh well, can't do anything now."

"I really feel bad," said Jeff. "Are you at least coming to *any* of Tia's party tomorrow?"

"No, I'm painting tomorrow, probably all day."

"What if you finish early?"

"Doesn't matter. My parents said I'm not going anywhere all weekend. That's the other part of my punishment."

"Wow, that's the worst," said Tommy. "This party is gonna be sick! I heard there's gonna be a hypnotist there to make people do stupid stuff."

"I didn't know you were friends with Tia," said Drew. "Do you ever talk to her?"

"No, I'm not, I mean, she's okay I guess. Everyone's invited, so it doesn't really matter. I dunno, it'll be cool," stumbled Tommy. "Anyways, I gotta go see if me and Caleb are riding to the party together. I'll see you guys later."

Jeff looked at Drew sincerely. "Is there anything I can do? You know, to make it up to you."

"It's fine, man," said Drew. "Don't worry about it. And this way you'll be able to work on your neighbor's house soon, get the money, and get your bike."

"Oh, I forgot to tell you. Last night my dad asked me how much I saved for the bike. After I told him I was only fifteen bucks short he was like, 'I'm proud of you for saving up for something you wanted.' And then he told me he wants to open a bank account for me and put in the money I saved, and at first I thought he wasn't letting me buy the bike, ya know? But then he took me out to the driveway and showed me the brand new bike he bought me! It's so awesome."

"That's great, man. I can't wait to take it for a test ride."

"For sure. It's so fast."

As the two walked home, Jeff talked about all the features of his new bike: the sparkling, navy blue paint, the 24-inch wheels, the handlebar brakes, and even a set of axle foot pegs.

All the while, Drew mulled over the recent events. He had originally stayed to take the blame so Jeff would be able to keep his bike money. Then Mr. Kaminsky didn't even ask for money for the broken window, and now Jeff's dad bought him the bike anyway.

Drew was happy that *someone* took the blame, because Mr. Kaminsky didn't deserve to have his window broken. *But,* Drew thought, *why does it have to be me?*

◆

Saturday morning Drew stood in Mr. Kaminsky's backyard staring at an unpainted wooden fence that might as well have extended forever. He tried to convince himself that this could somehow be fun, but standing there with the daunting task ahead was downright painful.

An open can of white paint sat on the ground. Next to it was a plastic package containing two brand new paintbrushes. Mr. Kaminsky opened the package and handed a brush to Drew. He took the other brush, dipped it in the paint, and showed Drew the proper fence-painting technique.

After his short demonstration, he set the brush down

and said, "You have everything you need. I have to go run some errands, but I'll be back in a couple hours." He lifted his sunglasses and scanned the entire fence. "Maybe you'll be done by then," he said in a tone Drew couldn't differentiate between sarcastic and sincere.

As Drew painted, each minute felt like ten. It seemed impossible that he would ever be able to finish. He occasionally stepped back to check his progress, but the white section of the fence seemed like a speck compared to what was still left to paint. Painting with his dad had been fun. This was not. Looking at the fence, he didn't see the beauty he saw in the ocean scene drawing, nor did he feel the same pride he felt when painting the swing set. Instead, all he saw was uneven paint dripping down the wood, and all he felt was frustration toward the whole situation.

I can't believe I'm doing this. I didn't even break the stupid window.

"Hello," said a voice from the yard next door.

A young boy's face peeked over the fence. Looking through the planks of the fence, Drew could see that the boy was standing on a patio chair.

"Hi," Drew nodded and continued painting.

"Whatcha doin'?" the boy asked.

"Painting this fence."

"That's Mr. Kaminsky's fence."

"Yeah," said Drew.

"Are kids even allowed to paint fences?"

"Yeah, kids are allowed to paint fences."

"How old are you?"

"Eleven."

"I just turned six." As the boy talked, his eyes went up and down with each stroke of the brush.

Drew looked up at him again. "Were you just eating a fudgesicle?"

"Yeah, how'd you know that?" the boy asked, sounding shocked that Drew could be privy to such secret information.

"You have chocolate all over your face," said Drew.

"Oh," said the boy. "Hey, can I do that too?"

"Do what?"

"Paint. I never knowed kids were *allowed* to paint fences. Can I do it, too?"

"Wait, you mean you *want* to paint this fence?"

The boy shook his head up and down.

"Wouldn't you rather go play or something?"

"I wanna play painting that fence. You get to do what grown-ups do. I wanna know what it's like to be a grown-up. Don't you?"

"I dunno. Wouldn't you rather just do kid stuff, though?"

"I was. I was running around pretending I was a airplane. See, like this ..." The boy stuck his arms straight out to his sides and glided around in a circle. "You ever been on a airplane?" he asked.

"Yeah, once," said Drew.

"Wow, I wanna ride on a airplane someday. What was it like?"

"It was cool, I guess. It was a while ago. I was about your age, maybe a little younger. I flew to the beach with my parents ..."

A brief pang of affection shot through Drew and quickly disappeared.

"It was weird because when we took off, my ears popped. It happens to some people on airplanes," he continued.

The boy covered his ears with his hands. "I don't want my ears to pop off."

Drew laughed. "No, your ears don't pop *off*."

"My mom says airplanes go fast. How fast did yours go?" The boy no longer seemed worried about his ears popping off.

"I'm not sure," said Drew, "but once you're up in the air, it doesn't even feel like you're going fast at all."

"Really?"

"Yeah."

"I bet we look like ants to people on airplanes," the boy mused. "I hope I get to go on one someday. But now I just pretend I am one. Can I help you paint? I'll do a good job. I'll be careful, I promise. I watched you do it. I'll do it the same way."

Drew looked at the second paintbrush lying next to the paint can. *What harm is there in letting the kid help if he wants to? Besides, I didn't deserve this punishment anyway. And if he helps, we can be done before Mr. Kaminsky even gets home.*

"All right, come on over. I got a brush for you and everything. By the way, what's your name?"

"Trevor."

"Okay, Trevor – wait, Trevor?"

"Uh huh."

Drew nearly dropped his paintbrush. He suddenly found himself thinking about Trevor Lambert and the cheat sheet. He remembered the saying Trevor had told him: Every time you don't get caught for something you did, you will get caught for something you didn't do. *I never got in trouble for planting that cheat sheet on Trevor, but then I got in trouble for breaking the window, even though it wasn't even me.* Drew remembered how free Trevor felt after serving his punishment.

"Can I have the other brush now?"

"Actually," said Drew, "I'm gonna paint the fence myself. I kinda have to."

Young Trevor's head hung low.

"Okay," he moped and returned to his side of the fence.

"You like pretending you're an airplane, right?" Drew asked through the fence.

"Yeah, it's fun."

"Then you should go ahead and do that. It'll be a lot more fun than painting this fence."

"Okay," said the boy. He stuck out his arms and resumed flying around his yard.

Each brush stroke on the fence was one step closer to finishing the job. Drew took a short break and backed away from the fence. He was just over the halfway mark.

"Looking good, look-ing good," said Mr. Kaminsky as he approached the fence with a big bag in his hands. "What do you say I grab us some iced tea and you can take a break?"

After putting the bag in the house, Mr. Kaminsky reemerged with two glasses of iced tea.

"You always want to make sure you cover the paint can when you aren't using it," he said. "It gets funky when you let it sit."

Drew nodded and covered the can. The two sat on the back porch and drank their iced tea silently. Just as Drew finished his drink and stood up to resume working, Mr. Kaminsky said, "You know I know you didn't break that window, right?"

Every bit of color Drew's face had gained under the morning sun disappeared at once.

"Listen, calm down. You're not in trouble," said Mr. Kaminsky. He motioned for Drew to sit.

Drew sat back down and remained silent. *Has Mr. Kaminsky known all along?*

The man leaned back in his chair and took another sip of iced tea. "Your story, it didn't add up. You said you *hit* the ball through my window. But you didn't have a bat with you. Where was the bat?" He turned the glass in his hand and looked at it for a moment. "In fact, you still had a glove on when I saw you."

"It's just I –"

"No, no." Mr. Kaminsky motioned with his free hand for Drew to stop. He leaned forward and his voice took on a sterner tone. "No explanation necessary. I want you to know, it takes a *man* to stick up for his friends. And that's admirable. But don't lie to your mom, all right? She doesn't deserve to be lied to."

Drew nodded. Mr. Kaminsky leaned back in his chair and smiled. "I guess your friends pulled off a real hit-and-run," he said, chuckling at his own joke.

Drew stared up at Mr. Kaminsky, who was just now finishing his iced tea. With his head tilted back and the sunlight reflecting off his glasses, he looked younger than before.

"This can be our secret, all right?"

"All right," said Drew, standing up again.

"Oh, just get out of here. I'll finish up," said Mr. Kaminsky, slowly getting to his feet.

"No," Drew said firmly. "I'll finish this. This is my job."

Mr. Kaminsky put his hands up as if to surrender. "Hey, no argument here."

Drew returned to the fence and continued to paint in the brush stroke Mr. Kaminsky had taught him. The sun was bright, and as Drew felt its heat on his face, he thought of the warmth he felt while looking at the drawing in his book. It was incredible to him that the little drawing managed to evoke so much emotion.

The air swelled with springtime music: the birds were chirping, the bees were humming, and in the distance a lawnmower was roaring. Even the bristles of the paintbrush passing smoothly along the fence blended into the symphony. Drew still wanted to be at Tia's party with Skylar and the rest of his friends; but he had to finish the job, and he did so with a smile on his face.

Anything to Win

Abigail Linwood. The mention of the name irked Drew to his core. Abigail was the best student in the fifth grade. She aced every test. She never forgot her homework. She always raised her hand, and she always knew the answer. In math class, she won the flash card competition. In language arts class, she won the spelling bee. And her project won first place at last month's science fair. Her name had become synonymous with academic success, so, of course, many of the other students referred to her as "the teacher's pet."

Drew sat in language arts class on a Friday afternoon in late April, doodling in his notebook as Mr. Frye introduced a new assignment.

"Write this down ..." Mr. Frye said as he thoughtfully stroked his brown goatee.

But Drew was hardly listening. Half of his attention was focused on his doodling, the other half on Abigail. He watched as she sat rigidly upright in her chair and drilled into her binder every word Mr. Frye said.

That binder, white with big yellow polka dots, was rather mysterious. She always used her arm to guard whatever she was writing in it. That wasn't out of the ordinary, though. Abigail always guarded everything, whether it was notes, a test, or even a simple in-class worksheet. What really made Drew curious was this: the binder had a lock on it. After Abigail would finish writing in it, or after she added important handouts to it, she would zip it closed, then pull a tiny silver key from her pocket and turn it in a lock attached to the zipper. After a brief glance around, she would slide the key back into her pocket. Whatever was in that binder, she didn't want anyone to see it.

"And definitely write this down ..." Mr. Frye said.

He was always telling the students to write things down. He rarely handed out papers at all. Instead, he had the students write everything in their notebooks. He said he had two reasons for doing so: it required the students to pay close attention, and it helped them remember the information better. Drew thought it did help a little, but it was a pain to stay so attentive.

It didn't seem hard at all for Abigail, though. She relentlessly copied Mr. Frye's words into her binder. How was she never tempted to steal a glance at the clock? And didn't she notice that Tommy, sitting right next to her, was chewing gum in class again? Didn't she wonder if Mr. Frye would catch him? Mr. Frye busted kids for chewing gum more than any other teacher and he had already caught Tommy three times in the past two weeks. But, as Tommy continued to chomp, Abigail continued to write. And Drew continued to ponder how a kid could stay so focused on class when there were so many other things to think about – like TV shows. And movies. And who was pitching for the Pirates that night. And the bee stuck in the ceiling light. And ruined swing sets. And broken windows. And Mystery Artists.

Drew sighed and looked down at his notebook. What had begun as a sketch of a zombie baseball player had deformed into a random series of crooked lines. He realized he better pay attention to Mr. Frye. The new assignment he was explaining was a special one. It was a contest he held every year called "If I Were Principal." The students would work in groups of three throughout the following week. At the end of the week, one student from each group would deliver a speech in front of the class.

"This really is a great assignment," Mr. Frye continued. "The winning team will receive a *special, secret prize*."

Heads perked up, and a wave of excitement rippled through the room. Ambitious looks were exchanged among friends, and silent plans already seemed to be forming.

"Dr. Linus will be here for the speeches. She listens to them every year. She likes to hear new ideas. When all the speeches are complete, Dr. Linus and I will choose the winner, and that team will receive the *secret prize*."

With this announcement, most of the students sunk back down in their seats. It was already likely that Abigail would win the contest – everyone knew that. But now that the principal herself would help choose the winner, it was a *guarantee* Abigail would win. Abigail was the student Dr. Linus wanted everyone to be like. There was one major way the other students knew this: Dr. Linus knew Abigail's name. Dr. Linus didn't know the names of many students. The ones she did know were of the kids who were sent to her office regularly for bad behavior, or the ones like Abigail, who were so exceptional that they demanded to be noticed. It was as if the principal was only familiar with the very best and the very worst students.

When Mr. Frye finished speaking, Abigail gently placed her pencil on her desk. She leaned back slightly with a barely hidden smile on her face, as if she were already plotting the defeat of her classmates. Or perhaps she was already preparing her victory speech and trying to figure out what her newest prize would be. Regardless, it was a foregone conclusion that she would win the contest, and it was likely that everyone in the class had silently accepted it – everyone except Drew. He was tired of Abigail being the best. Although he rarely talked to her and knew little about her beyond her academic success, he simply did not like her.

Perhaps the root of Drew's friction with Abigail arose last year when he was having a tough time with math class. He and his dad had spent hours studying for everything that could have possibly been on the upcoming test. When the students got their tests back, Drew turned his over and saw an 89%, his best grade in math all year. But the elation of success was snatched away when he turned and caught a glimpse of Abigail's 103% (she even got the bonus question right!). Seeing Drew's score, Abigail had said, "That's good, Drew. B's are really good for *some* people."

Now Abigail's mere existence taunted Drew. Every trifle of her being – from the freckles on her nose to the way she held her pencil to the way she protected that polka dotted binder – attracted his disdain. Fed up with feeling inferior, Drew decided it was finally time to knock Abigail off her pedestal.

Mr. Frye allowed the students to pick their own groups. As Drew, Jeff, and Tommy got together, Drew told them how much he wanted to beat Abigail and win the contest.

"I dunno, man," said Tommy. "Seems like a lot of work for nothing, 'cause Abigail will probably win no matter what."

He was staring down at his phone, which he had snuck out of his pocket and was hiding under his desk. He didn't appear to be texting or looking anything up, but rather mindlessly opening and closing apps.

Drew turned to Jeff. "What about you?"

Jeff shrugged. "I dunno."

"I'm telling you, we can do this," said Drew. "Abigail is always winning, always trying to prove how smart she is. This can be our chance. We can do this." He scanned his friends' faces, hoping to have uplifted their spirits, but

Tommy continued to play with his phone, and Jeff was staring down at a blank piece of notebook paper. Drew knew he'd have to find a better way to entice his friends.

"Tommy, you always wanna win prizes. Well, this could be huge! What if it's tickets to a Pirate game? Huh? What if the winner gets to meet some of the players, and instead of us going, it's Abigail?"

"Wait!" Tommy shot up, shoving his phone back into his pocket. "Do you really think we could meet the players?"

"Sure," said Drew. "It could be anything."

"That would be so sweet. What if we got to take batting practice at PNC Park?"

"So are you in?"

"Yeah, I wanna win. Can we, though? We don't got an idea, and anyways, I can't be the one to do the speech. Mr. Frye hates me for no reason. He'd never pick me as the winner."

"Well, it probably shouldn't be me," said Drew. "Teachers usually say I go off topic too much."

Drew and Tommy looked at the non-committal Jeff.

"Me?" he asked.

"It's gotta be you! You never go off topic like me, and Mr. Frye never yells at you. You're our best chance to win."

"Yeah, Drew's right. And we have to beat Abigail," said Tommy.

"And everyone would see me beat Abigail," Jeff said aloud but intended for himself. "Okay, I'll do it."

So Jeff wanted the glory, Tommy wanted the prize, and Drew wanted to beat Abigail. But all three agreed on one common goal: win the contest.

On Monday, Mr. Frye gave everyone the entire class period to begin working. After the boys had brainstormed for a while, a gleam of light seemed to flash across Jeff's mind.

"How about this ..." he started but then backed away.

"Go ahead," said Drew.

"Well, okay, what if the idea was to get the businesses around here to give us gift cards? Like, give us donations, ya know?"

"What would be the point of that?" asked Tommy.

"I mean," Jeff continued, "the school could get gift cards from all the places we go to. You know, restaurants like Rizzo's, and maybe Melia's, and places like that. And those could be rewards for kids for perfect attendance and things like that ..."

"Yeah," said Drew, "Mr. Melia is the best. He'd definitely do it."

"And getting free stuff is sweet," Tommy added.

"Yeah, and maybe for the places that donate stuff there could be a program where students volunteer at that place," Drew suggested. "Just to help clean up and stuff. You know, stuff kids can do."

"Exactly!" said Jeff. "See, it'll be good for the school because kids will work harder to get the gift cards. And if the school gets better, then all of Emerson gets better. And then more people would want to move here so their kids can go here. And that would mean more customers for the businesses here."

The boys noticed that Mr. Frye was standing next to them with an impressed smile on his face.

"I like what I hear," he said, tapping notes into his tablet. "It looks like this might be one of the best contests in a long time."

After he walked away, the boys noticed that Abigail and her partners, Lexi and Brooke, were looking at them. Tommy quickly guarded the paper on Jeff's desk and said, "What are you looking at?"

"Nothing –" Abigail began, but Tommy cut her off.

"Just mind your own business, Abby."

"My name is Abigail, not Abby."

"Really? I thought your name was Teacher's Pet," Tommy shot back.

Abigail sneered and shook her head. The two groups spent the rest of the period glaring at each other out of the corners of their eyes and discussing their ideas in whispers. It was war.

The next day, Mr. Frye gave everyone the second half of class to continue working on their ideas and begin preparing their speeches. At the end of the day, while everyone was getting ready to go home, Abigail was at her locker across the hall from Drew, Jeff, and Tommy.

"Time to go home and study for ten hours, right, Abby?" said Tommy.

"My name is not Abby. And it's not Teacher's Pet, either. It's Abigail."

"You sure?" said Tommy. "Maybe it's Suck-Up. Or is it Try-Hard?"

Drew and Jeff felt a bit awkward but laughed along nonetheless.

"That's not even clever," said Abigail. "You guys are so dumb."

"Yeah, well –" Tommy was interrupted as Lexi and Brooke came running down the hall.

"Abigail!" yelled Lexi. "We have to go or we'll be late!"

"Yeah, c'mon."

"All right, all right," said Abigail. She slid two books into her book bag and hurried up the hall behind Lexi and Brooke.

"That was weird," said Drew. "I wonder where they're going."

"Who knows," said Tommy, "and really, who cares?"

Drew and Jeff shrugged. The hallway was just about empty. A boy and a girl had been casually chatting about 20 feet down the hall, but they were slowly making their way to the door. The boys were also about to leave when something caught their eyes. It was as if all three of them saw it at the same time. A strange silence set on the hallway, as if the next move the boys made was of tremendous consequence. They glanced around; not a teacher was in sight. They looked at each other with widened eyes, and there was little question about what would happen next.

"Go go go go!"

"No one followed us, right?"

"I don't think so."

"And no one saw us back there, right?"

"No – I dunno – just keep going, man!"

The three boys hurried through Jeff's front door, up the stairs, and into Jeff's room as if a swarm of zombies were in hungry pursuit. Jeff locked the door and removed from his book bag the item they were so desperately trying to conceal. He examined it intensely, as if he still didn't believe such a valuable thing could be in his possession. Then he dropped it on his bed, as if he suddenly realized it could be dangerous. Drew and Tommy stood guard at the door.

"Are you sure no one can open this door?" Drew asked.

"Yeah," said Jeff, trying to catch his breath, "it's locked."

Tommy ran his left hand along the surface of the door and wiggled the knob with his right hand. "You sure? How strong is this lock? Your brother isn't gonna come barging in, is he?"

"No, this morning my mom said they were going to the store or something after school. And I'm pretty sure a six-year-old can't break down a locked door."

Tommy nodded. He and Drew stepped away from the door and stood on each side of Jeff. Jeff hadn't taken his eyes off the item on the bed. The three of them huddled next to each other in silence, staring down at the bright-ly-colored binder that seemed to stare right back. In bold, black letters on the front of the binder were these words: **PROPERTY OF ABIGAIL LINWOOD. DO NOT OPEN.**

"What the heck are we waiting for?" said Tommy. "Let's open it."

But as Tommy reached for the binder, Drew grabbed his arm.

"Wait," he said, "are we sure we wanna do this?"

Tommy switched his eyes from the binder to Drew and stared at him in disbelief.

"What do you *mean*? Why wouldn't we?"

"Because it's cheating, isn't it?"

"Oh, come on," Tommy scoffed. "It's not like we stole the binder. We just, you know, saw it sitting there. It's not our fault stupid Abigail left her locker hanging open."

"But how can we open it anyway?" Jeff asked. "It has that lock on it."

"That lock is nothing," said Tommy. "We can just bust it open with a hammer. Your dad probably has one in the garage, right?" He began scanning around the room. "Unless there's something in here we can use ..."

"Hold on," said Drew. Everything had happened so fast that he barely realized where he was. The last several minutes were a blur. "I don't think we should open it. We wouldn't want them to look at our notes if they found them, right?"

"Right," said Tommy, "but they *would* look."

"I dunno," said Drew.

"I guarantee they'd look," Tommy quickly added. "You saw how jealous they got when Mr. Frye said he liked our idea."

"Then why do we even need to look? We already have a good idea – Jeff's idea."

"Dude, why are you scared to open it?" Tommy asked.

"I'm not scared," said Drew. "I just don't think we should."

"You're thinking about this too much," said Tommy. "We got Abigail's binder right here in front of us. *You're* the one who wanted to beat Abigail so bad in the first place, right? All we gotta do is open the binder and steal – um, I mean use her ideas."

Drew looked from Tommy, to Jeff, to the binder, and then back to Jeff and asked what he thought.

"I dunno, I mean, I guess Tommy's right. It's not like we *planned* on taking the binder. It was just ... there."

"Exactly!" Tommy burst, his hands flailing in the air. "Sorry, Drew, but that's two versus one."

"Wait," said Drew, turning to Jeff. "We don't need to open it. We already spent so much time preparing. The idea you came up with is good. I think you're gonna win, and we don't have to cheat to do it. But if we do break that lock and look in the binder ... well, we *will* be cheating."

"But no one will even know! So what difference does it make?" Tommy said, almost yelling.

"Well," said Jeff, "Drew might have a point. I don't wanna be a cheater."

"Whoa," said Tommy, his voice taking on a defensive tone and his eyes darting back and forth between the two other boys. "We're not *cheaters*. Why would you say that?"

"We would be cheaters if we look in the binder," said Drew.

"No, this is different. Cheaters are people who are unfair and, like, do bad things on purpose. This is different.

We just ... look, this is *Abigail* we're talking about. You were the one who wanted to win so bad anyways, Drew. You wanted to beat Abigail, remember? Why should we care about her? Do you think she feels bad for us when we get in trouble, or get a bad grade, or get called on when we don't know the answer?"

"Maybe he's right," said Jeff, gazing at the yellow polka-dotted binder with wistful yet cautious eyes.

"Yeah, Drew," Tommy continued. "Think about how many times Abigail has done stuff to us. Like when she tells on me for chewing gum in Language Arts. Or when a teacher calls on somebody to read and they aren't paying attention, her arm shoots up and she's all like, 'Oh, *I* can read, *I* know exactly where we are.'"

"He's right, Drew," said Jeff. "She did that to you in Mr. Sawyer's class last week."

Drew seethed at the thought of Abigail's insult.

"See!" said Tommy. "Exactly my point." He turned to Jeff. "Didn't she do something to you once?"

"Yeah," said Jeff, gritting his teeth and shaking his head. "She bumped into me at recess and was like, 'Sorry, Jake.' And when Drew said, 'Uh, that's Jeff, not Jake,' she was just like, 'Oh, whatever your name is.'"

Drew sat on the edge of the bed and tried to think. Was Tommy right? Did Abigail deserve to be cheated? Or was there more to Abigail? He thought back to Trevor and how wrong they were about him. He remembered one of the lessons it taught him: don't judge a book by its cover.

Abigail probably doesn't judge books by their covers, he thought. *She probably reads every single word of every book (even the words in parentheses).*

"What if someone found out?" Jeff suddenly asked.

Tommy looked confused. "How would they? I closed Abigail's locker after I took the binder."

"You sure?"

"Yeah. I took it and put it in your book bag, then I made sure I closed the locker. So she probably won't even realize she left it open. The only way someone would find out would be if *one of us* told somebody. And I definitely wouldn't tell *anyone*. Would you?"

"Well, no, of course not," said Jeff, a bit defensively.

Tommy turned to Drew. "And would you tell anyone if we open the binder?"

Drew paused. A part of him wanted to say he *would* tell. Maybe then they would just decide not to open it. But he could sense that the three of them were losing trust in each other, and he knew friendship was nothing without trust.

"Look, I know none of us would ever tell anyone, but that's not the point."

He thought back again to what his dad had told him about baseball players using steroids, and how victories always felt better when you truly earned them.

"Because here's the thing," said Drew, standing back up, "if we look at this binder and then we win, the win wouldn't be, you know, authentic. I mean it wouldn't be a real win. Like in baseball, or any sport, you wanna win, but you wanna win on your own."

He was proud to have connected that idea to the current situation. He looked at Tommy and Jeff, expecting them to finally understand what to do. Instead, Tommy was looking at him like he had been speaking a different language.

"What are you *talking* about, man? This is about Abigail and the language arts contest. Why are you talking about baseball?"

"I ... never mind."

Tommy didn't understand, and Jeff still looked confused. Drew realized it was pointless to continue. Apparently he wasn't able to explain it the way his dad had.

A few moments of frustrated silence passed. Tommy fidgeted with a few quarters on Jeff's dresser, spinning them on their sides and sliding them around. All three boys periodically glanced at the white binder with yellow polka dots lying on the bed. Drew continued to search his brain for a way to convince his friends that they shouldn't open the binder. He wished his baseball analogy had worked, but suddenly he had another idea.

"Wait," he said. "What if Abigail *wanted* us to take the binder?"

"Huh?"

"What do you mean?"

"Think about it. Tommy, you said it's Abigail's own fault for leaving her locker open, but does that really sound like something Abigail would do? Since when does she make mistakes?"

"You might be right," said Jeff. "It does seem like something a girl would do. You know, act like they don't want you to look when really they do."

"Okay," said Tommy, "Drew *might* be right. But Abigail was in a hurry, remember? So if we can prove that this is her real binder ..." He walked over to the bed and grabbed it. A slight chill went down Drew's spine. "... then don't you think we should look in it and *guarantee* you win?"

"Well ..." Jeff paused for a moment.

Watching him think, Drew felt bad that he had put him in such an awkward position. Drew and Tommy had been playing tug of war with his allegiance, and the pressure was clearly weighing on him.

"It's up to you," Drew said. "It's your speech, so we'll go with whatever you say." He turned to Tommy. "Right?"

"Um, yeah, of course," said Tommy, setting the binder back down on the bed.

Jeff took a deep breath. "Okay, here's what we can do. We'll see if Abigail has a binder in school tomorrow. If she does, then this one is fake. If she doesn't, then we'll know this one is real."

"And if it is real?" Tommy asked eagerly.

Jeff thought for a moment then slightly nodded a few times, as if he had convinced himself he found an answer. "Then we'll bust it open."

Drew sighed, Tommy smiled, and Jeff buried the potential treasure under his bed.

The next morning, Abigail did not have her binder with her. The boys figured she could be keeping it in her locker until language arts class, so they waited until then to be sure. Mr. Frye told the class to work on their speeches, which were now just two days away. Drew, Jeff, and Tommy watched as Abigail, Lexi, and Brooke pushed their desks together. Abigail did not have her binder. In fact, she looked very distressed.

Mr. Frye walked over to Abigail and asked her what was wrong. A moment later he made an announcement.

"Listen up, everyone. Abigail's folder is missing. If anyone –"

"No," said Abigail. "It is not a folder, it is a binder. It is white with yellow polka dots, and it has a black zipper. And it has my name written on the outside."

"Okay," said Mr. Frye. "If anyone finds *that*, return it to her right away."

Eventually, Mr. Frye made his way over to Drew, Jeff, and Tommy.

"So how are things going in this group?" he asked. "You're going to talk about getting local businesses involved with the school, right, Jeff?"

"Um, yeah, we –" Jeff's words were halted as Tommy nudged at him under his desk.

"Actually," Tommy interjected, "we're thinking about

going in a different direction. We just have some newer ideas we're trying to figure out. That's okay, right?"

"Well, yes, that's okay, but I think you guys were on the right track before. Are you sure you want to change?"

"We just wanna change a couple things, that's all," said Tommy.

"All right, I do want you to keep improving on your ideas. But remember, the speeches are on Friday. You have to be ready."

"We'll be ready," said Tommy. "I mean Jeff will be ready. Right, Jeff?"

Jeff nodded. Mr. Frye eyed the boys somewhat suspiciously before turning his attention to a different group. Drew leaned over toward Tommy.

"What was that?" he asked in an angry whisper.

"That was us getting ready to win the contest."

Hundreds of emotions flowed through the boys as they walked home.

"This is perfect," said Tommy, hopping in front of Drew and Jeff to walk backwards while he talked. "We got Abigail's binder. Her actual, stupid, polka-dotted, girly binder. And she has no idea! All we gotta do is take all her ideas and say them before she does. The order for the speeches is already set. Abigail goes last, right?"

"Yeah," said Jeff. "Mr. Frye probably thinks he's saving the best for last."

"Then he's gonna be in for a surprise," said Tommy. "I wonder what our prize is gonna be. Maybe Pirate tickets ... or Kennywood tickets ... or free ice cream in the cafeteria for the rest of the year ..." He pulled out his phone as he continued to speculate.

How did all this happen? Drew wondered. All he wanted to do was defeat Abigail and win the contest. But everything had spiraled out of control – certainly out of *his* control.

As the boys made their way home, Drew tried to get a read on Jeff's thoughts, and he began to understand why it meant so much to gain the recognition that would come with winning the contest. Jeff often went unnoticed by people. He was a solid baseball player, but he never made the All-Star team. In school, he got B's on almost every test, whether he studied or not. He didn't raise his hand enough to reach "teacher's pet" status, but he wasn't quiet enough or "bad" enough to warrant any real concern from the teachers. In fact, a few weeks ago Mr. Frye forgot Jeff's name and replaced it with a hesitant point of his finger that must have poked at Jeff's self-esteem. But if Jeff's speech won first place, even Dr. Linus would be forced to know his name. And, perhaps most impressive, Jeff would be the kid who finally handed Abigail her first taste of academic defeat. Doing so would lift him from the shadows and transform him from average kid to legendary champion at Emerson Elementary. Still, Drew didn't think he had to resort to cheating.

"Anyways," said Tommy as he put his phone back in his pocket, "you guys ready to go open that binder?" The boys had reached the end of Jeff's street.

"Now?" asked Jeff.

"Yeah."

"Hold on," said Drew. He yet again found himself trying to slow things down. Then he realized he actually had a reason to stall. "I can't do it now. I have to get home because my mom is taking me over to my dad's."

"Is your dad taking you to our game tonight?" asked Jeff.

"Yeah," said Drew, "so I have to get all the homework done early, 'cause my dad wants to catch for a little before we leave. And we all wanna open the binder together, right?"

"Yeah," Jeff nodded.

Tommy paused for just a second before agreeing. The boys would wait until tomorrow, after Melia's, to open the binder. Once they viewed its contents, Jeff would spend the evening memorizing all of Abigail's plans for his speech.

The ball game was a nice distraction for Drew. His team won, he had three hits, and, while playing catcher during the second half of the game, he threw out two runners trying to steal second base. But as soon as the final out was called, his attention shifted back to the binder.

Normally, Drew spent the night at his dad's after a baseball game. He loved reliving the game, inning by inning, with him. But he decided to stay with his mom so he could stop at Jeff's house in the morning. He would swing by early and take the binder. He didn't know what he would do with it – maybe he could find a way to get it back to Abigail without her knowing who had taken it. He also didn't know how he would explain its absence to Jeff and Tommy, but he would cross that bridge when he came to it.

Drew got up early Thursday morning. When he got to Jeff's, he knocked twice, but there was no answer. This was not uncommon for the Gray family. The door had been unlocked, as it was every morning. He opened the screen door and waltzed in through the living room and into the kitchen.

"Hey, it's me," he announced.

Mrs. Gray was facing the counter, assembling the lunches for the day.

"Kelsey!" she yelled. "Do you want ham, turkey, or both?"

She turned to Drew and nodded toward the table with a smile. "Hi, Drew. Did you eat yet? There's fruit on the table."

"Turkey with spinach and no cheese!" The request came as a muffled shout from Kelsey's room upstairs.

Mrs. Gray listened to the response then nodded her head toward the cupboard next to the fridge.

"And I think there are Pop Tarts in the cabinet there," she said as she threw down slices of turkey and a handful of spinach leaves onto a piece of bread, then neatly arranged the items into a tidy sandwich.

A small football rolled into the kitchen past Drew's feet and wobbled to a stop. Zane came running in after it, wearing pajama pants and draped in Jeff's baseball jersey from last year.

"Hi, Drew," the little six-year-old said as he brushed past Drew and headed to the fridge, abandoning whatever game he was playing with the football. He reached in and pulled out a can of pop.

"Hey, Zane," said Drew.

"Milk or orange juice, Zane," Mrs. Gray said at the sound of the fridge opening.

He reluctantly put the pop back in the fridge and reached in with both hands to get the big jug of orange juice. He turned and, with all his might, hoisted it up onto the table. Mrs. Gray grabbed a cup from the cabinet above her head.

"Here. Don't spill," she said, extending the cup behind her.

Zane took the cup from her hand to the table and set it down. His eyes switched back and forth from the cup to the full gallon of orange juice. Just as he was about to attempt to pour it, Mr. Gray came into the kitchen.

"Careful there, big guy," he said, steadying the jug and helping Zane pour the juice.

Zane picked up the glass and chugged. Then he darted over to the cupboard, stood on his toes, reached up with an outstretched arm, and removed a pack of Pop Tarts.

"Hi there, Drew. I bet mornings are a lot calmer at your house, huh?" Mr. Gray said with a smile. Then, to Mrs. Gray he said, "All right, hon, I'm leaving." After the two exchanged a quick kiss, Mr. Gray told Zane to "be good" and headed out the door.

"Jeff!" Mrs. Gray yelled. "Five minutes! Let's go!"

Jeff came running down the stairs, and Zane zipped up them, bumping into Jeff on his way.

"Watch it."

"Sorry, Jeff!"

"You need to get dressed, too, Zane!" Mrs. Gray shouted to the little boy scrambling up the stairs.

"What's up?" Jeff greeted Drew.

"Just stopping by. Got up early this morning for some reason."

"Oh, cool. Hey, Mom, did you make –"

"It's right here," she said as she handed Jeff a brown paper bag.

"Thanks, Mom."

"You have all your homework done, right?" she asked.

"Pretty sure," Jeff answered, reaching into the cupboard. "I thought we had Pop Tarts ... Wait a minute ... Zane!"

Footsteps rumbled down the stairs, but they weren't Zane's.

"Bye, Mom, I'm leaving," said Kelsey as she headed for the door.

"Don't forget your lunch," said Mrs. Gray. She handed it to Drew, who passed it along to Kelsey.

"Thanks," said Kelsey, smiling.

Drew smiled back. It felt nice to temporarily be a part of the chaotic Gray family assembly line. "You're welcome."

"Hey, Jeff," Kelsey said, walking out the door, "I heard you had a big hit last night. First double of the year, right?"

"Right."

Drew turned back to the kitchen. Zane had come back down the steps without Drew even noticing. He had changed into jeans and a green t-shirt with a cartoon character on it that Drew didn't recognize. He stood next to Jeff while Jeff split a Pop Tart in half.

"Which half do you want?" he asked his little brother.

Zane considered his options, pointed, and Jeff handed him the chosen half.

"Zane, do you have your shoes on?" Mrs. Gray asked.

Zane looked down at his feet and frowned.

"No," he murmured.

Jeff rolled his eyes and shoved the last of his Pop Tart in his mouth. "C'mon, Zane, I'll help you."

Zane smiled and ran to get his shoes.

"I gotta help him, then brush my teeth, then we can go," Jeff said to Drew.

Drew saw his opportunity. "I'll come up with you guys."

While Jeff helped Zane tie his shoes, Drew set his book bag on the floor and sat down on the bed, directly above where Jeff had slid Abigail's binder Tuesday afternoon. When Zane went downstairs and Jeff went across the hall to brush his teeth, Drew reached under the bed for the binder. It wasn't there. He stuck his head under the bed. All he saw was a pile of action figures. No polka-dotted binder. For a second, Drew felt a sense of relief, as if the binder weren't there because it never had been – as if they had never taken it in the first place, and it had all been a bad dream. But he snapped out of that daydream when Jeff reentered the room and saw him looking under the bed.

"Where's the binder?"

"Um, Tommy has it," Jeff murmured.

"What? Why? When did ... Why?"

"He said he was worried Zane would find it. He

thought it would be safer at his house. I dunno, man. He called me yesterday and asked for a ride to the game. He came over here first and he took it. I didn't know what – I wasn't sure if he should take it, but I didn't wanna make a big deal, ya know?"

"Why didn't you say no?" asked Drew.

"I dunno. If I said no, he'd think I don't trust him or something."

"*Do* you trust him?" As soon as the question left Drew's lips, he regretted asking it. He wasn't even sure what he expected Jeff's answer to be, because he didn't know how he would answer the question himself. "Never mind. But, wait, he took the binder before our game? He had it at the field?"

"In his bat bag," said Jeff.

Drew could only shake his head. He couldn't believe Tommy would actually take the stolen binder out in public.

"I'm sorry, man. I didn't know what to do," said Jeff.

"Do you still wanna open the binder?"

"I just want to win. Just this one time, I want to win."

Drew hoped Tommy would mention the binder as soon as they saw each other at school, but he didn't. Drew figured he would wait until recess. If Tommy hadn't brought it up by then, he would.

The morning classes flew by without mention of the binder. Out on the playground during recess, Trevor invited Drew, Jeff, and Tommy into a game of rundown. They accepted, but first Drew pulled Tommy aside.

"Hey, why'd you take Abigail's binder?"

Tommy seemed slightly annoyed. "It's safer at my house, that's all. I got my own room, Jeff doesn't."

"But taking it to our baseball game where anyone

could open up your bat bag and see it? Is that safer than in Jeff's room under his bed?"

"Yeah," Tommy said with a simple nod, as if it were actually true. "Nobody goes in my bat bag. Look, rundown's starting. Caleb's playing, too. Let's go," he added, dashing off before Drew could muster a response.

After the game of rundown had gone on for a while, Drew, Tommy, Caleb, and Danny were standing to the side. Caleb was reminiscing about a hit he had in last night's game, reinventing most of the details.

"You shoulda seen it, Danny. I crushed it. It was my second at-bat. I walked my first time up ..."

Drew remembered that Caleb had actually struck out his first time up, but he didn't interrupt his story.

"... and I crushed a double over the left fielder's head."

Drew spoke up at this fabrication. "It went through the left fielder's legs, actually."

"What? Right, yeah, 'cause I hit it so hard."

Drew shrugged. "If you say so."

"Yeah," Caleb continued. "The only reason I struck – I mean the only reason I walked my first time up instead of getting a hit was 'cause of the bat I was using. I used Tommy's bat when I hit my double. Can I use it again next game?"

"Yeah," said Tommy.

"Sweet. Oh, I almost forgot, did you find a hammer? If not, I got one at home."

"A hammer for what?" Drew asked before Tommy had a chance to answer. "A hammer for what?"

"Relax, Drew," said Caleb. "It's to help you guys open the you-know-what."

Drew's mouth opened, but no words came out.

"I got one," Tommy said to Caleb.

"Okay. Hey, me and Danny are gonna go spy on those girls over there. You guys wanna come?"

"No," said Drew, "we have to talk about something."

After Caleb and Danny walked away, Drew burst out, "You told Caleb?"

"I knew you'd act like it was a big deal," said Tommy.

"It is a big deal!"

"No, it's really not."

"Yes it is!"

"Why?"

"Because it just is," said Drew. "Caleb's not in our group."

"So?"

"What if he tells someone?"

"He's not gonna tell anyone. He's not even in our language arts class."

"He probably already told Danny."

"Just relax, dude. This is why I had to tell him."

"What are you talking about?"

"Nothing. Are you gonna come over my house to open it with me and Jeff, or are we doin' it without you?"

Despite not wanting anything to do with the binder anymore, and despite regretting ever taking it in the first place, Drew agreed to be there. Frankly, he was surprised Tommy hadn't already opened it. He realized that he was no longer mad about Tommy taking the binder – after all, he had tried to do the same thing himself. But he still couldn't believe Tommy would let Caleb in on it. Drew, Tommy, and Jeff were supposed to stick together and trust each other no matter what. Since when did they need someone like Caleb?

The boys stopped at Melia's after school. Jeff had forgotten to bring money, but Mr. Melia said he could pick something out and pay him back next week.

After getting their snacks, they went to Tommy's. Tommy reached under his bed and pulled out the fateful binder, which was now covered with dirt. He reached under a second time and removed a hammer. Because Drew's dad worked with his hands, hammers had been around the house for as long as he could remember. But it was as if Tommy were holding an object Drew had never seen before. This was no tool for building; this was a tool for breaking.

Tommy tossed the binder onto his bed and extended the hammer toward Jeff. "It's your speech. You wanna do the honors?"

Jeff reluctantly accepted the hammer. He seemed to study it the same way he had studied the binder the first time he held it. He looked down at the binder and paused.

"Come on, just do it," Tommy urged.

As the hammer smashed down on the lock, all Drew could think about was how he never wanted to take something that didn't belong to him ever again. He scanned his friends' faces. Jeff's cheeks were pale and his nostrils flared, a sign of heavy breathing. Tommy wore an excited grin, as if he relished the moment. He pulled out his phone and began texting as soon as the lock was broken.

Inside the binder, the boys found notes from social studies class, a handout from Spanish class, and a few papers filled with words so big that the boys gave up on trying to figure out what they were. And then there were the papers for the "If I Were Principal" contest, brimming with detailed ideas.

"This is it. It's all here," said Jeff.

"This is perfect," Tommy gushed.

The boys had in their possession the exact words to Abigail's speech. She had even written "Pause for effect" at certain points.

The boys decided that Jeff would spend the night doing his best to memorize those words – Abigail's words. His idea about involving local businesses with the school was a distant memory.

It was Friday. The students filtered into Mr. Frye's classroom, bringing with them the bustling action from the hallway. All the clatter came to an abrupt halt, though, as soon as they saw that Dr. Linus was sitting in a seat in the front row sorting some papers on the desk. She didn't look up as the room began to fill, but she didn't need to – her presence alone could drown all the noise from the kids and turn the room into a sanctuary of well-behaved scholars.

When the bell rang, Dr. Linus made her way to the podium in the front of the room.

"Hello, class. Thank you for having me here on this exciting day. The 'If I Were Principal' contest has been going on for six years and is one of the most popular competitions we have here at Emerson Elementary."

As she talked about the importance of the project, Drew realized he didn't know much about his principal. In fact, this was the most he had ever heard her talk. When she walked through the halls, Dr. Linus silently patrolled with a sharp glare and a finger point – no words were needed.

"And finally," she continued, "this presentation is an opportunity for you to use all that knowledge you have gained all year, and put it into action with your own ideas."

Her final words rang in Drew's head: "your own ideas." It was as though they were carefully constructed to eat at Drew's conscience.

The first speaker was Mitchell. He dragged his feet to the front of the room, looking like he had just rolled out of bed, even though it was sixth period. He had remnants of his lunch on his shirt, cheeks, and, somehow, his forehead. He rambled for a minute or so about why students should be allowed to play video games in every class, and then returned to his seat.

Next was Erin. It was obvious that she had drawn the short straw in her group. Though she was a good student, her speech wasn't very convincing. She suggested that students should be allowed to wear pajamas to school, but she failed to offer any valid reasons.

Jonathan then waddled to the podium and made the claim that recess should be longer so the kids could get more fresh air and exercise.

Next Jake made his case that kids should be allowed to carry their book bags around all day instead of having to leave them in their lockers, but he talked so quietly that most of his speech was unheard by anyone not in the front row.

The fifth speaker was Mary Beth. She suggested that students should always have off school the day after Halloween. She added that students should be allowed to wear Halloween costumes to school any day in October. Zobby was in Mary Beth's group, and Drew could see her imprint all over the speech. Halloween was Zobby's favorite holiday.

Finally it was Jeff's turn. He looked to Drew and Tommy for a last bit of assurance as he stepped to the podium. Tommy nodded with a slight smirk on his face. Drew also nodded, but with a hint of disappointment he couldn't hide. But as he watched Jeff settle in behind the podium, he still found himself rooting for him. He knew how much a win would mean for Jeff.

Jeff began his speech with Abigail's first idea: The Abolition of Homework at Emerson Elementary.

"Kids already work so hard during school that we are exhausted when we get home. Also, we need time after school for other activities, like sports and clubs. Kids who play sports and join clubs become more well-rounded individuals, and everyone knows this. To allow for this, homework should be abolished."

Drew cringed. He could tell by the way he said it that Jeff didn't even know what "abolished" meant.

Using the pattern Abigail had laid out, Jeff moved on to part two of the plans from her binder. Drew wanted to watch Abigail as Jeff spoke to see her reaction, but she was in the back of the room. It was her seat in which Dr. Linus was sitting.

"Now, there is one item on the lunch menu that every kid loves: pizza," Jeff was saying. "If pizza was available to us every day instead of just once a week, kids would be happier and have fuller ..." He paused. Two, three, four quiet seconds passed. Then he continued abruptly: "stomachs. This way there will be no growling stomachs in the afternoon, and also all the kids will be happy, and happy kids are more willing to learn. And some people don't know, but pizza contains all the major food groups, so it is good for you ..."

As Jeff finished his speech, Drew felt that he had done a good job (minus that awkward pause), but something about him just wasn't right. Even though Jeff was standing up there, it was like he wasn't *really* there.

Mr. Frye thanked Jeff and announced that it was Abigail's turn to speak. Drew, Jeff, and Tommy stared as she slowly made her way to the front of the room. They half-expected her to walk right past the podium and run through the doorway and out of the building, crying all the way. But as she approached the podium, Drew saw that her stride was guided by confidence, not fear. She didn't seem rattled at all. The expression on her face was that of someone who had held a secret and was ready to reveal it.

"Good afternoon, everyone. Before I begin, I would like to thank Dr. Linus for being here. I would also like to thank Mr. Frye for allowing me this opportunity to speak in front of you today."

Drew, Jeff, and Tommy exchanged bewildered looks.

What was she possibly going to say?

"Interestingly enough, the topics of my speech are similar to those of the previous speaker. My ideas, however, are a bit different. First, we all know that most students don't enjoy homework. However, we also know that homework is imperative to the learning process, for it helps us to develop positive study skills and habits that will benefit us greatly in the future. I would like to suggest a compromise: the teachers should be allowed to reward students with homework passes. When a student completes ten consecutive homework assignments in a class, he or she would be rewarded with one homework pass for that class. Thus, students would strive to complete all their homework and still receive an occasional break. And if students are completing ten out of eleven homework assignments, that would be roughly ninety-one percent, which is higher than the school's average homework completion rate as it stands now. And although many of us have other activities after school, having homework to complete as well teaches us how to balance activities and manage our time, which, in the long run, will truly help us develop into well-rounded individuals.

"Secondly ..."

At this point, Tommy's fists were clenched upon his desk, and Jeff couldn't hide the redness that had rushed to his face and ears. It was as if the boys had dug their own graves by opening that binder, and Abigail was shoveling dirt over their coffins with each word she spoke.

"I'm sure everyone here is familiar with the phrase 'too much of a good thing.' Well, that phrase certainly would apply if, as was mentioned by the previous speaker, we had pizza for lunch every single day. I have an idea that involves the lunch menu, but it revolves around variety instead of monotony ..."

The three boys were too shocked and angry to hear

the rest of Abigail's speech. All they could do was sit in disbelief that she had actually set them up. Drew had been right. They had stolen a fake binder, a decoy.

After Abigail's speech, Mr. Frye and Dr. Linus convened by the doorway for a few minutes, whispering to each other and pointing to notes they had taken during the speeches. The class sat and waited for them to announce their decision, but they all knew exactly what they had known from the beginning: Abigail would be the winner. Their ears only remained attentive so they could find out what the secret prize was.

"There were several good ideas presented today," Mr. Frye said. "And every speaker should be very proud of his or her self. But there can be only one winner ..."

Dr. Linus picked up where Mr. Frye left off. "Yes, I was very impressed with what I heard today. There were a lot of creative ideas. Maybe some of you will become principals someday ..."

Just get it over with already, Drew thought.

"But there can only be one winner today," the principal continued, "and the winner is ... the team of Abigail, Brooke, and Lexi."

The rest of the students offered unenthused applause and waited to hear what the secret prize would be.

"And for their prize, they will each receive a twenty-five-dollar gift card to Melia's Market."

When the school day ended, Drew went straight to Abigail's locker. He didn't want to confront her or yell at her about tricking the boys. He just had one question to ask her. As he approached her, she was inserting her binder – her real, white binder with the yellow polka dots – into her book bag. Drew could see now that the binder they stole was pristine, while Abigail's actual secret binder showed signs of wear.

"Abigail –"

She turned from her locker. "Please do not say I did anything wrong. You were the ones who took my binder."

"I know, I know. But that's what I wanna ask you about."

"Oh. What?"

"Well, you set us up, I get that. You left that fake binder in your locker for us to see, but how did you know we would take it? And how'd you know we'd open it?"

"Honestly," said Abigail, "I wasn't sure if *you* would. And I wasn't sure if Jeff would. But I *knew* Tommy would."

Without Drew saying anything, she continued. It seemed like she felt the need to say more.

"I didn't even want to do it. It was Lexi's idea, and she convinced Brooke to do it. So I had to go along with it. But I didn't think I needed to. No offense, but I was confident I could win on my own."

"Well, the plan did work, and you did win."

"I know, but ..." she stopped and shook her head. Drew realized she didn't look as proud, or as satisfied, as he thought she would. In a way, she looked like she was the one who had lost.

"But what?" Drew asked.

"I don't know. I've won things before, and it always feels good to win. I work really hard."

Drew nodded. Despite the fact that some things came easier to Abigail, he had to admit she worked hard.

"And this win just doesn't feel as good," she said.

She shrugged at him in a sort of apologetic way and then left. Drew walked down the steps to where he, Jeff, and Tommy usually met at the end of the day. Jeff stood there with his hands plunged into his pockets and his head hanging low.

"I'm sorry, man," said Jeff. "I blew it."

"It's okay," said Drew. "So we didn't beat Abigail, and we didn't win the prize, but now you know that your original idea was actually really good."

Jeff lifted his head. "Yeah, I guess so. I guess we shoulda stuck with it. And we never shoulda taken that stupid binder."

Tommy came stomping toward them, shaking his head. He said he hated Abigail more than ever and he was going to burn the fake binder he had at his house. Then he said he didn't even care about the prize anymore because he could still go to Melia's whenever he wanted. He spotted Caleb about 20 feet away and said he had to go because he was going over Caleb's house. He strode toward Caleb, and the two of them took off down the sidewalk. Drew and Jeff watched as they drifted farther and farther then disappeared.

Melia's Market

The small bells hanging above the door chimed as Drew, Tommy, and Jeff entered Melia's Market. Mr. Melia saw them in the reflection of the big round mirror attached to the ceiling as he worked in the back of the store, where he was putting some meat through the grinder. He lifted his head, revealing his wrinkled face and welcoming smile, and said, "Check out the new merchandise. I just restocked this morning. I'll be up as soon as I package this last order."

"All right, Mr. Melia," said Drew. "Take your time," he added, though he knew he didn't need to. Mr. Melia had to be aware by now that the boys liked to walk around the store before buying their candy. Similarly, his practiced eye could always tell when someone was in a hurry, in which case he would immediately take his place at the cash register.

The boys began their traditional path down the first aisle. Proudly hung on the wall was the *Lifetime Achievement for Exemplary Community Service* plaque Mr. Melia received last year. Every time Drew walked past it, he was reminded of the party thrown last summer for Mr. Melia to celebrate his 40th anniversary as owner of the store. Mrs. Goyle, along with a few others, had coordinated the event. Drew was amazed at how many people showed up to celebrate the kind store owner. From the oldest residents to the youngest children, everyone respected Mr. Melia. Having someone call you by your name while you check out may have been a dying custom, but, for the people of Emerson, it was something worth hanging on to. Run by the family since Mr. Melia's father opened it over 60 years ago, Melia's Market was a family store that stood for more than convenience – it was for the good of the community.

"You guys doing anything this weekend?" Jeff asked as the boys continued down aisle one.

"I think me and Caleb are gonna go to the ice skating rink on Saturday for open skate," said Tommy.

"Cool," said Jeff.

"Yeah, it's gonna be sweet," said Tommy. "Caleb's cool. I don't know why Drew hates him so much."

"What? I don't – I don't hate him," said Drew.

"Yeah, you definitely do. It's like you hated him ever since we went to The Shack. But that wasn't even his fault. Besides, I stayed with you."

"I know," said Drew. He was surprised Tommy still realized how important it was that he had stuck with him and Zobby in the woods. He wondered if Tommy would do the same kind of thing now.

"And when that window got broke, we all ran 'cept you, so you can't blame him for that either," Tommy went on. "Even Jeff ran!"

Jeff's eyes quickly turned to random items on the shelves.

"I guess," said Drew.

It's not that I hate him, he thought. *I just don't trust him.* Caleb acted impulsively and without regard for those around him. That was what bothered Drew the most – other people had to face the consequences of Caleb's rash actions, yet Caleb didn't seem to care one bit. The Shack never would have been ruined if it weren't for Caleb. Mr. Kaminsky's window never would have been broken if Caleb hadn't taunted Jeff. And Drew, Jeff, and Tommy might even have won the "If I Were Principal" contest if Tommy hadn't convinced Jeff to open Abigail's fake binder. *Well, that one wasn't Caleb's fault,* Drew thought, *but it still felt like a Caleb decision more than one Tommy would make ... at least the old Tommy ... the Tommy before he started hanging out with Caleb so much.*

The boys reached the end of the first aisle. Drew peeked through the opened door into the back room to see if Mrs. Melia was there. The room was empty. That meant that today, like so many other days, Mr. Melia was by himself.

By the time the boys started up the second aisle, Tommy had moved on to a new topic.

"I can't believe we got *another* science quiz tomorrow," he said. "I hate Mrs. Steinbeck. School's practically over. Do we really gotta have another stupid quiz?"

"At least she doesn't give us homework on weekends," said Drew, remembering his talk with Alexus Ballentine.

"Come on, the quizzes are the worst. Caleb's right. He says she's definitely the meanest teacher ever."

"Anyway, I gotta study tonight," said Jeff, subtly changing the subject.

While the boys pretended to inspect the labels of the household cleaning products in aisle two, a pair of girls approached the register. Drew recognized them as sixth-graders but didn't know their names. Mr. Melia had just finished packaging his orders, so he washed his hands and made his way to the front of the store. The old man had a slow, methodical gait, which one is bound to acquire after so many years of working on his feet. Drew was always amazed that, although it was clearly difficult for Mr. Melia to move around on his feet all day, he never complained.

"Did you girls find what you need?" Mr. Melia asked, now standing at the register behind the counter.

"Yeah, just this, please," said one of the girls, setting a bottle of pineapple-flavored water on the counter.

"All right then," said Mr. Melia. "And did you need anything today?" he asked the other girl.

"Oh, I don't have any money on me. I didn't know we were stopping."

"Well," said Mr. Melia, "if you'd like a drink, too, go ahead and get one. You can pay for it the next time you're in."

"Really?"

"Sure. It's a hot one today. You've got to stay hydrated."

The girl smiled and picked out a beverage. Both girls thanked Mr. Melia and headed out the door. This was not an uncommon scene in Melia's Market. Mr. Melia always allowed kids to run a small tab if they didn't have any money on them. He would simply write himself a note in his little green notepad, and the kids could pay him back.

The boys moved on to aisle three. They continued to pull items from the shelf, scan the labels with feigned interest, and then put the items back. They appreciated that Mr. Melia gave them their space and let them take their time. The freedom he allowed them was the reason the old shop had become a rite of passage for so many kids in Emerson. They felt a sense of pride walking around the store without their parents. Though they were ultimately there to buy candy, they finally felt like they weren't viewed as little kids anymore. Melia's Market was a true bridge between adult privilege and youthful exuberance.

The boys were soon in the fourth and final aisle. Aisle three was the "boring" aisle. Its shelves were filled with things like vacuum cleaner bags, dust brushes, and other items no kid would ever be interested in.

"How much do you guys have today?" Jeff asked.

"Two bucks," said Tommy.

"Same," said Drew. "You?"

"Three bucks," said Jeff.

"Are you even gonna spend all yours, Drew?" Tommy asked.

"I dunno, we'll see."

Tommy and Jeff always spent every last dime given to them for candy. Drew, however, would often save a dollar here, a quarter there. He'd save money for weeks at a time and then trade all his change with his dad for the highest bill possible. He had been given money before (he always received a 50-dollar bill on his birthday from his Gran and Grandy), but he never felt like he earned it. After all, everyone has a birthday. And even though the money for Melia's came from his parents, he was proud of himself for having the restraint to stash some of it away.

After the boys finished examining the bread and frozen foods in aisle four, a woman with a baby in her arms burst through the door. She went directly to the frozen foods section along the wall, grabbed a family-sized bag of mixed vegetables, spun around, and set it on the counter.

"Ah, it's been one of those days. Can you tell?" she said, pointing with her free hand at her frazzled hair.

"Hectic days can get the best of us all, but you're hanging in there, Jenny," said Mr. Melia. "Need anything else?"

"No, that's it for today. I have chicken thawing out for dinner, but I realized I had no side dish, and my freezer is empty. Just about every edible thing in my house is baby food."

Mr. Melia chuckled. "Well, little Sophia's hair sure is getting dark. She looks more like her big sister every time I see her."

"When is this lady gonna get outta here?" Tommy whispered. "It's like we're never gonna get our candy."

"We've been walking around for like ten minutes," Drew whispered back. "If we were in a rush, we should've gone to the counter when we first got here. What does another couple minutes matter?"

"Whatever," said Tommy. He motioned with his head. "She's leaving anyways."

"So how was school today?" Mr. Melia asked as the boys came to the counter.

"Good."

"Good, good. How's baseball going?" he asked with the friendliest voice imaginable.

"It's going awesome," said Tommy. "We're five and one so far."

"Wonderful, wonderful. I'd really like to get down to the field for a game. Let me know if you have any games on Sundays, when the store is closed."

Drew could tell that Mr. Melia was sincere. Even the world's biggest skeptic would believe that when Mr. Melia said something, he meant it. Every word out of his mouth was so genuine that he could sell a broken down car to a used car dealer, but, luckily for the rest of the world, he was just too nice to lie.

"You still the ace of the staff, Tommy?"

"Definitely. I throw harder than any other pitcher in the league."

Mr. Melia nodded. "Jeff, how's the breakout season going?"

"Pretty good," said Jeff.

"You've been playing first base, right?"

"Well, yeah, but our coach puts me in the outfield a lot, too. Mostly right field."

"Nothing wrong with that," said Mr. Melia. "Maybe you're the next Roberto Clemente."

Jeff blushed and shrugged.

Mr. Melia turned his eyes to Drew. "And how about you, Drew? You still have that Gold Glove-type fielding?"

"I'm definitely trying. I practice a lot, throwing a tennis

ball off the garage. And I've been playing catcher in our last couple games. I like it."

"Ah, the catcher, the other half of the battery. You've got to be tough to be a catcher."

Noticing that Tommy was tiring of the conversation and his eyes were eagerly fixated on the candy, Mr. Melia then said, "Well, enough small talk. Let's get down to business. Are we going with the usual today?"

"Oh yeah," said Tommy immediately.

Drew and Jeff nodded along. The usual was for Mr. Melia to take the boxes of candy from the shelf behind the register, set them on the counter, and let the kids sort through and choose what they wanted for the day.

Mr. Melia nodded and placed seven boxes of candy on the counter, one by one. The boys leaned in to take a closer look, then began picking up different items, trying to figure out in their heads exactly what they could afford. Jeff and Tommy rummaged through the boxes quickly, but Drew patiently examined the candy. As Mr. Melia brought out round two, seven more boxes of candy, the phone rang.

"Woops, I left the phone in the back. Go ahead and pick out what you need, and we'll settle up in just a minute."

He hurried to the back as quickly as his old knees would allow. Mr. Melia would sometimes deliver groceries to people who were unable to get out of their homes to do their own shopping, and Drew figured it might be one of those people calling in an order.

Drew took out his cousin's old wallet. Though his mom had given him two dollars, he was only going to spend one because he knew he was having his favorite dinner, Sloppy Joes, that night. He set aside two packs of Boston Baked Beans and stepped back, satisfied with his decision. Jeff stacked candy in piles equal to one dollar to ensure his math was correct. Tommy, like always, had two dollars but set aside about four dollars' worth of candy. He would always choose what he wanted most that day and put back the rest. But this time was different. He looked to the back of the store. Mr. Melia was still on the phone, his back turned, taking down an order in his little green notepad. Then, unlike any other day before, Tommy quickly tossed about two dollars' worth of candy into his book bag. The looks on the faces of Drew and Jeff were identical. Both boys were astonished by their friend's actions, but neither could say nor do anything. They were motionless. Even breathing seemed impossible.

As Mr. Melia made his way back to the counter, Jeff kept his head down, but Drew stared at Tommy. Drew barely recognized the boy standing next to him as his good friend Tommy. It felt more like he was looking at Caleb.

"Sorry to keep you boys waiting. Do you have the math figured out for today?" Mr. Melia asked as he assumed his position behind the counter.

Drew and Jeff remained silent, both feeling ashamed for something they didn't even do.

"Yeah, we're good," Tommy said with a casual confidence that chilled Drew's spine. "I got two bucks' worth, Jeff has three, and Drew just a buck." He extended his steady hand holding the two dollars toward Mr. Melia.

"Thank you, Tommy," Mr. Melia said gratefully. He punched the amount into the register and placed the cash in the drawer.

"Sure thing, Mr. Melia," replied Tommy, and he calmly walked out of the store.

Jeff paid next. He handed Mr. Melia three dollars without looking up at the old man.

"Thank you, Jeff," said Mr. Melia. Jeff scuttled out the door without replying.

Drew pulled a crisp dollar bill from his wallet and slowly handed it to Mr. Melia.

"And thank you, Drew," he said with his friendly smile.

Drew tried to smile back but couldn't. He nodded and walked out of the store. Tommy and Jeff were waiting outside, Tommy with a proud grin on his face, Jeff still staring at the ground.

"Uh, you know what, go ahead without me," said Drew. "I forgot I wanted to ask Mr. Melia something."

"What?" Tommy snapped. Then, lowering his voice to a whisper, he said, "Come on, dude, we got away with it. Let's just go. It's no big deal."

No big deal? How could he say stealing from Mr. Melia was no big deal? And what did he mean *we* got away with it? *He* stole the candy by himself. Drew thought about asking him what he meant by "we," but it seemed like some sort of a trap. Was Tommy dragging Drew and Jeff into this? It seemed like something Caleb would do. But Drew realized that he couldn't blame Caleb for this. He couldn't blame Caleb for anything Tommy did. Caleb wasn't there – Tommy was. Caleb didn't steal the candy – Tommy stole the candy.

"I just ..." Drew's voice trailed off.

Tommy took a step toward Drew and, with sudden anger in his voice, said, "You're gonna tell on me, aren't you?"

Drew shook his head. "No, seriously, I forgot I needed to get something for my mom. You guys go ahead."

"So you promise you aren't gonna tell?" said Tommy.

"Yeah, man, of course."

"You promised! You can't tell now."

"All right, I know. Just go, guys. It's fine."

Tommy paused. With his suspicious eyes still locked on Drew, he said, "Come on, Jeff, let's go."

Jeff, whose head had jerked back and forth during

the confrontation as if he were watching a tennis match, didn't appear to know what to do. He nodded to Tommy but his feet didn't move.

"Seriously, Jeff, go 'head," said Drew. "It's fine. I just need to ask Mr. Melia something."

"Oh, uh ... okay."

Tommy and Jeff headed down the street, and Drew walked back into the store.

Mr. Melia was still near the register. He looked up from his notepad and said, "Yes, Drew? Did you need something else?"

"Oh, no. I, um, just wanted to see if you needed help putting the boxes back on the shelf. I know exactly where they all go."

Mr. Melia smiled, and dozens more wrinkles spread across his face.

"Sure," he said. "I didn't get a chance to straighten up yet. I always appreciate a little bit of help."

Drew stepped behind the counter and neatly placed each box in its proper place, periodically glancing at Mr. Melia, who had gone over to the second aisle to straighten up some boxes of tissues. Drew appreciated that Mr. Melia trusted him enough to walk away, rather than stand there watching over him to make sure he didn't make any mistakes.

"Okay, Mr. Melia, all finished. Have a good day."

"You too, Drew. Thanks so much for your help."

Drew walked out the front door then ducked over to the corner of the building, where he could look through the storefront window without Mr. Melia seeing him.

Moments later Mr. Melia returned to the counter and jotted something down in his notepad. Then he examined the boxes of candy. Drew wasn't offended – Mr. Melia often double-checked his own wife's work, too.

Continuing to peer through the glass, Drew watched as Mr. Melia removed the Cow Tails and Airheads from their homes. He sorted through the boxes casually at first, but soon his hands rummaged more frantically and his expression became more perplexed. He counted the candy, then recounted it, then recounted it again. Drew remembered what Mr. Melia had said when the boys walked into the store: "I just restocked this morning." That meant Mr. Melia knew how many pieces of candy should be in each box. Drew also knew that Mr. Melia was well-aware that Cow Tails and Airheads were Tommy's two favorites. He thought for sure that he would finally see Mr. Melia become angry. Instead, the man who was always smiling simply looked tired. In an instant, he seemed to age a decade. He pulled his glasses from his face and, with his head down, he began to weep.

Drew wanted to run into the store and console the old man, but he had made a promise. He watched through the window in helpless desperation.

Mr. Melia put the candy back in its place and wiped the tears from his face. As soon as he reapplied his glasses, something caught his eye. One of the boxes of Boston Baked Beans wasn't quite sitting flush with the others. Mr. Melia examined it further and found a ten-dollar bill underneath it.

Although Mr. Melia didn't know Drew was watching, the two shared a smile.

The Big Picture

Drew lay in bed staring at the ceiling. His alarm wouldn't ring for 18 minutes, but he was wide awake.

How could Tommy steal from Mr. Melia? he kept asking himself.

He hadn't been able to shake the images out of his head all weekend. Tommy deftly sliding the candy from the counter into his book bag. The cocky smile on his face while Mr. Melia rang him up. The threatening glare in his eyes when he warned Drew not to tell on him.

When Drew went back into Melia's, he hadn't been sure what he would do. And he still wasn't sure if leaving the money was right, or if he should've told Mr. Melia what happened. Was telling on a friend okay after promising not to? *Either way*, he thought, *maybe Tommy isn't who I thought he was.*

He rolled over and turned off his alarm before it rang. He went to his desk, where his science book lay open to page 139. After flipping to the front cover and reviewing the names, he opened his desk drawer, grabbed his wallet, and removed his handwritten list. He studied both lists, side by side, to see if somehow he had missed something.

He never imagined that playing detective would be so hard. He was nearly nine months into his search, and time was running out. There was only one week of school left, and it would be much harder to find the Mystery Artist once summer break began. *I will figure this out,* he said to himself. *I have to.*

Three names were crossed off: Jason Porter, Alexus Ballentine, and Skylar Jansen. Two names remained: Stacey Janofsky and Mike "Huddy" Hudock. Which of these two was the more preferable candidate? Huddy, the meanest and scariest kid Drew had ever met, or Stacey, the girl who had disappeared?

Part of Drew hoped it was Stacey. At least then he could hold on to the hope that the Mystery Artist was a nice kid who actually cared about what she drew in that book. It was a long shot, though. From what Alexus had told him, Stacey was similar to Abigail – the best student in her grade. Drew couldn't see someone like that drawing instead of paying attention during class (especially Mrs. Steinbeck's class).

But Drew knew Huddy was an artist. And even though he preferred a different kind of art, maybe when he was in fifth grade he wasn't such a tough guy. Maybe back then he liked to draw ocean scenes instead of motorcycles and skeletons.

What if Huddy isn't who he seemed to be? Drew wondered. *Sort of like Tommy – maybe nobody's who they seem.*

He slid the notecard back into his wallet. He began the day as usual, showering, packing his book bag, and eating breakfast. However, while his morning routine was standard, he vowed to do something much different by the end of the day: confront Huddy.

When he got to school, he walked down the corridor along the cafeteria and slipped through the double doors into the middle school. The hallways were different from the elementary school. Everything seemed less colorful, and the lockers were taller and thinner. Drew tried to act casual as he made his way through the unfamiliar halls, but nobody noticed him anyway – or if they did, they pretended not to. The kids seemed so big and business-like compared to the elementary kids. *This will be me in a few months?* Drew thought. *What if I don't know how to be a middle-schooler?*

He suddenly felt nervous. He checked his watch and realized he had to be back for homeroom in five minutes. Figuring he could give it another shot right after school, he turned and made his way back. But just before he reached the double doors, a familiar voice caught his ear. He turned and saw Huddy about 15 feet away, standing next to a smaller boy holding a stack of books. Huddy seemed to be smiling in a friendly way. Drew inched closer and craned his neck to see around a pair of girls who were blocking his view. Huddy patted the boy on the back with his right hand and reached his left hand in the air for a high-five. The way Huddy was smiling, he actually seemed approachable. Drew took another step toward him. But Huddy's arm came down swiftly and smacked the books out of the boy's hands.

"Have fun picking up your books, nerd," laughed the potential Mystery Artist.

Drew's courage plummeted faster than the books. He backpedaled, turned and rushed through the double doors, and bolted back to the elementary school. Each step made him feel farther away from finding the Mystery Artist.

Jeff was waiting for Drew at his locker. "You do the math homework?"

"Yeah."

"I didn't," said Tommy, standing with Caleb a few lockers away. "But who cares? We only got one week of school left."

"Yeah," said Caleb. "After that it's ..." He cupped his hands around his mouth and shouted, "summer BREEAAK!"

Tommy's face lit up with excitement.

"Sum-mer break! Sum-mer break!" Caleb chanted.

Tommy immediately joined him, and the two of them went clamoring down the hall.

Drew shook his head. He had hoped Tommy would be remorseful after stealing from Mr. Melia. Instead, he was acting like it never even happened. Drew felt an awkward tension around Tommy, and he could tell that Jeff did too, but Tommy didn't seem to feel it. With each passing inter-action, Drew was realizing that the old Tommy might be gone forever.

Throughout the day, while each teacher stressed the importance of doing well on the final tests, Drew tried to figure out if Huddy was definitely the Mystery Artist. He knew for sure it wasn't Skylar, Alexus, or Jason, because he had asked each of them directly. Skylar was the only one who even recognized the picture.

At least she remembered it, Drew thought. *Wait, if Skylar remembered the picture but Alexus didn't, that's prob-ably because the picture hadn't been drawn yet when Alexus had the book! It couldn't be Stacey Janofsky, because then Alexus would have remembered the picture. It had to be drawn after Alexus had the book. And only Skylar and Huddy had the book after Alexus, so it has to be Huddy.*

Drew was torn about his discovery. Now that he *knew* it was Huddy, he didn't know what to do. What *could* he do? Originally, he wanted to thank the person who drew the picture, and talk to them about what it meant – after all, if anyone could explain the power of the picture, it was the artist himself. But could Drew really ask Huddy, espe-cially after what he had seen that morning?

At lunch, the boys discussed scheduling plans for sixth grade.

"What are you guys gonna do for next year? Everyone's gonna take study hall, right?" Tommy asked.

"Wait, we get to pick?" said Trevor.

"Yeah," said Tommy, "in sixth grade you pick if you wanna take study hall or music or art. It's a pretty easy choice."

"Well, I dunno," said Drew.

"Not this again," Tommy scoffed. "Our classes are so much more tougher next year, and they're gonna give us more homework. Plus there's no recess. The least they can do is give us a free period."

"Well, it's actually study hall," said Jeff.

"Not really," said Tommy. "My brother says that either a substitute or the librarian is the person there. And they don't really care if you study. Some of the subs don't even care if you play on your phone. So all you gotta do is show up. It's way cooler."

"I guess," said Drew. But in fact, he realized how much Tommy's opinion had diminished to him.

"I'm just so excited for this year to be over. I just want these stupid tests to be over, hand in the stupid books, and get *outta* here," Tommy said, rolling his eyes and tossing his head back.

Just then, it occurred to Drew that he would have to give the book back to Mrs. Steinbeck in a few days. After that, he would never see the drawing again. He thought about ripping out page 139, or maybe taking a picture of it, but both of those options seemed to cheapen the experience. Part of the magic was to flip through the musty pages of the used science book. The thought of never giving the book back popped into Drew's mind for a second, and then it was gone. To take the book would be stealing, and, unlike Tommy, Drew couldn't do that.

He didn't know what to do. All he did know was that he hated the thought of losing the picture.

Drew felt more frustrated than ever. The thought of asking Huddy if he drew the picture was daunting enough; asking him without even having the picture to show him didn't seem like an option at all. *I can't just walk up to him without it. He might not remember if he drew it unless he actually sees it.*

Tuesday evening, Drew sat slouched at the dinner table, mumbling one-word answers to his mom's questions.

"Drew, you can't do this. I'm worried about you," Penny said.

"There's nothing –"

"There's nothing wrong, there's nothing wrong. That's what you keep saying. But there obviously *is* something wrong. And I am your mother and I need to know. You aren't getting up from this table until you tell me."

Drew kept his eyes glued to the chicken sandwich on his plate.

"Andrew David, look at me this instant."

As Drew lifted his head, he felt the tears well up in his eyes. He couldn't hold it in any longer. His mother put her arms around him. *At least I'm not crying in front of anyone from school*, Drew thought.

Finally, he explained the story to his mother. He showed her page 139 and told her about his constant pursuit of the Mystery Artist, his courageousness with Skylar, Alexus, and Jason, and his ultimate failure in uncovering the identity of the Mystery Artist.

Penny held the book in her hands and smiled. "This is a beautiful picture, Andrew."

Drew was glad she appreciated it.

"What does it remind you of?" she asked.

"What do you mean?"

"Doesn't this remind you of something?"

Drew could tell she was attempting to lead him somewhere – he just wasn't sure where. Penny closed the science book and set it down on the table next to the now-cold chicken sandwiches. She went to the closet in the living room and returned with a photo album Drew didn't recognize.

"Have you seen these pictures?" she asked.

"I don't think so."

"Well, years ago, when your dad and I were together, the three of us went on a vacation to the beach. I always went with my family when I was a kid. Some of my best memories are the times I spent there, and we wanted to continue the tradition with you."

Drew paged through the album slowly. "I know I've been to the beach, but I don't really remember being there, if that makes any sense."

"That makes perfect sense. You were only four."

Drew's eyes carefully traced each detail in the photos.

"Any of it look familiar?" Penny asked.

"Not really. I mean, I remember flying there on an airplane."

"That's right. We flew down to Orlando to spend a few days with my parents, and then we went to the shore."

"Oh yeah, that's right. I remember going to one of Peter's baseball games in Orlando."

"That's right, too. Do you remember anything else?"

Drew continued to turn the pages until something jogged his memory. "I remember this – the sandcastle!"

Penny smiled. "Oh, you do?"

"Yeah, a second ago I didn't think I did, but I do. I remember trying to build a sandcastle, and you and dad were helping me. Yeah, I had all those buckets and little shovels ..." The images were flooding back into his mind. He spoke faster and faster to get everything out before the memories disappeared again. "So we spent a ton of time making the best sandcastle – I remember I wanted it to be huge – and when we were almost finished, a wave came in and wiped it all away. I remember crying, and pushing my face into your leg, and ... um, I think maybe we built another one ...”

Drew was so intent on staring at the photo that he hadn't lifted his head while he recalled the scene. Now, when he did, he saw that silent tears leaked from his mother's eyes.

“That's absolutely right, Andrew. Absolutely right.”

Drew smiled at her. He felt a heaviness in his chest, and he wished his dad were there too.

“Maybe this is the reason I like the picture in my book so much. Maybe it's because I somehow remembered this. Could that be it?”

“I don't know, could be,” Penny said, wiping the tears from her face. “So, if you love this picture in your book, and you believe it's something worth pursuing, then keep going.”

Wednesday morning, Drew felt less anxious and more hopeful. He bounced to school, knowing just what he was on his way to do.

When he walked into the building, he found Caleb, who was standing with Tommy. “Hey, I need you to text Huddy. Tell him I need to meet with him after school today.”

Caleb pushed his hair out of his face and gave Drew a puzzled look. “Why?”

“Just do it. Tell him I'll meet him outside where the elementary school and middle school connect, right by the playground. And tell him that I have something of his that I think he'll want.”

“Huddy ain't gonna wanna talk to you.”

“Just text him. We'll meet right after school.”

At lunch, Caleb came over from his normal table and said Huddy would be behind the school this afternoon. He also told Drew that Huddy would be bringing a few friends with him.

By recess, Zobby had gotten word of Drew's plan. As Drew was about to be up in a game of kickball, she strode through the infield, directly toward him, and pulled him aside.

"This doesn't sound like a good idea. He's crazy, remember?"

"I know, but I just have to ask him something."

"What do you have to ask him? Why he's such a jerk?"

Drew didn't say anything.

"I know, it's another thing you don't wanna tell me," said Zobby. "That's fine, but I'm coming with you."

"No way. I'll do it by myself."

Zobby shook her head. "He's not gonna show up by himself, so neither are you. I'm coming."

Zobby's loyal bravery must have been contagious, because Jeff, Tommy, Trevor, and Caleb insisted they wanted to go, too. After their constant persistence, Drew said they could come, but he would have to talk to Huddy *alone*.

After school, they went around to the back of the building where the middle school and elementary school connected. Huddy was already there waiting with four other kids. Drew recognized one as the quiet boy from The Shack. But, to his surprise, Kris wasn't there. Drew had hoped Kris would be one of the kids Huddy brought, because Kris was the only one who was level-headed that day in the woods. But in a way, though he wasn't sure why, Drew was glad Kris hadn't come to support Huddy.

"This better be good, Daley," yelled Huddy. "I don't got all day either. 'Bout to go shoot some hoops."

Drew walked right up to him. He clenched his teeth

and breathed through his nose, trying his best to look calm and confident.

"So what did you *steal* from me? Huh? Hand it over before me and my boys beat up every one of you."

Huddy's four cronies, including the quiet boy, laughed brashly.

"I didn't steal anything," Drew whispered, unable to speak with authority.

"What was that, little girl? You didn't steal nothing, huh? Then why did Roey say you had somethin' of mine, huh?"

"Listen, I didn't steal anything from you, all right? I have something of yours that I found at The Shack."

"What? You're really gonna bring up The Shack? You got a death wish or somethin'?"

"Listen, I'm not trying to start trouble. We messed up The Shack and you were mad, I get it. But you messed with us, too. So we're even, okay?"

But as Drew said the words, he wondered if they were true. Were the kids even? Zobby's phone was replaceable – there were a million other phones just like it. But the artwork inside The Shack could never truly be replaced. And, although he knew there was no excuse for what Huddy did to Zobby, Drew now understood how devastated Huddy must have been when his comics and drawings were destroyed.

"Can I just talk to you for a minute ... alone?"

Huddy glanced at his friends. Drew could tell that Huddy had an image to maintain, and every move he made seemed to have that image in mind.

"Come on, just give me one minute."

Huddy gave a nod to his friends, and the two walked off about 20 yards away from the rest of the kids.

"What's this all about? What do you have?" Huddy asked, maintaining the sternness in both his face and his tone.

Drew set his book bag on the ground and pulled out a folder. From the folder, he removed a folded paper with the name "Mike Hudock" on the back.

"My picture!" Huddy exclaimed, snatching the paper from Drew's hand.

"Yeah, I found it in The Shack, but I didn't know it was yours 'til after we left."

"Yeah, it's mine, I was –" Huddy caught himself and changed his tone. "I mean, yeah, I don't care. I was just messing around with it. It was for art class a long time ago. I *had* to do it."

But it was obvious that Huddy did indeed care about the picture. He hadn't taken his eyes off it since he first unfolded it. Drew watched as Huddy seemed to trace the outline of the motorcycle with his widened eyes. He could tell that the way in which he appreciated this picture was the same way Drew appreciated the picture in the science book.

"Well, it's good. You're a good artist," said Drew.

As though he realized his friends were watching him, Huddy suddenly switched his focus from the picture back to Drew. He squinted his eyes and molded his entire face into a scowl.

"Yeah, I'm good at a lot of things. So this was it? Seriously? That's why we had this stupid meeting? Come *on*!"

He made sure he exclaimed the last part loudly enough for everyone to hear. Then he turned to face his friends and carefully slid the picture into his back pocket. In that moment, Drew realized that there really was another side to Huddy.

With another gust of nerve, Drew responded, "No, that's not all."

Huddy turned back around. "Then what?" he barked.

An entire school year of searching helped Drew to find his courage, and he turned to his book bag on the ground and pulled out his science book. In a flash, he opened to page 139.

"I just need to know – you drew this, right?"

Again the hard exterior of Huddy vanished. He slid next to Drew to get a better look. His eyes drank every detail of the drawing.

"No, that's not mine. I would've remembered drawing something like that." The boy's words were soft and heartfelt. They were also whispered so his cronies couldn't hear his vulnerability.

A wave of disappointment crashed over Drew. *How could it not be Huddy? He's a good artist. He cares about his pictures. He had the same book. It all adds up – it has to be him!*

"But –"

"I didn't draw the stupid picture!" Huddy snapped.

He grabbed the textbook and flung it behind the two of them. Drew didn't move. As all of Huddy's friends – including Caleb – laughed, Huddy picked up Drew's book bag and dumped everything out. "That's for wasting my time ..." He turned and stepped so close to Drew that he cast a shadow over him. "Don't bother me ever again. You hear me? If you do, you'll get *much* worse than this."

Drew didn't budge. He stood toe to toe with the bully, refusing to bow down to his intimidating glare. After several seconds, Huddy scoffed and returned to his friends, who were all still laughing.

Before leaving, he said, "Hey, you wanna hoop with us, Roey?"

"Yeah, but I was gonna hang out with Tommy ..."

"I'll come, too," Tommy said eagerly.

Huddy motioned with his head, and Caleb and Tommy followed the older boys. Now, Drew and his friends were left to clean up the mess. It was Zobby who first began to pick up all the loose items. Jeff patted Drew on the shoulder while Trevor jogged over toward the science book. Drew thought someone as big as Trevor would have done something, but he actually looked more shaken than anyone.

"What was that all about anyway? That picture of the beach?" asked Jeff.

Drew nodded.

"You all right?" Zobby asked.

Drew gazed out across the empty playground for several seconds. "Yeah, I'm okay."

He had taken so many risks – approaching the most popular girl in school, going to The Shack, throwing a snowball at an eighth-grader, talking to Tommy's scary older brother – and now, after all this time, he had gotten nowhere. What was once a promising adventure turned out to be nothing but dead ends.

Zobby and Trevor walked home toward their houses while Drew and Jeff headed in the other direction.

"Man, I'm sorry about all that," said Jeff, after the boys passed the closed bridge.

"Thanks," said Drew. "I just wanted to find out who drew the picture."

"Well, I'd be glad it wasn't that kid," said Jeff. "Seriously, he's crazy."

Drew smiled. Jeff had a good point. And truthfully, underneath all the confusion, Drew did feel a little relieved that his beloved picture wasn't drawn by Huddy.

On Thursday, Mrs. Steinbeck gave the students a few minutes to review notes and ask questions before the final test. Drew leafed through his book, half-heartedly reviewing the information. Along with the picture, he realized he would also miss the book itself – the familiar smell of the worn pages, the distinct rustling sound they made as they glided through his fingers, and even the handwritten names inside the front cover. He couldn't believe he only had it for one more day.

At lunch, Tommy took his normal seat as if he hadn't ditched Drew and Jeff yesterday. He popped a tater tot into his mouth and casually struck up a conversation about summer activities.

Jonathan passed by and said, "Surprised to see you here today, Daley. I figured you woulda been crippled by Huddy." He set his lunch down on the table. "Seriously, did that really happen? Did you wanna talk to a scary kid who's two years older *and* twice your size about some stupid drawing?"

"Lay off, man," said Jeff.

"I got this," said Drew. He turned to Jonathan and said, "Yeah, I did talk to Huddy about a drawing. And guess what? Huddy likes art, too. I doubt you'd make fun of *him* – or, if you want, you can go tell him how stupid art is. Want me to arrange a meeting for you?"

After a moment of stunned silence, Tommy yelled "Mic drop!" and everyone at the table roared a collective "Ohhh!" The clamor rippled through the cafeteria, and Jonathan was sent scurrying away by the sweeping chorus of jeers.

Although Jonathan was gone, Drew still felt like stepping away from the table himself.

"I'm gonna grab another chocolate milk," he said.

When he got in line, someone asked, "Hey, what was all that about?"

Drew turned around and saw Skylar. "Huh? What was what about?"

"All the yelling."

"Oh, uh, that was nothing," he said sheepishly.

Skylar playfully nudged his shoulder. "Come on, tell me."

"Well, remember that drawing we talked about a long time ago?"

"The one in the science book?"

"Yeah. I thought I finally figured out who drew it. I had it down to two people, and one of them is this girl Stacey Janofsky – I guess some people called her 'Red' ... You don't happen to know her, do you?"

"No, I don't think so."

"I figured. She doesn't live here anymore. Anyway, you're not gonna believe this, but I thought it was Mike Hudock, you know, Huddy? Anyway, I found out he liked art, and I had crossed off everyone else, so I figured it was him. Then when I talked to him about it he just said, 'I would've remembered a picture like that,' or something. Then he dumped everything out of my book bag and threw my science book, then Jonathan was making fun of me about it. I don't know. It has to be Stacey, but I have no clue how I'll ever talk to her. But anyway, that's why everyone was yelling and stuff."

Skylar responded, "That's awful! I'm sorry he messed with you. Michael is such a jerk sometimes! But ... you said he's an artist?"

Hearing Skylar say Huddy's real name sounded strange. It was like his nickname made him seem larger than life, while the name Michael showed that he was just a regular kid.

"Well, I don't know if he's an artist," said Drew, "but I do know he likes to draw. He's good, too. Probably not better than the person who drew the picture in the science book, though. They're the best!"

"Wow. That's surprising. A cool kid like him into drawing," said Skylar, seeming to drift off for a second. "But hey, I'm gonna get back. Bye, Drew."

Even though it was a Melia's Thursday, Drew doubted the boys would make the trip to the convenience store. The three of them hadn't talked about the Melia's situation, but they all knew that things had changed. Not even

Tommy brought up wanting to go back.

At their lockers at the end of the day, Jeff explained that Zane's kindergarten graduation was today and he would be staying after school for that. So it was just Drew and Tommy walking home together.

"Look!" Tommy exclaimed. "The bridge isn't closed anymore. We can walk right across now. We'll get home twice as fast."

But when the boys were a step away from the bridge, Drew slowed down. He felt like his feet were stuck in the pavement.

"I don't think I wanna go this way," he said.

Tommy looked at him blankly.

"It's just we walked the other way the entire year, and I think I'm gonna keep doing that." He paused for a moment and said, "Come with me, man."

"No," said Tommy. "It makes no sense. We'll get home faster by the bridge. It's like a shortcut."

Drew shrugged. "I know, man, but I'm still just gonna go the long way."

"Whatever."

Tommy didn't seem to have the faintest idea what Drew was talking about. They said their goodbyes, and Drew took the long way home.

As Drew approached Skylar's house, she and a woman who appeared to be her mom were sitting on the front porch. Drew waved and gave a subtle head nod to Skylar as he passed.

"Hey, Drew," she yelled.

"Who's that?" Drew heard the woman say.

"That's Drew. He goes to my school," said Skylar. She shifted her attention to Drew. "Hey, come meet my mom."

"I was just going to get Skylar and me some lemonade. Would you like to stop for a few minutes?" Mrs. Jansen asked.

"Um, sure, thanks."

"Let's wait inside. It's way too hot out here," said Skylar.

They walked inside and Mrs. Jansen went into the kitchen to get the lemonade.

When Drew walked into the house, he felt a similar sensation to when he would open his science book to page 139. The living room wall was covered with framed artwork. To the left was a picture of a moonlit forest, drawn with dark shades of blue, purple, and green pastel. On the opposite wall was an illustration of the Jansens' front porch, sketched in pencil. With a triumphant rush of joy, Drew put the pieces together.

"These are ... yours."

Before Skylar could respond, her mom returned from the kitchen.

"Oh, they are all hers," she said, handing Skylar and Drew each a glass. "But she hardly draws anything anymore. I can't even get her to take art class, can you believe that? She has real talent – much more than her father and I ever had."

"Mom, stop."

"I'm serious. Aren't these good, Drew?"

"They're unbelievable."

He turned to Skylar, who took a swig of lemonade and looked away.

"Thank you for the drink, Mrs. Jansen. But I have to get home now."

"Thank you for stopping, Drew. You're welcome here any time."

Skylar silently walked Drew out to the front porch.

"Well, I have to get going, bye," said Drew, hurrying down the sidewalk.

"Drew, wait."

He turned around and waited for her to continue. She opened her mouth but didn't say anything.

Finally, Drew asked the question he needed to ask. "The picture in the science book. It was you all along, wasn't it?"

Skylar hesitated. Clasping her hands behind her back and looking down at the ground, she said, "Yes. But you have to understand ..."

"Understand what?"

"I dunno. When you asked me right away, I didn't know you. I didn't know you'd make it like your mission or whatever to find the person who drew the picture."

"Why didn't you tell me after we became friends?" Drew asked.

"I dunno."

"It doesn't make sense," said Drew.

Skylar didn't respond. She was normally composed, but now she seemed unnerved.

Drew paused and realized he had a more important question to ask her: "Why do you think I love the picture so much?"

"What do you mean?"

"I've shown it to a bunch of people, and none of them cared about it as much as I do. Something about it is special, but I can't figure out what."

"I dunno," said Skylar. "It's just a picture."

"Not to me. And I know it's special to you, too. When I first mentioned it to you, your eyes lit up. Why?"

"Drew, I ... I guess because it's something simple. Or maybe it took my mind off science class. That's probably why. But I have no idea why *you* like it so much."

Drew paused. "Okay," he said finally. He realized she was right. She had drawn the picture, but she wasn't responsible for Drew's reaction to it.

Drew turned toward the street but stopped again.

"One other question. Why don't you draw anymore? You're really good."

"No, my parents are the only ones who think I'm good. I do it for fun or whatever. It's no big deal."

"Well, I'm telling you, you are good. Do you know what I was thinking about when I walked by your house this afternoon?"

Skylar shook her head side to side.

"I was thinking about what I should do with my science book tomorrow. I have to hand it in, and I might never see that picture again. It meant a lot to me this year. I still don't know *why*, but I know it's my favorite picture. And tomorrow it'll be gone. I just ... I don't get why you wouldn't wanna keep taking art and making more pictures."

Skylar shrugged and slightly tilted her head. "All my friends take study hall. So I just decided to do that instead. That's all."

"That doesn't even make sense. I can tell by the pictures in there that you like doing it."

Skylar blankly stared at Drew. She seemed to be growing more and more uncomfortable.

"Uh, it's fine, never mind," said Drew. "But I do have to go."

"All right."

Before Drew got to the curb, he turned around. Skylar was still on the porch. Drew thought for a moment and said, "I'm glad it was you."

Skylar smiled and went back inside.

It was officially the last day of fifth grade. Drew couldn't believe he had finally found his Mystery Artist.

For the most part, the last day of school was a breeze. The teachers allowed the students to play games and sign each other's yearbooks. Of course, Mrs. Steinbeck still conducted a regular class, teaching a lesson from the last chapter of the book and preparing the students for some of the topics that would be covered next year.

Even though he knew she was a good teacher, Drew was relieved to get out of Mrs. Steinbeck's class altogether. He hated being nervous every time she called his name.

"Mr. Daley."

"Huh? Yes?"

"Your book, Mr. Daley."

He had decided to hand in the book without making a copy or ripping out page 139. Finding the artist made it a lot easier for him to give up the picture he loved. He found a great deal of happiness in it, and he hoped the book's future owner would, too.

As he extended the book toward Mrs. Steinbeck, he hesitated and, for a brief second, second-guessed his decision. But she took the book, opened to the inside cover to verify the book identification number, and nodded. It was over.

At lunch, Drew looked for Skylar, but she wasn't at her normal table.

"Everybody signed up for study hall, right?" Tommy asked the group.

"Yeah," said Trevor. "I need all the extra studying I can get."

"Me too," added Jeff.

"I signed up for art," said Drew.

"Are you serious ..."

Before Tommy could finish his insult, Drew snapped back, "Yeah, I am serious. I like art. I like to draw. And guess what, so does Huddy, even if he won't admit it. And Skylar likes it, too. But even if no one else liked it, I still would. So I don't care if you think it's stupid. 'Cause it's not stupid to me."

Tommy was stunned. In fact, all the boys were, including Drew himself. A few seconds later, Trevor broke the tension by bringing up a water park his family planned to visit next week, and the boys didn't rehash the art-versus-study hall discussion. Drew had officially closed that debate.

Mr. Sawyer tried to do a bit of teaching, but he knew as well as the students did that it was time for summer break to begin. He went around the room and asked the students to name their favorite thing about the class. Many kids talked about multicultural week. A few others, including Drew and Jeff, talked about their field trip to the museum.

When all the students had answered, Abigail raised her hand and asked Mr. Sawyer what his favorite moment was.

"Well, you know I'm proud of all of you for the hard work you did this year. But there is one presentation that sticks out to me. At the beginning of the year, you had to talk about a role model of yours, remember?"

Everyone nodded.

"And Drew talked about the runner who picked up a flower holder the wind had blown over. More than the awards or accolades, the money or appreciation, I love the idea of someone doing something regardless of how it will be perceived. Or, better yet, even if it might never be seen at all. Those things we do when no one is watching – that's how we know who we are."

Mr. Sawyer paused for a moment. Then he continued:

"A lot of things will change when you get to middle school next year. Things like peer pressure may play a bigger role. But remember to always be yourself, no matter who's watching. Now, I know you've heard this before and you'll hear it again, but remember: it doesn't matter what others think they see. It's what's on the inside that counts."

"You mean that a lot of things around us will change, but we shouldn't change, right?" said Abigail.

"Well," said Mr. Sawyer, "no, you will change. That's inevitable. I'm certainly not saying you should live in the past. What I'm saying is there are some things you should leave in the past, and some things you should keep forever. Don't let the world change you completely. We've all got a youthful spirit within us. Make sure you never lose yours. Don't forget what it's like to just be a kid."

The final bell of the school year rang as he finished his sentence.

"Have a good summer. And don't forget to visit me next year. Just because you're big middle schoolers now doesn't mean you're too cool for me."

Every student was up and out of the room before Drew got up from his seat.

"Did you mean all that?" he asked Mr. Sawyer.

"You know I did, Drew. Sometimes people make choices for the wrong reasons. You're a really good kid. Trust your instincts. And always remember to be prepared for a presentation," he joked, referencing the infamous "States" project.

Drew laughed. "Yeah. Thanks for everything, Mr. Sawyer."

He walked out into the hallway, where Jeff and Tommy were waiting for him.

"Hey, man, Roey said he's going to play some street hockey. You in?" Tommy asked.

"Probably not today."

"Come on, man, it's summer now!"

"No, but thanks, though."

"You sure you can't go either, Jeff?" Tommy asked.

"Yeah, sorry."

"Suit yourselves. I'm goin' straight to Roey's house. See you at our game tomorrow."

With empty book bags on their backs, Drew and Jeff started home. When they got to the bridge, Drew explained to Jeff that he still wanted to take the long way home. To his surprise, Jeff said he would join him. They walked down and around the bridge, the way they had done nearly the entire school year.

"Did you understand what Mr. Sawyer meant?" Jeff asked. "He was talking about holding on to things. Do you think that means you should've held on to that picture?"

"I don't think so. I think I just need to remember how it made me feel, that's all."

"Yeah," said Jeff. "Mr. Sawyer's probably right. A lot of stuff will probably change in middle school. Some things already started changing, I think."

"Drew!" Skylar was hurrying down her sidewalk.

"Hey, I didn't think you'd be walking this way," she said, standing in front of him. "You know, because that bridge is open. But I'm glad you did ..."

Taking his cue, Jeff said, "I gotta get home. I'll catch up with you later."

The boys exchanged a subtle wink, and Jeff headed down the road.

"I wanted to say I'm sorry," Skylar continued. "I know I said it yesterday, but I want you to know that I really am."

"Don't be," said Drew. "I should be thanking you for drawing the picture."

Skylar smiled. "Did you hand in your science book today?"

"Yeah, 'fraid so."

"Did you rip the drawing out, take a picture of it, anything?"

"No, nothing. I left it there and handed it in. Maybe someone will like it as much as I did," said Drew, happy with his decision.

"I was hoping you'd say that," Skylar replied. She pulled a large notepad out of her book bag, opened it, and carefully tore out the first sheet.

"I thought maybe you'd like this," she said, handing the sheet to Drew. "I worked on it all last night, and I finished it today during lunch."

In Drew's hands was a larger, more detailed version of the ocean scene drawing. Drew stared into it, and it had an even stronger effect on him than the picture in the book had. An old memory seemed to arise from a shadowed corner in his mind. He remembered being at the beach with his parents when he was four years old. He recognized it as the same memory captured in the photo album his mom had shown him.

But now, as his eyes remained fixated on the picture, the memory became so vivid that he felt like he had traveled back in time and was standing on the beach. He could see the movement of the waves, the way they would rush toward the shore and then wash away in gentle retreat. He remembered how the tide varied according to the time and the wind, and he thought, for a moment, about how we are always inevitably changing.

In the closet of their beachfront condo, Drew had found an old set of sandcastle tools, containing a small sand shovel and three differently-shaped buckets. Standing by the curb in front of Skylar's house, Drew could sense the excitement he had felt when he took those tools to the beach.

He continued to gaze into the picture. Now he could hear the sounds of the beach: the waves, the music, the people milling about, the cawing of the sea gulls. Strangely, though, none of those sounds served as distractions. Rather, they joined together harmoniously as background noise to allow the moment to be captured. Drew had spent what felt like hours building the biggest, best sandcastle he could – digging, piling, molding, shaping. And now he recalled the moment when a wave came to shore and knocked over his kingdom in the sand. He remembered what his parents said to him in that moment, and it seemed very important.

"Don't cry, Drew," his mother had said, putting her arm around him.

"We'll build another one, bud," said his father.

"But I liked this one," young Drew whimpered as tears streaked down his cheeks. "And now it's ruined."

"Nothing is ever ruined," said his mother.

"But it was perfect."

"I know it was. So we'll just have to build an even better one," his father said, smiling at his wife.

She smiled back.

"It's all we can do," she said as she wiped Drew's tears.

Drew looked up at his parents' smiling faces and stopped crying. He stooped over, picked up his tools, and began building another castle.

"Do you like it?" Skylar asked.

In a hushed voice, Drew said, "It's perfect. Thank you."

Skylar blushed and brushed her yellow hair from her face.

"Seriously, I can't believe you did all this –" Drew's words were cut off by a different voice yelling from the front door.

"Hey, Mom, it's him! I knew it! It's really him!"

Sprinting from the front porch toward Drew was an elated little kid. "You saved me!"

Skylar looked to Drew, who shrugged to show that he was just as confused as she was.

"Who? Drew? Was it Drew this whole time?" asked

Mrs. Jansen, following her son down the sidewalk.

As he got closer, Drew finally got a good look at the kid's face. It was Brady, the kindergartener he had guided to the art room on the first day of school.

"What do you mean, he saved you?" asked Skylar.

"Come on, remember!" Brady implored.

"All year Brady has been talking about his savior," said Mrs. Jansen, smiling at Drew. "The six-foot tall hero who saved him and got him back to his class. It's all we've heard about."

"You're *him?*" asked Skylar.

"Um," said Drew, "I don't know about the six-foot tall stuff or anything about a hero, but I did help Brady find the art room on the first day of school."

The once bashful Brady threw his arms around Drew's waist. "You're the best. Thank you!"

"I told him if he ever ran into you again, make sure to thank you," said Mrs. Jansen. "So often people do good things but never know what real impact they make."

Drew's mind sprinted to the runner, the person he looked up to, the person who helped him launch his quest for the Mystery Artist in the first place.

Mrs. Jansen lured Brady back inside with the promise of a juice box and a snack. As Skylar and Drew stood in the Jansens' front yard, Drew couldn't help staring down at his brand new picture. Even though Skylar hadn't seen the drawing in a full year, she had somehow recaptured all its beauty.

"So," Skylar said, "you helped my little brother find the art room, did you?"

"It was no big deal. He was just a little mixed up. It was his first day."

"Well, the picture wasn't the only thing I wanted to talk to you about. We had class signups today. What did you take, music, art, or study hall?"

"I took art. I guess you're taking study hall again, right?"

"Not this time. I took art. And what's even better is because I didn't take it this year, I'm in art-one next year ... so we'll be in the same class."

"I ... don't know what to say."

"You don't have to say anything."

"But I do. Thank you, Skylar. The picture in the book. Now this. This is awesome."

Skylar smiled and walked back up her sidewalk, and Drew continued down the street.

All the bad things from the past year – the storm, the broken window, the cheating, the bullies, the defeats – seemed small and distant, and Drew was glad to leave them buried in the past. But, looking down at the picture, he knew there were also some things worth holding on to.

He also knew that some questions still remained. Was the old Tommy really gone forever? And though she wasn't the artist, what really did happen to Stacey Janofsky? And, most of all, he wondered what kinds of changes middle school would bring.

But for now, as he headed home with the picture in his hands, Drew had victory in his heart and a brand new summer before him. He carefully rolled the picture into a cylinder. Then an extra burst entered his stride, and his feet moved faster and faster. He turned the corner and ran toward Ernest Way without looking back.

Matt Fazio

Matt Fazio is not a bestselling author, but he hopes to be one someday. He teaches Composition and Communication courses at various universities in the Pittsburgh area and is a marketer for an accounting and consulting firm.

When he isn't writing, teaching, or marketing, he's likely researching fantasy baseball stats (2012 League Champion), playing songs on guitar (exclusively early 2000s pop punk), or quoting Willy Wonka (the Gene Wilder version, of course). He received a BA in English Studies from Robert Morris University, an MA in English Literature from Slippery Rock University, and a PhD in Rhetoric from Duquesne University.

Matt lives in Pittsburgh, PA, with his wife, Erica, and two daughters, Thea and Josie.

Follow Matt at:

www.detoursanddesigns.com
www.facebook.com/DetoursandDesigns
Instagram: @detoursanddesigns
Twitter: @fazio_matt

Josh Malacki

J osh Malacki lives in Pittsburgh, PA, and received a
BA in English from Robert Morris
University. He is left-handed.
His hair is brown. He is terrible
at writing third-person author
bios, as you likely figured out,
or at least suspected, when he
told you he was left-handed, or
certainly no later than when he
informed you of his hair color
(brown). Nevertheless, he promises you that *Detours and
Designs* is a lot better than this bio.

Although Josh's poetry and short fiction have appeared
in a handful of publications, he is best known for his fifth-
grade D.A.R.E. essay, which won first place in a landslide.
Detours and Designs is his first novel.

Follow Josh at:
www.detoursanddesigns.com
www.facebook.com/DetoursandDesigns
Instagram: @detoursanddesigns
Twitter: @MoshLajacki